"Let's get one thing clear, Conner. I'm your attorney. Anything personal is out of place."

A dimple appeared on his right cheek as he smiled. "Okay. When did you become a lawyer?"

Before she could say a word, he stopped her. "That's an appropriate question, Counselor, since you'll be defending me."

"Of course." She caught his eye. "I passed the Virginia bar this summer. If what you want is a seasoned attorney, it's in your best interest to say so now."

Conner seemed to weigh her words carefully. His eyes never left hers.

"You'll do just fine, Counselor."

Audrey pretended to ignore the silky smoothness of his voice, but she couldn't lie to herself about the shiver running down her back.

A mantra of support echoed through Audrey. *He's my client; I'm his lawyer.* She focused on what was at stake for Conner and for herself to keep her emotions at bay. She had to offer him the best defense she could. More was at stake than anyone knew....

Dear Reader,

The verdict is in—LEGAL THRILLERS are a hit! And in response to this popular demand, we bring you another of Harlequin Intrigue's ongoing LEGAL THRILLERS. Stories of secret scandals and crimes of passion. Of legal eagles who battle the system...and undeniable desire.

Gay Cameron met the world of law through her training as a private investigator. The inspiration for the story grew from many trips to the Rappahannock River, where wonderful people and spectacular scenery continue to fill her imagination with tales of romance and suspense. This is Gay's second book for Harlequin Intrigue, following *His Brother's Keeper*.

Look for the LEGAL THRILLER flash for the best in suspense!

Regards,

Debra Matteucci
Senior Editor & Editorial Coordinator
Harlequin Books
300 East 42nd Street
New York, New York 10017

The Defendant
Gay Cameron

Harlequin Books

TORONTO • NEW YORK • LONDON
AMSTERDAM • PARIS • SYDNEY • HAMBURG
STOCKHOLM • ATHENS • TOKYO • MILAN
MADRID • WARSAW • BUDAPEST • AUCKLAND

In memory of Commander Edward Tabb Justis, Jr.

For sharing their knowledge and expertise, I sincerely thank
Lyndon Howell, lawyer, neighbor and friend; Commander
Laura Omer, U.S. Navy, Director of Continuing Education,
Uniformed Services University of Health Services, neighbor
and friend; and Louis C. Roy, Director of Operations, Gold
Shield Investigations & Security, Inc.

ISBN 0-373-22404-4

THE DEFENDANT

Copyright © 1997 by Gay Cameron Snell

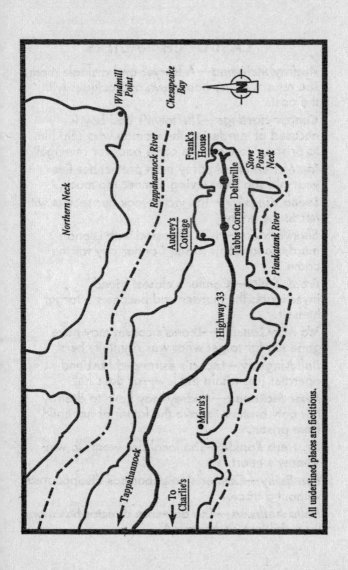

All underlined places are fictitious.

CAST OF CHARACTERS

Audrey McKenna—A lawyer and a single mom, she returns to her hometown and collides with the past.

Conner Hastings—The town's bad boy is accused of murdering the woman who sent him to prison. Now had he come back for revenge?

Ian McKenna—Audrey must protect her five-year-old son from loving Conner too much.

Leona Kingsley—The victim took her secrets with her to the grave.

Sheriff Parks—He is obsessed with Leona's murder and wants to see Conner pay for the crime.

Frank Smith—Conner's closest friend investigates the murder and becomes a target himself.

Ida May Lansing—Leona's cousin may have gone too far to get what was rightfully hers.

Bull Kingsley—Leona's estranged husband operates just within the law—or does he?

Peter McKenna—Audrey may have to destroy her only brother to save the father of her child from prison.

Dr. Herb Rankin—The local doc wants to win Audrey's heart.

Ben Reilly—Conner's neighbor has disappeared without a trace.

Della Andrews—The day-care director has more than children on her mind.

Prologue

Conner Hastings poured his first cup of morning coffee, opened the front door and stared into the barrel of a .45.

"What the—"

"Gotcha this time, boy."

Sheriff Parks slapped a cuff on Conner's wrist, knocking the cup from his hand. Hot coffee burned a trail down his side. He sucked in his breath.

In one smooth motion, the sheriff holstered his gun, twisted Conner's arms behind his back and clamped the cuffs closed.

"What do you think you're doing?" Conner struggled to get free.

"Don't try any games on me, boy." Parks forced Conner's arms higher while he searched him, then spun him around and pulled out his gun again. "'You have the right to remain silent. Anything you say or do may be held against…'"

The Miranda rights. Conner blocked out the words. What the devil was going on? His insides twisted into knots. His side, scalded from the steamy brew, burned like a blaze from hell. Already he had visions of ending up in prison—again.

"Head for the car." Parks poked him down the steps with his gun. "Come on, git."

"You are going to tell me what's going on, right?"

"You made a big mistake this time, boy. Figured you could sneak back into Tabbs Corner and do away with Leona. I don't think so."

"What in the hell are you talking about?"

Conner knew Leona Kingsley, all right. The Kingsley family had run this town since he was a kid.

"I'm taking you in for the last time, boy. They'll throw away the key on this one, and I'll be right there helping them."

The sheriff shoved him forward. Conner tripped over a dead branch and Parks caught him by the cuffs. Gritting his teeth, he refused to acknowledge the pain that shot through his shoulders.

Parks pushed him into the police car, the gun still trained on him. "Even if you had a lick of sense and a dime to call your own, you couldn't be half the kind of person she was. Leona Kingsley was good people, not scum like you."

Conner blocked the door with his feet. "Spit it out, Sheriff. What's got you rattled this time?"

Parks pinned him with accusing dark eyes. His finger slid back and forth over the pistol's hammer. Short salt-and-pepper hair made him look like a throwback to the fifties. The wiry build carried a potbelly that hung over his belt.

He pulled a sheaf of documents from his pocket and waved the pages in front of Conner. "You didn't even have the guts to do it face-to-face." His expression became a neutral reflection of his office. "You're under arrest for the murder of Leona Kingsley. I have a warrant for your arrest and—" he shook one of the documents in Conner's face "—a warrant to search the premises. That includes your truck, boy." He grabbed the door and slammed it shut.

Conner was shaking. He knew the routine and still he was shaking. He should have realized the sheriff would be out to get him, but never would he have guessed that the woman who'd sent him to jail once could do it again from the grave.

Chapter One

Audrey McKenna rounded the corner of the courthouse hallway—and ran smack into the solid chest of an over-sized male. She struggled for balance, relieved as strong hands stopped her fall.

She glanced up at the man helping her. "Thank...*you!*" Her heart almost stopped its beating.

Conner Hastings dropped his hands and backed off. Astonishment overtook his face.

Audrey couldn't take her eyes from him. He was as tall as she remembered, and as sinfully handsome. His half smile was both sexy and wicked, and bore witness to the arrogance he carried like a shield. The town had once dubbed him the "Terror of Tabbs Corner," and aptly so. He attracted trouble. And after six years, he still attracted her.

"You never know who might be haunting the halls of justice. Right, Audrey?"

His expression changed from astonishment to indignation. Those dark, secretive eyes that had hounded her dreams became sharpened daggers aimed point-blank at her. She stepped back, overwhelmed by the anger she saw. What gave him the right to be so angry? He was the one who had destroyed their future.

She fought to be civil and called on every bit of inner

strength she possessed to retain her composure. "Is this your latest thrill? Crashing into people?"

"Absolutely. Especially when she's a sexy lady with fire in her eyes."

The sarcasm didn't escape her. Neither did the shadows that briefly touched his eyes.

"Then I'd say you'd better watch your step. Fire has a way of consuming whatever is in its path."

"Is that a threat or a promise?"

The cocky look on his face sent a lump to her throat. Audrey forced herself to swallow. "Merely a statement of fact."

She stared at the man she had loved so completely. His once-bronzed face was pale from his time in prison. Thick, dark hair formed a slight widow's peak that looked all too familiar. His eyes were a stormier blue than she'd ever seen them.

"Excuse me." Wishing she had left by the back exit, she edged around him on wobbly legs and headed down the long hall.

She didn't want to see Conner. She had loved him desperately a lifetime ago, but she wanted nothing to do with him now. That part of her past had no place in the present.

Her hands were shaking. She hid them in the pockets of her suit jacket. She could handle this, she repeated to herself forcefully, increasing the tempo of her gait with each repetition. She had handled more debilitating problems before.

But she wasn't prepared for the pain. She thought she'd laid the past to rest, but her rapidly beating heart and her trembling fists told her it had always been there, hiding inside, waiting and hoping for some sort of resolution.

And what about Conner? Had he thought of her even once in the past six years? Was he watching her walk away? Tempting as it was, she wouldn't give him the satisfaction of turning around to see.

THE VISION OF CONNER standing in the hall stayed with her as she clicked along the sidewalk toward her office, her salvation, her first day in her first position as an attorney. She found herself wishing she'd been able to stay in the mountains longer with her brother, Peter, and the rest of the family. Then maybe she wouldn't have run into Conner.

But, no. Instead she'd left before dawn to make the long drive back to a hometown she'd avoided for the past six years. She hadn't even taken time to stop by the cottage that would be her new home.

And maybe she should have. The cottage sat at the mouth of a creek that protected it from the harsh storms that hit the area. From her front porch she could see not only the other side of the small creek, but across the Rappahannock River, as well. The river had a way of smoothing away her troubles. The gentle lapping of the water against the Virginia shoreline was just what she needed right now. She'd returned to Tabbs Corner to embark on her career, only to find it shattered before it could begin.

Three women she vaguely recognized exited the gift shop and came to a dead stop when they saw her. They stared—just as people used to do when she was dating Conner. Audrey sent them a dazzling smile and called, "Good morning."

She'd encountered the same reaction earlier after she'd dropped off her car at the garage and walked to the law offices. At the time she'd thought perhaps the townspeople hadn't recognized her, which seemed odd. They had known her and her brother during their teenaged years. Her grandfather had known everyone in town. Yes, she'd left without explanation six years ago. She'd been young and foolish enough to think she'd found true love with Conner. His betrayal had devastated her.

She'd never dreamed they were curious because of Conner. The fact that they were both back in town had resurrected the past. She had hoped enough time had passed for the town to forget her relationship with him. She didn't relish being known as the former sweetheart of a convict.

She turned the corner at First Street and let herself into the brownstone three buildings down. Regal, Thompson and Lutz had converted the house into offices, and the fact that it had once been someone's home had made it feel comfortable earlier this morning. No longer. Seeing Conner had destroyed her ability to find joy in something so simple. She felt like a mass of nerves.

"Did you deliver the brief?" Lori Thompson sat behind a desk, leafing through a huge stack of papers. She appeared as harried as she had an hour ago when Audrey left.

"Yes, no problem." No problem that she cared to mention. Being a relative newcomer to town, Lori might not know about her former relationship with Conner.

Lori set down the papers and pushed her brown hair from her face. "I'm sorry to send you off running as soon as you walked in the door. I promise you, I didn't bring you in to run errands. It's just that things are such a mess around here. Adam's mother had a stroke and he flew home to Minnesota to help her out. I tried to talk Mr. Regal into filling in for a few weeks, but he's off on one of his fishing trips." She raised her hands in exasperation. "Heaven help anyone who tries to interfere with his fishing trips."

Audrey remembered Mr. Regal. Adam Lutz she had never met.

"And to make matters worse, Judge Walker refused to assign another court-appointed lawyer to the case Adam was handling. Right now, you are a godsend."

AUDREY'S OFFICE was the first one on the right down the hall from the front door and provided the privacy and quiet she needed to make the most of her time. The morning sped by like lightning. She was absorbed in her work three hours later, when some internal radar called her attention to the hall.

Conner walked by her office door, and her heart tightened like a fist. She pushed back her chair and marched around her desk, worried he'd come to cause trouble.

"What are you doing here?" she demanded when she reached the hall.

If she hadn't been so shocked to see him, she might have laughed at his expression. Total surprise slid across his face as his disbelieving eyes found hers. His first attempt to answer failed. He quickly recovered.

"I might ask you the same question."

Lori interrupted a potentially explosive scene. "Audrey, I'm glad you haven't left yet for lunch." She held out her hand. "You're Mr. Hastings. How do you do? I'm Lori Thompson. Mr. Lutz had a medical emergency and had to go out of town. We've had to turn your case over to another attorney."

"I understand." Conner eyed Audrey with a frown.

"Please understand, Mr. Hastings, we're new to your case, so bear with us. This is Audrey McKenna. She'll be your attorney of record."

Conner's face turned bone white. He glared at Audrey. After a long pause he responded in a flat voice, "We've met."

Lori's eyes darted back and forth from Audrey to Conner before she asked, "Is there a problem I should know about?"

Audrey wanted to bolt, but she'd vowed never to run from anything again. Even if she were to break that vow, curiosity would have prevented her from moving. What had Conner done now?

Conner's blue eyes never strayed from Audrey's face. "That depends on Ms. McKenna here."

"Audrey?" Lori stepped forward, her impatience obvious.

Audrey cleared her throat and glanced around, feeling lost. "Lori, could I have a word with you? Privately?"

Lori frowned. "Certainly. Excuse us for a moment, Mr. Hastings."

Once they were in Audrey's office, Lori closed the door and turned to Audrey. "Do you mind telling me what's going on? The tension in the hall is hot enough to burn the paint off the walls."

Audrey braced herself to be candid. "You need to know that Conner and I were once...Conner and I...have a history."

"When were you involved with him?"

"We started dating when I was in high school."

"Puhleese, puppy love doesn't count."

If only that were all, thought Audrey, digging her nails into her palms.

Lori waited for Audrey to continue, and when she didn't, the creases from her frown deepened. "Wait a minute here. Are you suggesting that because you and this man have a history, you can't defend him?"

Audrey didn't know how to answer the question. Three weeks ago she'd had no job offer she could accept, no established home and a student loan to repay. Her only choice then was to move to Tabbs Corner to her grandfather's cottage on the Rappahannock River, where the rent was free, and hope she could find a position somewhere in the area. Working as an attorney for Regal, Thompson and Lutz meant salvation. And not just for her.

Lori needed an attorney who could do the job without question. And it would not bode well for Audrey if she declined her first client.

"Well?" Lori perched one hand on a hip.

Audrey didn't want to defend Conner. The challenge could very well destroy her. She didn't want to be reminded of the passion they'd once shared and have her emotions shredded on a daily basis. But she saw no other

choice. Her only hope was to do everything she could to
maintain her professionalism for the duration of the case.

She threw back her shoulders and summoned every
ounce of willpower and gumption she had stored up for
the past twenty-seven years. "I can certainly maintain the
necessary attorney-client relationship with Mr. Hastings to
give him a solid defense. As long as he agrees, I see no
problem."

Lori gave a short sigh, relieved. "Good. Then let's get
to work." She handed Audrey the folder she'd been holding and turned to the door. "You'll find everything you
need in the file. Once you've reviewed the facts and had
a chance to talk with Mr. Hastings, we'll discuss the case.
You'll see that Adam performed every trick in the book to
get him out on bail. Adam's shoes are pretty big to fill,
but I have every confidence in you. The trial is scheduled
to begin in a week and a half."

She paused before opening the door. "Mr. Hastings
pleaded not guilty of the murder at the preliminary hearing. If you can convince him to change his plea, you may
be able to save him from a life sentence. I think the prosecutor would be willing to bargain."

Her statement pulverized Audrey. Conner was charged
with murder? An excruciating numbness paralyzed her.
Only when Conner came in and closed the door could she
make herself move to her desk.

"Please, have a seat." The words croaked from her
mouth.

A mantra of support echoed through her mind: *He's my
client. I'm his lawyer. Get a grip. Get a grip.* She dug
deep inside to find the control she needed to achieve the
necessary professional objectivity. She focused on what
was at stake for Conner and for herself to keep her emotions at bay. She *had* to offer him the best defense she
could. More was at stake than anyone knew.

"First, I want to review what we know." She hid her
trembling hands. "Feel free to interrupt at any time."

"When did you become a lawyer?"

Conner's face hadn't relaxed. Stress lines still creased his forehead.

"A little background seems appropriate, since this is a small town and a jury could be influenced by your record."

"You didn't answer my question."

Audrey slammed down the papers on her desk, relieved to have an excuse to release some of her tension. "Let's get one thing clear, Conner. I'm your attorney. Period. Anything personal is out of place."

A dimple appeared on his right cheek as he smiled. "Okay. When did you become a lawyer?"

Audrey jumped from her chair.

Before she could say a word, he stopped her. "That's an appropriate question, Counselor, since you'll be defending me."

Audrey sat down. "Of course." She caught his eye. "I passed the Virginia bar this summer. If what you want is a seasoned attorney, it's in your best interest to say so now."

Conner seemed to weigh her words carefully. His eyes never left hers. His jaw muscle tightened and his face became disturbingly pensive. She prayed he wouldn't opt for another attorney, then caught herself abruptly.

The lines still furrowed his brow when the words rolled off his tongue. "You'll do just fine, Counselor."

Audrey pretended to ignore the silky smoothness of his voice, but she couldn't lie to herself about the shiver running down her back.

"Then let's continue." She held on to her pencil for dear life. Hopefully, her trembling didn't show. "Six years ago a jury found you guilty of attempted armed robbery, malicious wounding and resisting arrest. You were sentenced to ten years in prison." She looked up at him. "I presume you got an early release for good behavior."

"That's right. But I've been better...with you."

She refused to take the bait. Yes, maybe so, but that was in the past.

"You really believe I was guilty, don't you?" The shadows of pain in his eyes forced her to look away.

"What I believe is irrelevant." She twisted the pencil in her hand. "Your guilt or innocence is not the question. I am merely reviewing the facts as they are listed."

She continued to peruse the file. One fact jumped out at her. She raised her head and looked him square in the eye. "Is this correct? You were arrested on suspicion of murder less than two weeks after your release from prison?"

"That's right." A hard edge coated his voice.

Wishing she'd seen the file before he'd come in, Audrey continued to read about the woman who'd been shot in the back of the head. After a long, pregnant silence, she pushed back her chair and twirled the pencil between her fingers. She looked at him closely.

"Motive, Mr. Hastings. Leona Kingsley was the prosecution's star witness against you six years ago. She, essentially, is the person who won the case for the prosecution and sealed your fate."

"I didn't kill her."

Audrey gritted her teeth and continued. "Evidence, Mr. Hastings. Sheriff Parks found your gun at the scene of the crime. Can you explain that?"

"Audrey, I was in prison for six years."

"The gun, Mr. Hastings."

"I thought the gun was where I always keep it—on the gun rack in my house. Anyone could have broken in and stolen it while I was away."

"With your mother there? Did she report a break-in? That would help your defense."

Conner looked decidedly uncomfortable. "My mother moved to Florida two years ago."

"And the house has been empty since then?" At his nod, she said, "I see."

"No, you don't see." He sprang from his chair. "Prison is an ugly place, Audrey. I have no intention of going back."

"Sit down, Conner. We haven't finished."

She struggled to keep her voice—and her attitude—objective. Just as she'd feared, it was impossible to separate Conner's reason for being there from her heightened awareness of him. Hiding that awareness was becoming more difficult by the minute. A virtual war raged inside her.

He ignored her request to sit down and instead looked out at the beautiful, blue August sky, a sky that matched the color of his eyes—which at the moment held a vulnerability that made her want to weep. The longing for freedom in his eyes rendered her speechless.

He turned to her slowly, as if giving himself time to regroup. A steely determination had replaced the shadows in his eyes. He went back to his chair.

"By all means, Counselor, continue."

Audrey cleared her throat. To regain her composure, she reread the notes in front of her. "Opportunity, Conner. Where were you at the time of the murder? The file simply states, 'no alibi.'"

He looked at her hard and long. "That's correct."

She hadn't missed his hesitation. It made her wonder if he would open up more easily to someone he didn't know. He wasn't offering much help. Yet, knowing him as she did, she understood that a stranger would get even less help. Conner always wanted to take care of Conner. She wouldn't have been surprised if he'd refused the help of counsel. That arrogant stubbornness was like a double-edged blade—it had helped him survive the poverty of his childhood, but it played against him now.

Audrey felt the resolve swell inside her. "Where were you? Point-blank, no hemming and hawing, no excuses, just a simple statement of where you were at the time of the murder. Period."

A grin touched his lips. She put on her most professional facade to hide the aching she felt.

"You want to know where I was? It won't help, Audrey. I drove into Tappahannock to buy roof shingles. I made a couple of stops on the way home. The very hour Leona was killed, I was on the road. Alone."

"The very hour?"

He caught her eye. "Stinks, doesn't it?"

Audrey shifted her gaze. "Go on."

"That's it. I have no alibi."

"Where did you stop? Someone will remember seeing you. We'll coordinate times." Audrey was beginning to feel desperate.

"No one saw me, Audrey. Trust me."

If only she could. But she had trusted him once and he had betrayed that trust. From everything she'd learned so far, it appeared the only man she'd ever loved was going to be convicted of murder.

A shudder racked her body. The thought of Conner being found guilty was almost more than she could bear.

CONNER FELT the worst of the tension dissolve once he escaped from the law office. He'd thought nothing could shock him more than literally running into Audrey at the courthouse that morning, but he'd been wrong. Meeting her at Adam Lutz's office— as a lawyer, no less—had tied his tongue in knots and kept him speechless for a moment.

He climbed into his truck and drove the short distance to the hardware store. He left the windows wide-open, as if begging the summer breeze to cool him down. Audrey McKenna had him burning with a fever he couldn't control. On top of that, she'd screwed up his thinking. How could he be so furious with her and so attracted to her at the same time? He didn't trust her; that was for sure. Any normal person in her shoes would be out for revenge. He had to be out of his mind to let her defend him.

For six years he'd lived with one goal in mind—to get

out of prison in one piece. Always his eye had been on the future. His memories of Audrey's faith in him had spurred him on to pursue his degree in prison so he could leave with at least something of value.

But he hadn't planned on seeing her again. Being with her without being a part of her life was enough to drive him insane as it was, but he sure as hell didn't want to get involved with her. He'd pushed her out of his life once; he knew he could never do it again.

He parked in front of the store and headed for the paint section. The majority of the roof shingles he'd bought in Tappahannock the night Leona was murdered were still stacked beside his house, but he needed to buy the paint now. For some reason, he believed that if he had materials on hand, he'd be around long enough to finish fixing up his house.

About ten people were browsing in the store, and every one of them watched him weave his way through the aisles to the shelf in the back. He managed to get the paint he needed, but he was so preoccupied with thoughts of Audrey and his house that he almost ran down Herb Rankin on his way to the checkout counter.

"Conner Hastings, nice to see you." Herb Rankin, better known as "Doc," retreated a step.

"How are things, Doc? I hear you took over your father's practice."

"Two years ago, yes. But then, this would be news to you now, wouldn't it?"

Whether the insult was intentional or not, Conner chose to ignore it. An awkward moment followed.

"You seem to have survived prison just fine. I'm glad to see that, yes." Doc nodded almost absently, his eyes wandering from Conner.

"It's not the kind of experience you want to try, Doc. Believe me."

"No , I suppose not."

Doc had been two years ahead of Conner in school.

Everyone had always known he was going to follow in his father's footsteps someday. He and Conner were about the same height and build, with similar dark brown hair, but the resemblance stopped there. Up close there was no question of who was who. On top of that, Doc dressed in the latest fashions, a habit Conner had never esteemed, much less been able to afford.

"This new business is atrocious." Doc's neck flushed. "You didn't murder that poor girl, did you? No, of course not. We sorely miss her at the center, you know. She was always there when we needed her."

"The center? Is that the new building on Main Street I passed coming in?"

Doc nodded. His eyes lit up. "That was my father's one desire—to build a recreation center for the people in town. He donated the funds for the building the year before he died, you know. We've put it to a different use since then. The senior citizens in the area can have a full day at the center, and if they elect, they can become involved with the day care facility that operates in the left wing. It works out quite well, actually."

"That was generous of your father."

"Ah, yes. Wasn't it?" Doc's eyes focused on some invisible spot to the right.

Conner had always thought of Herb Rankin as an okay guy. Strange sometimes, but okay. It felt good to find someone who believed in his innocence. Based on the hostile looks of the other customers, none of them did. He damn well knew Audrey thought he was guilty. He'd seen the doubt in her eyes. Remembering that hooded, questioning expression in those sea green eyes sent a stab of anguish through his gut so cutting he sucked in his breath to lessen the pain.

"I was sorry to hear what happened to Leona." Conner struggled for normalcy.

"Yes, it was a tragedy. I'm confident justice will be

served." Doc moved aside. "But here I am delaying you. Forgive me. I was on my way out, also."

"No problem, Doc."

They were at the checkout counter, when Doc leaned close and said, "I hear your girlfriend is back. Romantic, really, the sweetheart waiting for her lover to get out of prison."

Something in his tone struck a sour chord in Conner, and he recalled the mad crush Doc had had on Audrey one summer. He formed his words carefully and stated them emphatically. "You're wrong. Audrey is her own person."

"Oh. Well. I apologize. One does tend to presume things."

Outside, Conner loaded the paint in his car and headed home. His mother had sent him some cash when he'd told her he was being released. She'd sounded happy when she called. He probably had her new husband to thank for that.

For the price of one dollar, she'd sold him the house before she left. One dollar—that was about what it was worth. But it had some potential. Even with the trial hanging over his head, he was sticking to his decision to fix it up and put it on the market. The work would keep him sane.

He refused to have his phone connected. No matter which way the jury ruled, he didn't plan to be in the house long enough to need it. Public phones suited him just fine. He stopped at the gas station on the edge of town and slipped his money in the slot to make a call. With his life hanging in the balance, he was going to need Frank Smith's help.

It was still hard to believe his closest friend had left the police force in Richmond and was carving out a successful life as a free-lance investigative reporter. Frank knew everything going on from Fredericksburg to Richmond and down to Tabbs Corner. He was the brother Conner never had. For six years Frank had visited him every few weeks in prison. Not many people had buddies like that. Yet he hadn't heard from Frank since his arrest, and that seemed strange.

When Frank didn't answer the phone, Conner hung up, more confused. Normally, Frank stuck to a rigid schedule. He wrote in the morning and did his field research in the afternoon. Frank should be home. So why wasn't he answering his phone?

Conner returned to his car and continued down the road, his mind wandering in the past just as if it were yesterday. She'd let her hair grow longer, that gorgeous, rich brown hair that turned auburn in the sun. His fingers itched to let the soft, natural curls tease his fingers again. Her deep green eyes held more mystery than before. He would have smiled remembering her sassy comebacks if the pain of regret hadn't been so great. If he had any sense, he would send her packing.

But not even the cold walls of prison could make him stop needing her, wanting her.

Chapter Two

The full moon caressed the beach in a seductive glow. The gentle rhythm of the waves sang of sensuous delights, teasing them, calling them to taste the magic of their love. Conner's arms wrapped her in a cocoon of enchantment. His hands blazed a path of desire over every inch of her body. She yearned for him, ached for him. She explored every part of him. Their tangled bodies sought pleasure and gave pleasure in return. And when their love exploded in a sparkling burst of light, it redefined their world forever.

Audrey threw her purse in the desk drawer and slammed it shut. No wonder she'd been late for work this morning. She couldn't get that blasted dream out of her head. She'd been telling herself since the sun had come up that it didn't hurt to dream a little, as long as she remembered the past was over. But when she tried to dismiss the dream, it clung to her conscious mind, daring her to let it go.

She grabbed some files from the next drawer up and closed it with a bang, mentally demanding the stubborn part of her mind to get the message.

Her efforts were in vain, for when she looked up, the object of her dream was standing in the doorway, leaning against the jamb, one thumb hooked in the belt loop of his jeans. For a fleeting second she thought he had materialized out of her dream, and a trembling excitement coursed through her body.

"You're late." His denigrating tone overpowered the amusement suggested by his stance.

This was no dream. Things had happened and time had passed. This Conner Hastings was not as safe as the Conner of her dreams. Standing there in tight-fitting jeans and a royal blue T-shirt, he was definitely more intriguing, more tempting, more...man than any dream figure.

With an effort of will, she redirected her thoughts. Not about to offer excuses, she answered simply, "Yes, I'm late."

She averted her eyes. Still, she could feel his ever-changing eyes following her movements, as she hung up her jacket and sat behind her desk.

"That presents a problem."

She was glad to have to look at him then, but she regretted it when she did. From deep within sprang a longing to touch, to taste, to feel his body next to hers. She straightened her spine. "What problem?"

He strode to her desk. No doubt he could read her thoughts in her eyes, for his own looked back at her playfully.

"I scheduled several deliveries at the house for late this morning, thinking I'd be finished here in plenty of time."

"We can't afford to play around, Conner. We need to discuss your defense."

"It'll have to wait."

"Wait for what? The trial's in less than two weeks. This is your life we're talking about." Was the man crazy? He acted as though he were postponing a trip to the races.

"We'll have to talk about it this afternoon, that's all."

"I need all the time I can get, Conner."

"Then we'll talk at the house while I wait for the deliveries."

With the dream so near the surface of her thoughts, Au-

drey hesitated to agree. Dealing with him in her office was
bad enough. On his own turf, it would be harder.

"Having second thoughts, Counselor?"

He reached across the desk and touched her cheek.
Slowly his fingers trailed a hot path along her jawline to
her chin.

The effect was scintillating. If ever a man held a woman
captive, it was now.

"Not at all," she insisted.

"Good."

He backed away and paused at the door. Audrey re-
trieved her purse from the desk drawer and rose, then
grabbed her briefcase. The look Conner sent her made her
knees feel weak.

"You're mine, Counselor. Let's go."

AUDREY GOT in her car and thanked heaven she was driving to his house by herself. Yet it felt strange to follow
behind him. He was an ex-convict, a man now accused of
murder—a man who could turn her upside down without
a thought.

The road leading to his house was much worse than it
used to be, with a checkerboard of potholes that made
driving a straight line impossible. A barrage of memories
invaded her mind: picnicking in the woods; studying away
from prying eyes; whitewashing the outside of the house—
and the way she'd collected for her help.

The car's sudden jerk caught her by surprise. She'd
driven right into a pothole the size of a tractor tire. She
eased her way through it and realized Conner's truck had
stopped up ahead. A delivery van was coming toward
them. Conner had left his truck and was talking to the
driver. When he returned to his vehicle, Audrey followed
him into the yard and parked.

"I'll be right there." Conner stepped out onto the road
to guide the van up to his house.

A hot breeze rustled the leaves as she looked around the

yard. She couldn't believe the change. The place was a mess. Broken furniture and split trash bags littered the ground. The weeds were knee-high. The woods, which took up the majority of the property, were crowding into the yard.

"What in the world happened here?" she called to Conner.

As the two workmen lowered the back panel of the van, he came up beside her. The shiver of awareness made her feel weak all over. The sensual pleasures of her dream flooded her imagination.

He looked uneasy as he followed her gaze. "It was never much anyway, but it's mine."

Coming from "the wrong side of the tracks," as he called it, had always bothered him. She shouldn't have said anything.

Don't get personal, she chastised herself. *Remember, you're his attorney, not his guest.*

His house sat on the edge of two acres of land. The surrounding houses, most of them well-kept but well-worn, were scrunched together on smaller lots. The addition of several beat-up trailers down the road hadn't enhanced the area.

"Your mother always kept things pretty nice, Conner."

"Old man Reilly down the road was supposed to be watching the place after she left for Florida. I guess he moved. I haven't seen him. Meanwhile, everybody and his brother has been using it as a dumping ground."

She searched for something positive to say, desperately wanting to set him at ease. She could see where he'd replaced the shingles. The old ones were stacked beside the house, their neatness a sharp contrast to the rest of the landscape. "The roof looks great."

"It's a start."

She felt regret yet tremendous relief when he failed to smile. She couldn't seem to stop wanting what she couldn't have. Being here with him on familiar territory was not helping.

Conner glanced at the workers. "Look, this will take a few minutes."

"Don't worry, I'm fine."

She found an old stump off to the side and used it for a stool, watching as he rolled up his shirtsleeves and helped the men unload several boxes. She was taken with his profile—the high cheekbones from some distant Indian ancestor, a classical nose that had miraculously escaped being broken, eyes the color of a tropical ocean. The man was drop-dead gorgeous, and no amount of wrestling with her mind could slow the frantic beating of her heart.

Thirty minutes later, he led her into the house. Conner headed for the kitchen. Audrey dropped her jacket on the overstuffed chair, put her briefcase down and looked around. There was no clutter in here, like outside, but the room was a drab reminder of the poverty of his youth. The arms of the sofa and chair were worn to threads. The walls were spotted with water leaks, and the wallpaper had faded beyond belief. The short table in front of the couch had lost its finish. Nevertheless, the place was clean.

"What are all those boxes?"

She walked through the L-shaped room to get a closer look. The boxes were piled together in the far corner, where she remembered a dining room table sitting long ago. These walls had been stripped of their paper and painted a soft off-white that made the room look inviting. "Is this computer equipment?"

Conner appeared in the kitchen doorway and handed her a tall glass. "Lemonade, with a twist of lime."

"You remembered."

He lifted her chin and his dark eyes caught and held hers, as if searching for some truth. She felt a moment of panic—there was so much they hadn't discussed. But the momentary panic faded when the fire burning from his touch blocked out any other thought. Raw passion smoldered beneath his intense gaze. She needed to turn away; she wanted to pull back and demand that her body stop responding to this man accused of murder; but she couldn't.

His fingers trailed a sensuous path along her lips before he broke the spell and let her go.

"Nothing personal. Right, Counselor?"

Audrey stumbled back into the living room on legs less than steady. "Right. We have work to do."

She couldn't help it if her voice betrayed the frustration of her body. Intentionally, she chose the chair instead of the sofa. She sipped at her lemonade while she gathered her thoughts. She needed a clear head. He wasn't going to like what she was about to suggest.

"So, how about it, Counselor? How do you plan to keep me out of prison?"

Audrey sucked in a deep breath and plunged ahead. "Lori believes the prosecutor will bargain. Have you considered changing your plea to guilty? It would mean—"

Conner leaped from the couch. Before she knew it, he was across the room, locking her into the chair with his arms. His face was inches away, his breath a sweet mixture of sugar and lemon.

He made no effort to hide his anger. His words came out in a snarl. "I...am...not...guilty."

His anger did wonders for her self-control. She grabbed on to her professional self like a lifeline, refusing to acknowledge her personal doubts about his innocence. "As your attorney, I have an obligation to present you with your options."

"Pleading guilty is not an option."

"Fine. That's certainly your choice."

She was still locked in his gaze. She would not be the first one to look away. If she was ever going to defend him successfully, she needed to reclarify their relationship right now. She would not be intimidated by him. Standing her ground was the only way to counter his overbearing manner. No matter how much she wanted to reach up and stroke his rough face.

Without breaking eye contact, he released his hold on the arms of the chair and stood. "Come up with some other options, Counselor. Somebody murdered Leona. Let that person pay the price."

All thumbs, Audrey searched her briefcase for a notebook, relieved to escape his scrutiny, yet tempted to let his eyes draw her in again. "I'm at a disadvantage here, since I've only just arrived back in town." She crossed her legs and balanced the notebook on her lap. "Who else had a motive to kill her, Conner? Who would benefit?"

He ran his hand through his hair, a gesture that sent her eyes straight down to her notebook.

"She was killed one week and five days after I returned, as you know. And, as you know, I'm not exactly welcome in the gossip circles around town. Your guess is as good as mine. I do know she inherited the family fortune last year." At Audrey's questioning look, he added, "Frank told me."

Frank Smith, a friend from the past. He and Conner must have kept in touch during the past six years, Audrey thought. A tinge of envy surfaced that Frank had been the one to stay in contact and not her.

Audrey recalled that Leona's family owned large tracts of riverfront property, as well as a lot of stock in a nearby paper mill. She made a note to find out more about Leona's inheritance. "I'll research the records. We may need to bring in an outside investigator, too. We don't have much time. I'll check with Lori to see whom the firm usually uses."

She was about to continue, when someone shouted from the yard. Conner strolled to the door, his long gait absorbing her attention. She forced her eyes away and peered out the window. Frank Smith was standing in the middle of the yard. She moved to follow Conner, but stopped at the doorway when she saw Frank's eyes darken as he joined Conner.

Conner reached out to greet Frank with his usual slap on the shoulder, then he drew back, puzzled when his friend pulled away. "What happened? I've been trying to reach you."

"You know what happened—Leona Kingsley." Frank's voice was a mixture of pain and frustration. "I thought you got over being angry at her. Six years is a long time to hold a grudge. I had you pegged a little differently, pal."

"What are you saying? I never held a grudge against the woman. She made me angry as hell and her assumptions were wrong. But I knew six years ago she just told the court what she thought she saw. I never denied being near the convenience store that night. Not six years ago, not now."

Audrey didn't want to hear this. She had enough to worry about with the murder charge. Rehashing the armed-robbery conviction would help no one. Yet there was, of course, a connection. If Leona Kingsley hadn't testified against Conner, he might not be the prime suspect in her murder. Except that Sheriff Parks had identified Conner's gun as the murder weapon.

She focused again on Conner, trying to discern the truth. He was pacing, his eyes as cold as ice. And then he stopped. The curiosity in his face disappeared and a neutral mask slipped into its place. He stared at Frank as if the man were a stranger.

"You think I killed her."

Frank watched him steadily, his eyes searching, questioning. When Conner tried to speak again, Frank cut him off. "You and I have been friends for a long time, old buddy. I have to give you the benefit of a doubt. But for the past few days I've been doing my damnedest to make sense of everything, and it comes down to one basic question—who else wanted Leona dead?"

Conner stepped back. The sunlight hit his face. Audrey

cringed at the pain in his eyes. His jaw clenched in a grip of fury that she could feel from inside the house.

Her heart ached for him. He and Frank had been closer than brothers for years. When Conner got in trouble, Frank was always there to back him up and smooth things over. They stuck together like the best friends they were. It must be killing him to know Frank might have lost faith in him. He would rather lose an arm.

"Is that all you came to say?" Conner's voice was a monotone. He hadn't moved.

Audrey's patience snapped. This had gone on long enough. Conner shouldn't have to endure this abuse from Frank.

She charged out the door. "Stop it, you two." In the space of a heartbeat, they both froze, their shock at her interruption evident.

She shook a pointed finger at Frank. "You have no right to talk as though Conner is guilty. He's innocent unless proven otherwise. Period."

Frank caught her pointing finger and held it tight. His straight, dark hair fell over his forehead and his mouth turned up in a sad grin. "Ah, come on, Audrey. Is that any way to greet an old friend?"

She stood before him, one hand slapped on her hip. "Frank Smith, if you're such a good friend of mine or Conner's, why don't you look into those doubts of yours and stop listening to all the gossip?"

Frank turned to Conner. "She hasn't changed much, has she?"

She'd loved Frank like a brother, too. Before he had left for the police academy, the three of them had seen a lot of one another. Frank's gentle teasing reminded her of better days.

Conner nodded his general acceptance of Frank's comment. Although some of the tension had left his face, he still looked as hard as stone. Having diffused the situation this far, Audrey was determined to smooth it out all the way. She grabbed Frank by the arm. "Come on in and have something cool to drink, and tell us whatever theories are lurking in that probing mind of yours."

After Conner brought drinks from the kitchen, and after Frank offered Conner what served as an apology, they spent a few minutes inspecting the new computer equipment.

The adrenaline brought on from her anger at Frank had subsided. As they sat down to talk, she attributed her outburst to habit. She and Conner had been an inseparable couple for four years before she'd left Tabbs Corner. Her grandfather had threatened daily to kick her out of the house if she didn't break off with him. There was no future with him, her friends had warned—and they'd been right. Yet back then she'd defended their relationship whenever challenged. Old habits died hard, she told herself, clenching her hand.

"Somebody stands to inherit a lot of property," Conner was saying.

"It sounds like a viable motive to me." Frank rubbed his chin in thought.

"What was she doing with herself? Who were her friends? Who worked for her over the past year? If nothing else, you can lay that out for us." Conner's earnest interest in clearing himself held Frank's attention.

His enthusiasm caught Audrey. "You could save us a lot of time by running the names through the police files once we have them," she remarked.

"Frank's not a cop anymore," said Conner.

Audrey turned to Frank, her enthusiasm dampened. "You're not? What happened?"

"That's a separate story." Frank's eyes wandered. "But don't worry. I still have my contacts."

"Frank's a free-lance investigative reporter now. If anybody can dig out some answers, he can."

"Right." Frank shifted uncomfortably in the wake of Conner's praise and refocused the conversation on Leona.

"Maybe we should ask around about her marriage, too. She and Bull split, you know."

"What?" Audrey and Conner expressed equal surprise.

"I don't think it was a legal separation," Frank continued. "Leona kicked him out about five months ago. I heard she was sleeping around, but I never caught any names. That was a while back, too, so I may be behind in my facts."

"It could also be why they separated." Audrey's mind spun with possibilities.

"Maybe, but Bull's no angel, either." Frank paused, as if trying to remember something. "She was still living in that big house her grandfather built on the Piankatank."

"That's a beautiful place." Audrey remembered it clearly.

The Piankatank River was south of the Rappahannock and much smaller, more private. Audrey pictured Leona's gorgeous home set atop a hill, with its lovely terraced gardens in full bloom all summer. When she and Conner had had a whole day to themselves, they used to spend the morning fishing around Stove Point Neck, then cruise up the peaceful Piankatank past Leona's family home, and fantasize about their future. The water, the small boat, Conner standing at the helm, guiding them through a fantasy wonderland, were so real that Audrey now found herself digging her nails into her palms to bring herself back to reality.

"That's where they found her body—down the hill from her house."

Frank's comment flattened the fantasy. She knew where they'd found Leona's body, but hearing it said aloud shocked her all the same.

"I can't picture Leona taking care of that big place by herself." She forced her hands to relax.

Conner nodded. "Neither can I."

Frank set down his glass. "Leona probably did hire outside help. I also heard she was organizing a fund-raising campaign to raise money for a swimming pool at the center. Which gives us two more angles to work on."

Audrey gasped. She couldn't help it, the sound just escaped. Mention of the center took her off guard.

Conner and Frank looked at her strangely. No doubt they would know her secret before long. As soon as her brother returned from the mountains. The thought brought on another kind of tension.

She purposely ignored their curiosity and pretended she hadn't been ready to jump out of her skin. "That's the new building on Main Street, the one that doesn't match anything else."

"That's right. Audrey, are you okay? You look a little pale." When Audrey nodded he turned his attention to Conner. "You know what I really want to find out? How the hell did your gun get involved in this? If it wasn't for that damn gun..."

Audrey saw Conner stiffen, and spoke up before things regressed. "We don't know, but we intend to find out. If we can prove someone stole Conner's gun, we've got a chance."

"I agree." Frank nodded. "Did old man Reilly see anyone snooping around?"

Conner hadn't totally relaxed, but the anger had left his eyes. "I can't find him."

"You're kidding." Frank appeared truly amazed. "That old man has lived his entire life within a thirty-mile radius of Tabbs Corner. Somebody must have seen him."

"Nobody I've talked to."

"Based on the condition of the property, I'd say quite a few people trespassed after Conner's mother left." Audrey recalled the scattered trash. "They could have easily broken into the house and taken the gun."

"Then we keep looking for Ben Reilly." Frank leaned back on the sofa. "Let's consider the possibilities for a minute. What have we got?"

Audrey picked up her notebook and listed the options

they'd discussed. "Leona's wealth could have provided someone with a motive to kill her. Conner and I can follow through on that. I'm curious to see who the legal heir is, especially since she was estranged from her husband."

"And we'll talk to the neighbors again," Conner added. "Maybe someone will finally remember seeing old man Reilly. Even if we find him, chances are slim he'll be of much help. No one can watch a house twenty-four hours a day."

Frank strolled to the door. "I've been out of town for the past week, so it'll take a few days to catch up on the gossip. But I'll definitely see what I can find out about Leona Kingsley's life." He turned to Audrey. "You were right, Audrey. I need to check into every possibility before jumping to conclusions. Three or four days should do it. Are you staying at the cottage?" After her confirmation he added, "I'll call you."

Conner followed him to the door. "Anything you find might help."

Frank slapped him on the back. "We'll work this out, old buddy. Don't worry."

With Frank gone, Conner began pacing. To think of him as a vulnerable, lost soul was ridiculous, because he didn't look that way at all. He looked tempting and alluring, especially with his thick, dark hair, which just touched his collar, brushed back. But his face was so pale. She wondered if it would have a chance to tan before they sent him back to prison.

His stormy eyes had darkened and now hid his emotions. The muscles in his arms bunched as he clenched his fists, an obvious sign of tension. Still, he paced with an authority that declared he was in control of his life.

Every fiber of her being longed to console him, to put her arms around him and feel his heart beating next to hers. She wanted to see the laughter return to his eyes and hear the teasing in his voice, yet she had to stay objective.

She had to keep her personal feelings out of matters. Maintaining her distance was the only answer.

She returned her notebook to her briefcase and rose to leave. Conner came up behind her and put his hand on her shoulder. He smelled of the woods, fresh and clean. Her body burned with needs long forgotten.

"Audrey..."

His voice shattered the moment, thank goodness. She pulled away and fought for some semblance of control. Swallowing the knot in her throat, she walked quickly to the door without turning around. She couldn't. One more look at him and she'd be lost.

She dug deeply to find the professionalism she needed. "I'll see you tomorrow."

As she drove away from his house, her hands clutching the steering wheel, she fervently prayed that Conner was not a killer. He just couldn't be.

Chapter Three

Conner picked up a three-legged table and threw it into the trash pile with a vengeance. In spite of the hurricane warnings, the sun burned hot on his bare back, like the fever burning inside him. He had tried setting up his new computer. He'd cleaned up the packing mess. Nothing seemed to douse the fire Audrey had ignited.

For six years her image had kept him alive. The fantasy of holding her again had dominated his thoughts. How could he ever forget the smell of heather in her hair, the softness of her breasts pressed against him, the very feel of her in his arms? But Audrey McKenna was strictly off-limits—now, tomorrow, forever. She deserved better than an ex-convict. Knowing that didn't stop him from wanting her, though, and the thought of her in his bed, in his life, was more than he could bear.

A slight crunch of gravel registered somewhere in his mind as he hefted an empty oil drum into the pile.

"I seen you was back."

He didn't recognize the voice, but there was no mistaking the round face and unkempt blond hair. "My God, boy, you've grown up since I last saw you. You must be, what, twelve years old by now? Holy cow."

"Be thirteen next month." Ernie Covington raised his chin as if it would make him taller.

Conner wiped the dirt from his hands and shook Ernie's
hand. "So, how's your mom and your brother?"

"Mom's okay. She's still working down at the Laundro-
mat. Billy got hisself a job at the gas station."

"All right, good for him."

Jenny Covington was not much older than he was, Conner recalled. To think she had two boys, twelve and fifteen,
was unbelievable. Her husband had run out on her when
Ernie was only a baby, and she'd been living in a trailer
across the road, struggling to make ends meet, ever since.

"I do yard work, you know." Ernie's voice cracked as
he spoke.

"Do you, now?"

"Looks like you could use some help."

Getting used to Ernie as a young man was taking some
effort. What he remembered was this little kid tagging
along behind him everywhere he went. Jenny had let Conner take Ernie fishing when the boy had turned five. And
then there was the time Conner had let him shoot his rifle.
They'd bagged a deer that day. Jenny had been so excited
to get a whole season of food that she'd hugged him and
cried, something that embarrassed Conner even now.

Conner took a deep breath and realized that some of the
sizzling tension he'd felt when Audrey had been at the
house had dissipated. Thank God. Maybe now he could
function better.

He surveyed the yard, a slight smile on his face. "I think
you're right. You wouldn't have some time available this
afternoon to help me, would you? As long as you let me
pay you, of course. This is hard work. I couldn't let you
do it for nothing."

Ernie's pleased expression broke down into a frown.
"Mom wouldn't like me taking money from you."

"Hey, sport, I'd rather pay you than give it to somebody
else. I can't do all this by myself."

The boy's pale blue eyes widened as he glanced around

the yard. "Yeah, I can see that. Okay, yeah, sure. I'll help you."

Ernie's chunky body was all muscle, Conner discovered quickly, and having his help was the best thing that could've happened to him this afternoon. Thoughts of Audrey faded to an uncomfortable ache as he and Ernie worked in relative silence. In that respect Ernie hadn't changed—he'd never been a talker.

Conner grabbed the last piece of large furniture from behind an oak tree. The yellowed stuffing from the upholstered chair littered the woods like clumps of used snow, and Conner made a mental note to have Ernie pick up the stuffing the next time he came. Right now the sun was so low in the sky Conner knew it was time to quit.

He looked around at the yard, satisfied he'd done all he could to prepare for the hurricane creeping up the coast. Anything he'd missed, he'd take care of tomorrow.

"The next step is to load the junk into the back of the truck so we can take it to the dump. But not today," he told the boy.

Ernie left, and an unusual loneliness settled over Conner. Seeing the boy had resurrected his greatest regret. At one time, he'd looked forward to having his own kids—his and Audrey's. But after the devastating turn his life took six years ago, he knew it would never happen. Audrey was the only woman he'd want to have children with, and that possibility had been snatched from him forever.

He fixed himself something to eat and ate his dinner, all the while trying to push Audrey from his mind. But everything he did, everything he touched, stirred up more memories, like the lemonade in the refrigerator with the lime beside it. The five hours he spent setting up his computer were no better. He used more energy trying to force her image from his mind than he used connecting his equipment. Finally, exhausted from the emotional strain, he called it a night, knowing that in his dreams he could relinquish the battle.

AUDREY PULLED UP beside Conner's house late the next afternoon. Researching the settlement of Leona's estate had gone more quickly than she would have thought, thanks to the file clerk. Mrs. Bracken had also given her some other information that could prove to be even more relevant. Before she shared it, though, she needed to verify it.

Spotting Conner coming down the road, she noted the broad shoulders and slim waist that fit so perfectly with his long, masculine stride. The wind tousled his hair as he joined her in the yard.

"My life would be a whole lot easier if you would get a phone, Conner."

"Why? I would have missed seeing your beautiful face."

The smile that touched his lips made Audrey's stomach flutter. She ignored the teasing compliment and brought her thoughts back to business.

"Climb in. We're going to visit the woman who inherited most of Leona's estate."

He slid into her car and closed the door. "You've been busy."

"Most of the information I wanted is a matter of public record," she stated, turning toward the main road. "Of course, a few discreet inquiries helped, too. Evidently, passing down the land through the female side of the family is a tradition in the Lansing family. A cousin inherited the majority of her estate."

"I didn't know Leona had a cousin."

The surprised look on his face reminded her of an earlier Conner, a young man who had had no prison record, one who had taken each day as it came until she'd convinced him to enroll in a nearby community college.

She slammed on the brakes a little too hard at the stop sign and willed herself to halt the reel of memories intruding on her thoughts. She couldn't afford to be distracted from Conner's defense. Nevertheless, the film continued to roll through her mind as if it had a will of its own.

"Her cousin's name is Ida May Lansing. She lives not too far from here."

"I don't know her."

"There's no reason you should. She's in her forties, lives by herself on several acres in Hartfield. The file clerk at the courthouse knew something about her, a Mrs. Bracken, a nice, older lady who said she's lived here all her life."

"I remember Mrs. Bracken. My mother used to talk about her."

"She thinks Ida May is Leona's second or third cousin on her mother's side and that she bought the farm in Hartfield about ten years ago."

"I'd bet the shirt off my back Leona's will didn't make Bull Kingsley very happy."

The thought of Conner stripped to the waist was one worth savoring. Yet Audrey blinked the image away. She didn't want to see Conner half-naked. She didn't want to see him at all except as a client to defend. There was no possibility of a personal relationship here. He'd hurt her too badly in the past to risk that pain again. She needed to concentrate on making a good life for herself, not on past mistakes.

"According to Mrs. Bracken," she said, "Bull stormed into city hall wanting to know who had forged Leona's will. Bull claims Leona left everything to him, but that's not the case. He did inherit the house, the property it sits on and most of the money. Ida May inherited the paper-mill stock and the riverfront properties, mainly because of the way Leona's mother set up the paperwork before she herself died."

"Hmm. If Bull really believed he inherited everything, that gives him a solid motive. But if he knew about the cousin, I don't think he'd want Leona dead before he convinced her to make some changes."

"My thoughts exactly. But if Ida May believed Leona

might change her will or find a way to get around what was already in place, that gives her a solid motive, too."

Conner stretched against the back of his seat, his arms behind his head, the T-shirt taut across his broad chest. "This is getting complicated."

Audrey kept her eyes glued to the road. "I think you have a real ally in Mrs. Bracken. She was really anxious to tell me anything that would help you. She said Leona's death is a real loss to the town."

"Mrs. Bracken always went to the restaurant where my mother worked. They became pretty good friends over the years."

"She told me all this gossip about Leona and how she'd just reneged on two real estate deals." Audrey turned onto Ida May's long drive. "Unfortunately, we were interrupted before she could give me any names. It's a bit farfetched, but we may have two more suspects to add to the list."

She parked in front of the house beside a new Cadillac Seville and pocketed her keys, then caught Conner's arm before he opened his door. "Let me do the talking."

Conner grinned and Audrey melted a notch.

"Whatever you say, Counselor."

She loved the dimple that showed itself when he smiled. Heaven help her, she would always love it.

"That's what I say," she replied quickly, and stepped from the car.

They reached the porch and Conner took her arm. "Watch out for the broken step."

Ida May's small porch fronted an old, two-story farmhouse plunked down on the edge of acres of wilted-looking cornfields. The outside of the house needed a fresh coat of paint and the porch boards were falling apart.

Ida May opened the door. "You must be Audrey McKenna." She glanced at Conner. "And you..." She rounded on Audrey. "I cannot believe you brought *him* with you."

Audrey flinched at yet another attack on Conner. "Yes, I understand that. May we come in?"

Ida May's back stiffened. Her nose shot up a notch. "Certainly not. I have no intention of inviting my cousin's murderer into my home."

"I'll wait in the car." Conner left before Audrey could offer a consoling glance. Even though his tone of voice was gruff, she had to admit he'd handled the rejection courteously, something he wouldn't have done when he was younger.

"I want that man off my property." Ida May demanded compliance. Her eyes followed Conner as he walked toward the car.

"I'll take care of it." Audrey hurried from the house to catch up with him.

She reached him at her car. "There's no sense in you waiting. Why don't you go on?" She handed him the keys to the vehicle.

"I'd like to know what the woman says." He spoke gruffly.

"Then wait for me at the end of the drive."

He looked at her closely. "All right." His voice was cold. He still stung from Ida May's rudeness.

Audrey turned back toward the house and saw Ida May watching them from the doorway, before the woman redirected her attention to a handyman rounding the corner. Audrey reached the house just as Ida May was issuing instructions.

"You might as well start with all the branches that have fallen." She indicated several problems.

The old man shuffled away.

Ida May let out a sigh of disgust when she noticed Audrey. "I suppose we might as well get this over with."

She turned from the door, leaving it open for Audrey to follow her in. Audrey caught a glimpse of an emerald ring set in old gold that covered half an index finger.

She was glad she'd handled the preliminaries of condolences and explanations on the phone. Ida May Lansing was not what she'd expected. At a glance, one might describe her as elegant, sophisticated. Tall and lithe, she wore an expensive-looking cream-colored suit with matching heels and delicate pearl earrings, but the style was way out-of-date. Her dyed hair swept up in stiff wisps, and on inspection gave the impression of a mannequin's wig.

Ida May sat on the edge of a wingback chair in what looked like a former parlor. Audrey was surprised to see the blue velvet upholstery sun-bleached along the back and threadbare on the arms. The rest of the room matched the chair's shabbiness.

Ida May scowled at her. "You have some nerve bringing that man here."

Her haughty voice was in keeping with her surprising appearance, Audrey noted.

"I wasn't trying to offend you, Ida May. Conner is innocent until proven guilty. With his life at stake I feel he has a right to participate in the preparation of his defense, if that's what he prefers."

She diplomatically avoided mentioning that Conner would stick with his not-guilty plea at the trial. There was no point in alienating Ida May further. Obviously, she'd already made up her mind about his guilt. Unless she was hiding something.

The woman raised herself higher in the chair, her posture stiff. "What is so important that couldn't be handled on the phone? I really have no time for this."

"I'll be brief, Ida May. Were you close to your cousin?"

"What is this? An inquisition?"

"No, no, not at all. You see, I didn't really know Leona." Audrey spoke in the warmest tone she could muster and kept her eyes on Ida May. "I'm trying to learn more about her, that's all."

"Well, I don't like it one bit."

"I don't blame you." Audrey paused for effect. "I

would feel the same way in your situation. Did you see Leona very often?"

Ida May interlaced her fingers in her lap. "From time to time." She frowned. "I wasn't welcome in Bull Kingsley's house. Can you believe that? My own grandparents' home, and I wasn't welcome."

"You didn't get along with Bull."

"He didn't get along with me, and I know why. You see, I know he married Leona for her money."

"What makes you think that?"

"Do you know Bull Kingsley?"

"No, I've never met him."

"Consider yourself lucky. He's uncouth and surly. I don't think he's put in an honest day's work in his life. Why, if the sheriff didn't have the goods on Conner Hastings, I'd have no doubt that Bull murdered my cousin in cold blood. He's certainly capable of it."

Audrey added one more strike against Bull Kingsley as a viable suspect.

"Did you tell Leona how you felt?"

"I tried. She wouldn't listen to me. She had her own way of thinking. I am the oldest living Lansing left. The oldest has always held the position of authority."

Audrey caught the resentment in her voice. "I understand you've inherited Leona's vast real estate holdings."

"Yes, as is my due. Property rights have been handed down through the female side of my family for several generations."

"Forgive me for sounding so stupid. I'm just trying to understand. If you're the oldest, why did Leona inherit before you? Shouldn't the property have been passed on to you?"

"You are absolutely right. I am so glad to find someone who understands."

"What happened?"

"The fault of birth. My mother was an unwed teenager when she became pregnant with me. Grandmother was a cranky old woman. She never forgave my mother for refusing to marry my father. She claimed my mother publicly humiliated her, so she broke with tradition and altered her will to leave everything to her youngest daughter, Leona's mother."

"I can see why you would resent that."

Audrey decided a little baiting might produce some results, and she hadn't forgiven Ida May for being rude to Conner. "Did you know Leona was considering changing her will and leaving everything to her husband?"

Ida May's gasp was audible, though she tried to hide it. "The idea is preposterous. Leona wouldn't have broken with tradition."

Audrey wasn't about to point out that Leona would have been following the precedent set by her grandmother.

"When was the last time you saw her?" Audrey carefully observed the way Ida May lowered her eyes.

"Let me think. I'd guess five or six months before she was murdered."

"So, possibly you might not know about a new will."

"Leona had every intention of divorcing that man. She wouldn't have cut me out. I'm her only cousin, for heaven's sake." Ida May stood. "I really must end our talk. If you have no further questions, I'll show you to the door."

Audrey followed and noticed the suitcases semiobscured in the dining room. With a big, friendly smile, she said, "You must be going on a trip. How exciting."

"Yes, isn't it?" Reserved hesitation entered Ida May's voice. She opened the front door. "My travel agent assures me he can book me on a cruise to the islands within the week. Perhaps even tomorrow."

"How nice."

Yes, how nice, thought Audrey. And convenient. If Ida May had any part in her cousin's murder, she would be difficult to reach in the islands.

Audrey paused by the door. "By the way. I understand you already sold that one hundred acres on the other side of town to the Peeble Corporation for development. Isn't that the parcel of land Leona promised to donate to the town?''

Ida May cut into her with a glare. ''My business is none of your concern.''

Oh, yes, it is, Audrey thought, smiling as she slipped through the doorway. She turned around, but before she had a chance to thank Ida May for her time, the door slammed in her face.

CONNER STOPPED drumming his fingers on the steering wheel the minute he saw Audrey strolling down the drive. Her radiant smile matched her quick step. In spite of his lingering anger at Ida May's slap in the face, he felt his mouth curl in a smile.

Audrey hopped into the car, all freshness and heather, and he eased onto the road. ''I take it you had a successful interview.'' The rosy glow in her cheeks fascinated him.

''It was a hundred times better than I expected.''

Encouraged by her enthusiasm, he urged her on. ''So tell me.''

As she summarized the meeting, he listened for the twist that would explain her excitement. Hearing none, he felt his spirits drop.

''I find it odd that she's going to the islands at this particular time. I would think she would want to be here for the trial.'' Audrey's voice was as animated as before.

Conner turned the car to the right and let out a sigh of regret. ''Audrey, I hate to burst your bubble, but so far I haven't heard you say anything that could help the case. So the woman's going to the islands. Big deal. After her reaction to me, she must figure the trial is only a formality.''

Audrey reached across the seat and grasped his shoulder, as if she knew that the touch of her hand could stop his downward slide. Eyebrows arched over sparkling eyes. ''There's something else.'' She told him about the hundred-acre land deal. "Ida May never confirmed the deal, understand. This is based strictly on rumor and instinct. But I couldn't believe her negative reaction."

"So you hit a sore spot when you brought it up."

"Definitely. She was livid. She actually slammed the door in my face."

He would expect Audrey to be insulted, but she actually looked pleased. There was even a touch of mischief in her deep green eyes.

"Why would she sell that land? How did she find a buyer so quickly?"

"Someone must have been waiting in the wings." Conner tried to guess in which direction her sharp mind was going.

"Doesn't that make you wonder why? If Leona had turned down an offer—which, according to Mrs. Bracken, she had—and she'd already agreed to donate the land to the town, why didn't the developers find another location?"

Her excitement charged the very air around them. She made him feel so alive. But he gave up trying to follow her logic. "You tell me."

"I think Ida May knew she was going to inherit the Lansing properties. She knew she would get title to that land."

Her words stunned him. "You think she killed Leona?"

"She certainly had a motive. She'll be a rich woman once she sells her inheritance."

Conner felt a spark of hope ignite deep inside.

"And another thing. When I told her Leona was thinking about changing her will, she adamantly refused to consider it was a possibility."

Conner finally realized the logic behind her excitement. "Maybe Bull was right. Maybe there is another will. And maybe Ida May found out what her cousin was up to."

"If that was the case, she'd put a stop to it before she was robbed of her rightful inheritance."

Her comment hung in the air as he pulled up in front of his house. Conner suddenly felt very awkward. Their suspicions could prove to be unfounded. The hope he clung to could quickly be lost. Only Audrey's belief in possibilities kept him from going crazy.

Feeling a tenderness toward her he didn't dare show, he rested his arm across the top of the seat and let his fingertips lightly touch her windblown curls.

"You did good today, Counselor."

He was about to say more, when a black Acura stopped on the road by his house. Ernie Covington got out on the passenger side and waved to him.

Conner frowned when he couldn't see the driver through the darkened windows. "I wonder who that is." He opened the door and got out.

He knew plenty of new residents could have moved into the area in the past six years, people he wouldn't know, but he also knew darkened front windows were illegal in the state of Virginia.

"Hey, Conner." Ernie shoved some money in his pocket as he came closer. He smiled at Audrey as she joined them in the yard.

"This is Audrey." Conner kept his voice pleasant. "She knew you when you were younger."

"I remember you." Ernie's blond hair tumbled down his face.

"You've grown awfully tall since I last saw you." Audrey shook his hand. "You're almost all grown up."

Ernie blushed and looked up at Conner. "Want me to work on your yard now?"

Conner watched the Acura drive away, then zeroed in on Ernie. "Who was that?" His patience was wearing thin.

"I don't know." The boy shrugged. "Just some guy."

"You don't know who he is? Then why were you in his car?"

"That's the good part." Ernie beamed and pulled a fistful of bills from his pocket, oblivious to Conner's rising anger. "I was down at the gas station with my brother. This guy pulls in and says he'll give me twenty-five bucks to deliver a package to Mr. Bull Kingsley."

Bull Kingsley? "And?"

"So I did." Ernie watched Conner from the corner of his eye as he tucked the money away.

"Ernie." Conner placed his hands on the boy's shoulders and hoped that what he said got through. "We get a lot of strangers through here at this time of year. If you don't know somebody, you don't do him favors, you don't take his money and you sure as shootin' don't get in a car with him."

"But..."

"No buts." Conner forced back his anger. "Understand?"

"I guess."

"I mean it. I don't want you getting into any trouble."

Ernie stared at him with wide eyes and a resigned face. "Can I keep the money?"

Conner didn't know if he wanted to throttle the boy or hug him. "You can keep the money. Now, how about earning some more loose change by cleaning up the remains of that chair over there in the woods?"

Ernie looked where he pointed. "You got it." They slapped hands. "I'll do a good job, too."

"I know you will. Go on inside and get yourself a soda, then you can get to work. I'll be through here in a minute."

He waited until Ernie reached the house before speaking. "Why in the hell would some stranger want a kid to deliver a package to Leona's husband?"

"That's a good question." She gazed at him as though she didn't know him. "Did you notice the dark windows? The man didn't want anyone to see him. That much was obvious."

"Yeah, and the muddy plates. I'd like to know what was in that package. Have you seen a black Acura around town?"

"You're asking the wrong person."

"Maybe Frank will know who owns it." He hoped Ernie would take his advice and stay away from strange people with mysterious packages to deliver.

"I need to get back to the office." Audrey moved toward the driver's side of her car.

Conner shook off his concern for Ernie and followed.

She paused by the fender. "I'd like to know where Ida May was the night Leona was killed."

"Why don't we ask her?"

"Oh, we will. We know she had a motive. She very likely had the opportunity. But how do we connect her with your gun?"

The evidence against him still stung. "She could have been the one who stole it. Or maybe she had help. I say we keep an eye on her. See how she reacts to our visit."

"That's an excellent idea. I doubt she'll do anything today, though. It's almost dark, and the weatherman is sure that hurricane moving up the coast will be here sooner or later."

"Then tomorrow." Conner was anxious to follow any lead. "If it's not here by tomorrow, we can hit her place early."

Audrey turned away abruptly and jumped in the car. "Not tomorrow." Her voice was sharp. "I'm tied up tomorrow."

"I see."

But as she started the car and squealed out of the yard, Conner knew he didn't see at all. What had just happened? Why was she suddenly in such a big rush to leave?

Chapter Four

Audrey came out of the grocery store Saturday morning and found all four of her tires slashed.

"Oh, no!" She circled her car to make sure her eyes weren't deceiving her.

The freckle-faced clerk gaped at her car. "Ma'am, if you'll keep hold of the basket, I'll go call somebody to help you."

Audrey grabbed the second grocery cart. "I'd appreciate that. Do you know that old garage outside of town?"

"Yes, ma'am. James lets me help him on my days off. He the one you want? We got a new gas station that's closer."

Actually, that was where she'd left her car on her first day in town, but those people were very slow. With Peter due back from the mountains late this afternoon, she didn't have time to waste. "I'd rather you call James."

The clerk returned to the store to make the call. Audrey let out a sigh of exasperation and unlocked her trunk to load the groceries and the box of bottled water.

The day was turning into a series of minor catastrophes. First the well pump had broken; now her tires were flat. And from the looks of the sky and the feel of the wind, the hurricane could hit before nightfall. Whatever else was going to go wrong, she hoped it happened soon. Once Peter got back, he would insist on taking care of all these little problems for her, and the last thing she wanted was to begin her new life dependent on her brother.

James arrived twenty minutes later. He climbed down from his truck, and Audrey saw he was as short as she remembered, with a little less hair. His smile was still friendly, his manner somewhat shy.

He looked at her tires. "Got yourself a problem, I see."

"It's good to see again, James."

Audrey had to smile at the man. He was much more comfortable around cars than people. Still, their history dated back to the time that he'd fixed race cars for Conner and Frank.

"I heard you'd moved back." He stooped low and examined the next tire.

Frank came around from the side of James's truck and joined him. "How'd this happen, Audrey?"

"Somebody slashed them." James peered more closely at a cut.

"Frank, I don't believe you're here."

"I was at the garage checking on my race car, when the clerk called, so I thought I'd drive over with James to take a look."

"You're still racing?" Audrey pushed back her wind-blown hair.

Frank actually blushed. During the time she'd dated Conner, the two of them had to put up with her complaints about their racing.

"Not exactly. James found a driver for me. He's been trying out my car on that track down the road."

"Boy, somebody did a total job on those tires," James declared.

"You don't think this could be related to Conner's case, do you?" Sincere concern softened Frank's frown.

Audrey felt a chill up her spine, but logic overcame her emotional reaction. "Let's hope not. More than likely it was some kids who came down for the weekend to sail and got bored with the windy weather."

"Give me a hand with these new tires, will you, Frank?"

Audrey watched as they unloaded the tires and the equipment and carried them to her car.

Frank took her aside when he finished helping James. "My next stop was your place. I wanted to bring you up-to-date." He hiked himself up onto the bed of the truck.

Audrey propped her arms along the flatbed's side, anxious to hear Frank's progress. "I'm listening."

"I talked to a few people who work at the country club Leona belonged to, the fancy one in Tappahannock. Came away with some juicy stuff." He wiggled his eyebrows and smiled. "Leona was definitely having an affair, but she never brought the guy to the club."

"They don't know who it was?"

"No, but I have a few out-of-the-way places to check yet, places that don't list their numbers in the phone book."

Leave it to Frank, she thought, as James carried a flat tire past them and tossed it into the truck.

"I also spent half a day at the center talking to anybody and everybody. The old-timers are really upset about Leona's murder."

Audrey's pulse hit a hard beat at mention of the center.

"I had this one weird conversation with an old woman who looked about ninety. She wanted to know if Leona left Doc everything like the others."

"That's an odd thing to say."

"I thought so, too, until she said she didn't have time to talk to me anymore—she had to go meet with Leona about the swimming pool plans."

"Oh, the poor thing." Audrey remembered how illogical her aunt had become before she died. "Her mind must be slipping."

"Several of the seniors had fuzzy minds, but they all loved Leona. They wanted to tell me everything they could. They talked about Della Andrews, the woman who runs the day school for the kids. According to several regulars, she and Leona were always at each other's throats."

"About what?"

"Nobody seemed to know. I introduced myself to Della and asked about Leona. She talked about Leona's wonderful ideas and her skill at fund-raising, but I didn't pick up a clue to what they argued about."

"Doc Rankin might know." Audrey remembered reading that Doc took care of the medical needs at the center.

"Yeah, I thought of that. I made an appointment with him for this afternoon."

"Conner and I paid a visit to Ida May Lansing." She filled him in on the details and told him about her suspicions.

"Sounds like she could have had a real, live motive."

James tossed two more dead tires into the truck. "I'll be through here in just a minute." He lumbered back to Audrey's car.

Frank nodded and continued. "There's one other thing. Did you know Bull Kingsley was pushing for a reconciliation with Leona? That's what this girl said who works in the office where Leona worked."

"Boy, you covered a lot of ground."

"But Stacy—that was her name—Stacy didn't think Leona would go for it. She said even if Leona wanted to get back together, she wouldn't have done it because of Bull's shady deals."

"What shady deals? Is he involved in something illegal?" She thought of the black Acura and the mysterious package Ernie had been paid to deliver to Bull.

"Not that I know of. She said Leona was afraid Bull would—how did she put it—eat up all her money and leave her with nothing but scraps. That's when Della Andrews interrupted us and hauled Stacy away to help her move something. I don't think Stacy knew anything else anyway."

"Bull's the one who found her body, you know."

"That's what I heard. I think there's a lot more on Leona that hasn't surfaced yet. I'll keep digging, but it wouldn't hurt for you and Conner to hunt down Bull Kingsley."

"We'll do that."

James walked to the truck loaded down with equipment.

"Hold on, James. I'll help you with that stuff." Frank patted Audrey's shoulder. "Don't worry. We're making progress. I'll get back to you on Monday or Tuesday."

But as Audrey helped them clean up around the car, she knew she didn't feel as optimistic as Frank. To bring in a not-guilty verdict, they had to find the real killer. She just wasn't sure they could do that in the week they had left.

AUDREY DROVE HOME and felt her heart crash against her ribs when she saw Conner's battered blue truck parked behind the cottage.

This couldn't be happening, she told herself as she slammed out of the car. Not today. She had too much to think about before she saw him again. And Peter would be furious when he found out she was defending Conner. She didn't want Conner around when her brother arrived.

She found Conner in the well pump pit on the side of the house. "What do you think you're doing?"

The noon sun edging around the clouds glanced off his dark, almost black, hair as he looked up to answer her. "Your pump's broken."

"Yes, I know." Did he think she was blind?

He stooped lower to examine the pump and she caught her breath. His forest green T-shirt stretched tightly across his back. Those rippling muscles...

"It needs a valve. I think I've got one in the back of my truck."

He literally sprang out of the pit, his body as agile as ever, and started searching the toolbox in the bed of his truck. Audrey closed her eyes and took a deep breath. Already she could feel her body responding to this man. Already her heart beat faster and her legs felt shaky.

"Conner, I can fix the pump. You don't need to do this."

"Here we go."

He held out a rusty valve for her inspection. He was so close she could smell his mint-flavored breath. She wanted to slip her arm around his waist and pull him closer. She couldn't stop herself from letting her fingers brush his when she reached for the valve. Such brief contact shouldn't cause the delicious tingling up her arm.

Quickly she withdrew her hand, under the pretext of examining the valve. Giving in to these personal impulses had to stop. "Will it work? It looks awfully old."

She was too close to miss the devilish gleam in his deep blue eyes. He knew what he did to her.

"It'll hold for a while." He winked. "But you need to replace it with a new one."

She could have bought one when she'd gone into town, but the only thing she knew about pumps and wells had to do with the end result—water from the spigot. She wasn't about to admit this to Conner. "I'll take care of it."

"No doubt in my mind."

He reached for the valve and captured her hand in his. She wanted to retrieve her hand, but hesitated. One look at his face made her feel weaker than a kitten. The need shining through the shadows in his eyes made her heart explode with desire. He wanted her. Plain and simple. And right now she wanted him more than he could ever know.

He relinquished her hand, only to pull her close. His lips caught hers in a white-hot frenzy—unyielding, demanding, like the man himself. Their tongues tangled in a dance of passion, plunging, seeking, needing. Sweet, hot passion turned every feeling into pure need.

She tore herself away and fought for control. "That can't happen again, Conner. Not if we're going to work together."

He stepped back, a sharp glint in his eye. "No. Of

course not." A hard edge tinged his voice. "But then you didn't exactly mind, did you, Counselor?"

"We need to stick to business."

He stared at her, and his gaze was unsettling.

"You are absolutely right. Strictly business."

After another long moment he turned back to the pit and said over his shoulder, "But if you want to hear the latest, I expect that business to include some of those crabs out back."

"I forgot!" She ran toward the back of the house. She'd left a big pot of crabs slowly steaming outside on the propane stove when she'd driven to the store. They would be overcooked by now.

"Don't worry," he called from the pit. "I turned off the burner and drained them."

She came to a halt, but not before registering the humor in his voice. Audrey felt none of his amusement. She felt caught between a rock and hard place. Conner couldn't stay, but she couldn't very well tell him to leave after he'd saved the crabs and fixed the pump. Besides, she wanted to hear what had brought him here in the first place.

She carried the groceries inside and checked the clock to make sure her watch was right. There was just enough time for him to eat lunch and leave before Peter returned. As long as she didn't let him linger.

He finished with the pump as she put the last item on the shelf. "Grab those newspapers." She pointed to the rack. "We'll eat outside."

"I'll carry the crabs around."

Sitting out front under the tree while they talked would be much easier than staying inside. Rational thinking around Conner was difficult enough without being enclosed in a small room with him for any length of time.

She mixed some lemonade and sliced a lime. She put the utensils they would need in her pocket, picked up the fresh loaf of bakery bread and two beers and carried everything out to the picnic table that overlooked the creek.

She sat down on the opposite bench and handed Conner a beer.

"I thought you'd rather have this than lemonade."

"Looks like we both have good memories."

And there it was—that dimpled smile she loved so much. Her arms felt like limp spaghetti and she almost dropped her drink. It had been natural to bring Conner a beer. He always drank beer when he ate crabs.

They settled down to eat their meal. Audrey's nerves had her jumping at every unusual sound. Conner seemed confident and relaxed.

"I talked to every person up and down that road again." His blue eyes darkened to the color of the clouds overhead. "No one has seen Ben Reilly in days."

Audrey felt too uptight to eat, but she kept up appearances and selected her first crab. "Did you try to get the names of any relatives? It seems to me Ben Reilly has a daughter somewhere."

The shadows in his eyes kept shifting as he moved his head, and Audrey found herself fascinated by the changing hues of blue.

"Jenny Covington said she might have her name and address somewhere, but she's not sure." He picked up another crab.

Audrey had no doubt Jenny Covington would turn her house upside down to find the information. That was the effect Conner had on certain people when he set his mind to it. That was the effect he had on her, except her response was based on feelings she didn't want to consider.

"I did narrow down one thing." He cracked open a claw. "Stan Perkins, remember him? He lives in that shack on the river, way back in the woods at the end of the road." When she failed to respond he smiled and added, "The guy who used to come after us with a shotgun every time we stepped on his property."

Audrey warmed to his smile and laughed at the memory. "How could I ever forget him? I can still picture his old, wrinkled face when he was waving that shotgun at us. But it wasn't very funny then. I used to lie awake at night thinking of possible explanations for coming home with my backside loaded with buckshot."

"You did? I never knew that. I always figured Mr. Perkins was all talk and no action."

Talking about the good times she and Conner had shared made Audrey even more nervous. She gazed at the trees lining the shore across the creek that fed into the Rappahannock River. Those memories were so potent she would be lost if she met Conner eye-to-eye now. Yet she could feel him watching her, as if trying to delve deep into her mind. She fought the urge to look at him again and instead broke off a chunk of bread.

The silence that followed was so filled with tension Audrey could feel the static in the air. The second he looked away, she knew the difference.

He cleared his throat and continued. "Mr. Perkins saw old man Reilly two days after Leona was murdered. He said Ben was wired beyond belief."

He played with the beer can in his hands, rolling it back and forth across his palms, a dead giveaway to a discomfort Audrey hadn't noticed before. Two worry lines furrowed his brow.

"What do you mean 'wired'?"

He looked up at her, his eyes loaded with other kinds of questions she hoped he didn't ask. "Nervous, worried about something. Perkins said he wasn't acting normal at all. Ben told him he might go away for a while."

"It looks like he did that all right. He didn't happen to mention where, did he?"

"I wish."

Audrey smiled to herself. She wished for a lot of things, too, and most of them had nothing to do with Ben Reilly. "Let's hope Jenny can find the name and address of his daughter."

She wiped the spices from her fingers, then broke off another piece of bread and tossed it into the creek for the ducks hovering nearby. The effort did little to help her shaky hands.

"By the way, I ran into Frank. He thinks it's urgent we talk to Bull. I agree with him."

"He can be hard to find. Maybe you could put that investigator you talked about on him."

"No such luck. Lori said the firm can't afford an investigator right now."

"I'll ask around and see if anyone knows where he's living." Conner took a swig of beer and finished off another crab.

Audrey glanced at her watch. Sea gulls circled above the pier, hoping for handouts. The tide swished against the bank. It was an idyllic setting, even under threatening skies, but it did nothing to ease her mounting tension.

Conner leaned against the tree trunk behind him and stretched out his legs beneath the table. "Those were perfect, Audrey. You always did know how to steam crabs. I haven't had any crabs since...well, you know since when."

She did. Since prison. It was a cold reminder of his betrayal six years ago—and what she'd discovered after she'd left town. But those thoughts couldn't take over right now. In less than forty-five minutes Peter would be back. It was time for Conner to leave.

She stood up and began to clear the table. Conner took the hint and helped her. Although it seemed like forever, only ten minutes elapsed before she was telling him goodbye behind the cottage.

They stood so close together their breath intermingled, and Audrey was sure he would try to kiss her. Before she had time to consider what to do, knowing full well she couldn't resist him if she tried, he stepped back.

"I'll try to find Bull." His eyes sparkled with mischief. He gave no indication of leaving.

"Maybe Frank will have more on Leona after the weekend." Audrey released a nervous sigh and walked toward his truck so he would follow. "Stop by the office Monday, say two o'clock, and we'll decide when to pay Bull a visit."

They reached the driver's side and he started to open the door. Audrey felt her nerves begin to settle. Until he stopped and turned around.

"I forgot to tell you one thing. I kept a lookout at Ida May's this morning. There was a parade of traffic in and out of her place—construction crews, a van from some decorator service, a landscape service—but she never left the house."

Right now, Ida May was not Audrey's main concern. "We'll decide what to do about Ida May on Monday."

He opened the door of his truck, and she breathed a sigh of relief. Too soon.

Peter's green van drove up beside Conner's truck. Audrey closed her eyes in dread and wished the earth would swallow her whole.

Peter jumped out. When he saw who was standing beside her, his eyes flashed from shock to bitter hostility. This stranger who was her brother looked as if he wanted to murder Conner with his bare hands. Peter opened his mouth to speak. Instead he snapped it shut, unlocked the side door of the van and picked up two suitcases to carry inside.

Audrey's heart pounded against her chest. Her body broke out in a cold sweat. No matter how much air she gulped in, she couldn't get enough. There was no avoiding the inevitability of the situation.

Ian, Audrey's five-year-old son and the love of her life, jumped down and ran toward her shouting, "Mommy, Mommy." He beamed with happiness. The dimple creasing his right cheek was a carbon copy of Conner's.

She knelt to catch Ian, knowing his usual flying leap into her arms would pulverize her this time. She hugged him for as long as he would let her and told him how much she'd missed him. Then she staggered to her feet.

Conner gaped at her in disbelief. The blood had drained from his face. The confusion and pain and fury in his eyes shook her to the core. It was impossible to tear her eyes away from him until he turned to his son in awe.

Ian tugged at her hand. "Come on, Mommy. I want to show you what Uncle Peter got me."

Her feet wouldn't move. She thought for sure her body would shatter if she budged an inch. She'd never intended for Conner to learn about Ian this way. Never.

Ian sensed her resistance and dropped her hand. He followed her gaze and tilted his head up to meet Conner. "Who are you?"

Several seconds passed before Audrey found her voice, and when she did, she spoke in a harsh whisper. "His name is Conner, Ian. He's an old friend of mine."

Conner couldn't take his eyes off Ian's face. Except for the curly hair and green eyes, the boy looked just like him.

He stooped and held out his hand. "How are you, big guy? It's awfully nice to meet you." The words came out in a hard choke.

Ian shook his hand and giggled. "You can come, too." He grabbed Audrey's hand and made a path for the van.

A fierce riptide of emotion surged through Conner as he watched the small boy lead Audrey to the van. The swell of raw emotions threatened to reduce him to a bumbling idiot. He stumbled along slowly behind them, half-numb from shock, not sure he believed what he could see with his own eyes. By God! He had a son!

Ian scooted into the van and pulled an underwater mask over curls just like Audrey's. "See?" He showed Audrey the mask. "It works real good."

Audrey leaned over to see. "What have we here?" She fingered a snorkeling tube and a pair of flippers. And eyed Conner with every other breath.

Her hands were shaking. Her face was pale. All through lunch he'd wondered why she was so nervous and now he knew.

"I didn't think you'd mind." Peter surprised them both by coming up from behind. He tried to edge Conner out of the way. "He was so taken with Roger's set, we went ahead and got him one, too."

Audrey examined the snorkeling tube, unaware of the tug-of-war for space. "Does he know how to use this thing?"

"We bought it the day after you left." Peter watched Conner from the corner of his eye. "He's used it in the swimming pool every day since."

"Can I try it in the creek, Mommy? I didn't get to go swimming today." Ian had picked up all of his equipment and was ready for a swim.

Peter drilled his eyes into Conner. "Obviously, we got back earlier than I'd planned." He shifted his attention to Audrey. "Helen didn't want to get caught in the hurricane and have to stop halfway home. Roger wasn't very happy—you know kids."

Audrey ran her hand through Ian's curls. "Maybe we can try it out at the beach later," she told him. "It's not so deep there, and you'll be able to wade right in and..."

She rambled on without making any sense. That she was tied in as many knots as Conner gave him a brief moment of diabolic pleasure.

Ian stood up in the van and turned to Conner. "Want to go s-norkeling with me?" Green eyes as bright and inquisitive as Audrey's met him squarely.

"You can bet we will." With a quick look, he dared Audrey to say otherwise.

Peter glared at him and placed a protective hand on Ian's shoulder. "You'll get in plenty of snorkeling time with Roger, Ian—don't worry."

Conner challenged him eye-to-eye and wondered what had set his fuse. He acted as though he wanted to string him up to the nearest tree, yet they hardly knew each other.

After Audrey and her brother had moved into their grandfather's house, Peter had left for the army within the week. He and Peter barely knew each other's names. Did Peter realize Ian was his son? Did he think he was protecting Audrey and Ian from some cold-blooded killer? Or had old man McKenna poisoned him with unfounded lies about his granddaughter's involvement with the town's black sheep?

Conner glanced at Audrey, torn between wanting to strangle her for her betrayal and wanting to kiss her hand for this precious gift. Her eyes darted between him and Peter. Perspiration had broken out on her forehead. She was wringing her hands as if there were no tomorrow. She looked ready to collapse.

She grabbed him by the sleeve. "Excuse us for a minute, Peter." She didn't wait to catch his reaction.

Conner didn't know what he would say to her, but whatever he said would be unfit for Ian's ears. Anger burned inside him like acid. Only the fact that she'd given him the most unbelievable gift of his life soothed him.

She led him the few feet to the truck before saying a word. "Conner, I..."

But Conner would have none of it. "I guess I now know why you were too tied up to work on the case today."

She had betrayed him in the worst possible way. He tempered the unspeakable pain that sliced through him as he turned away from her, climbed into his truck and drove slowly down her drive.

Chapter Five

"You're sure you don't mind keeping Ian for the day?"

Peter's wife, Helen, smiled and patted Audrey's hand. "Don't you worry for one minute. Even with such an age difference, he and Roger have a grand time together, especially when they start in on the computer games." She looked out at the dark sky. "The weatherman said the rain and wind from the hurricane will be with us for another day or two. I'll be glad when it clears up."

She took Audrey's arm and guided her gently to the door. In a soft voice she said, "Go on, now. I've kept you long enough."

Meeting Conner consumed Audrey's thoughts as she drove through town to the state highway. The most important problem right now was getting his cooperation so she could prepare his defense. After yesterday, that might be impossible.

The rain was now so heavy that the dirt road in front of Conner's house flowed like a river. The only way she could get close was to go with the skid of the car and follow the rivulets of mud cutting through his yard.

The downpour drenched her as she ran to the house. She knocked loudly three times and then banged on the door with her fists. Conner opened it, looking more virile than ever—wet hair, no shirt, tight jeans unsnapped at the waist. The sight threatened to undermine her purpose in coming.

He stood there silently.

"Are you going to ask me in or what?"

"Nobody invited you here." He was blocking the doorway and rubbing his wet hair with a towel.

If she hadn't known him, she would have bristled at his sharp tongue. She'd learned long ago that this brusqueness hid an angry pride as great as her own.

"Too bad. Let's just say I invited myself. We need to talk." She could be stubborn, too.

"About what? The fact that I've had a son for five years and didn't know it? Or about the ambitious young defense lawyer set on making her reputation by defending a lost cause?"

"That isn't fair and you know it."

A gust of wind blew rain inside the house and Conner stepped back. The water clogging the gutter overhead splashed onto Audrey's neck. She welcomed the cold trickles. It cooled her off in more ways than one.

"Look, Conner." She tried to reason with him. "This is sort of stupid, don't you think? You're standing there getting soaked, I'm standing here getting sprayed and the rain is about to flood your house." And controlling her temper was becoming a lost cause.

His fierce, dark eyes attacked her. "Well, just maybe I want to know why you kept my son hidden from me all this time."

"I did not hide him from you."

"I don't know what else you'd call it." He had twisted the towel around his neck and was pulling it back and forth.

"As I recall—and I remember your exact words—you told me to get out of your life."

"I didn't know you were pregnant, for crying out loud."

He stopped pulling at the towel. He gripped the ends in white fists and pierced her with his gaze. "For what it's worth, they convicted an innocent man six years ago."

"Oh, yeah, sure. Any other 'truths' you'd like to throw in?"

"That I didn't kill Leona Kingsley?"

"As your attorney, that's a moot question."

"As your client, it's not, not for me. Once upon a time, it wouldn't have been for you, either."

"Forget once upon a time," Audrey snapped through the downpour.

"Once upon a time kept me alive for six years."

"Conner, if you're going to keep dwelling on the past, I can't help you."

"How about this, then." He scooped her up and carried her inside before she could open her mouth.

"Put me down this minute!"

"Whatever you say, Counselor."

But he didn't exactly put her down. Instead he shifted her against him and let her slide down his hard body, one slow inch at a time.

"You have no idea how hard it is to keep my hands off you with those raindrops slipping down your cheeks."

Before her feet touched the floor, he licked the raindrops from her lips, then crushed his mouth to hers and demanded everything she couldn't dare give. She tried to resist—she knew she did. But the hardness of his body pressing against her had a storm raging inside her that matched the one raging outside.

She snaked her arms around his neck and made her own demands very clear. Her hands traveled across the corded muscles in his shoulders, down his well-defined back, over smooth skin that felt like heated stone. Her tongue explored his mouth just as his fought to explore hers. She molded her lips to his and felt an aching passion swell in every feminine part of her.

His crushing mouth became tender, loving, more sensual and seductive. Waves of need washed through her before she registered the change.

She had no chance to stop him as his warm mouth left

hers. He set her firmly on the floor. Hard, steamy blue eyes stared back at her with the same passion she herself felt in every fiber of her being. Yet his gaze was unsettling, distancing.

"You'd better go dry off." His husky voice was not quite convincing.

Only when he turned her away by the shoulders and nudged her down the hall did she realize what she'd done. She rushed into the bathroom, away from Conner, away from the needs she thought she had under control. One glance in the mirror told her too much. Her face was flushed, alive; her eyes smoldered with passion.

This would never do. She shook out her wet jacket, then grabbed a towel and rubbed at her hair until her scalp tingled. Even with her head hurting and her arms cramping, it took several more minutes to recapture some element of professionalism and put things into perspective. Finally, drawing in a deep breath, she opened the door to face him.

She found him at the kitchen window, gazing at the rain. "Let's get this out of the way before we go any further. Tell me now if you want another attorney. I would certainly understand."

"Ha!" He spun around and glared at her. "Don't trouble yourself with understanding anything. I definitely do not want another lawyer. I figure you have as much stake in this as I do."

"What's that supposed to mean?"

His dark eyes trapped hers. "Neither one of us wants Ian to grow up with a convicted murderer for a father."

Audrey gasped. She flung her hand over her mouth. She had worried about Ian and the effect the trial would have on him, but hearing Conner express her fears made them real. She realized in her heart she'd never thought of him as a murderer. Yet at this point she couldn't dispute or dismiss the damning facts.

She tried to control the new anxiety creeping through

her fingers as she walked back into the living room and sat down. "You might be much better off with an experienced trial lawyer, Conner. Seriously."

It was impossible to read his eyes when he sauntered into the room, but there was no mistaking where they were directed. She could feel them stabbing her and searching every inch of her face.

"I may be angry as hell at you, Audrey, but I have complete confidence that you will win me an acquittal."

Although his words were not quite a vote of trust, she was surprised at the relief she felt. "Then I suggest we get to work."

He leaned his back against the wall, his arms folded in front of him. "Oh, no, you don't, Counselor. We still have some unfinished business—our son."

"Look, Conner, I didn't know I was pregnant that last time I saw you. If I had known, maybe I would have handled things differently."

An uncomfortable silence followed that made her wish she'd never come. She could feel herself being drawn in again. The curl of his damp hair intrigued her. The set of his broad shoulders had her reliving the feel of him.

She broke the silence in self-defense. "Can we leave the past behind for now? I had every intention of telling you about Ian. I just hadn't figured out how. I've dreamed of the day when you could see him—"

"And I intend to keep seeing him," Conner interrupted, his voice firm and direct, his face sincere and intense.

"I wouldn't have it any other way."

Audrey fought a smile. He was always his most appealing when he struggled to hide his feelings. Yet she could read the frustration simmering in the depths of his eyes. She wanted to smooth the lines on his brow, but she knew it wouldn't help. Neither one of them could undo the past.

The best she could do for all of them would be to win him an acquittal. That meant she had to stop allowing him to overwhelm her and cloud her thinking. She would encourage him to develop a friendly relationship with Ian. Not with her—the survival of her sanity depended on that point.

The bottom line was quite clear: Conner had cast her aside once and could do it again. Cruising into a relationship with him without trust in the future would be like sailing on a river without water—it just wouldn't work.

"ARE WE there yet, Mommy?" This was the fourth time in twenty minutes Ian had asked that question this morning. His first day at the center's day care had him raring to go.

"You bet."

Audrey parked the car and unlocked the back door. She caught Ian's hand before he could race across the center's parking lot, then straightened his shirt and tried to smooth down his curls. He continued to twist and wriggle to get free from her hold.

"Are you ready?" she asked at last.

"You bet."

His mimic made her smile. He was such a great little guy.

She had made several visits to the day care at the seniors' center while Ian was up in the mountains. She was very impressed, just as Helen had said she would be. When she'd learned Della Andrews, the director of the day care, had a background in nursing, she'd felt confident placing him here for the few weeks before school began. For Ian's sake, she was thankful no one in town knew he was Conner's son.

Della Andrews greeted them inside the door. Audrey guessed she was in her midthirties. A big woman, she wore a neat, practical, navy suit that enhanced her homely features and actually made her somewhat attractive.

Della's smile was welcoming, although it seemed a little

forced. "This must be Ian." Her bearing was erect and tense as she took them down the hall.

"Mrs. Tompkins will be Ian's teacher. She's wonderful with the children." She introduced the woman who joined them.

Mrs. Tompkins, a middle-aged woman with a kind smile, led Ian off to meet the other children.

Della watched him go down the hall. "The youngsters draw the seniors to the center like flies. Another sweet face is always welcome." She reached to shake Audrey's hand. "I'm so glad you decided to let Ian join our little group. You can rest assured he'll be just fine."

Audrey thought it strange that Della's first priority as day care director was attracting seniors to the center, but she dismissed the thought and watched Ian at play. Mrs. Tompkins gave him time to adjust to his new surroundings, and fifteen minutes later he sat on the rug to build block towers with two other little boys and waved her a hasty goodbye.

She was almost to the front door, when someone called her name. She stopped midstride and turned around. A tall, good-looking man dressed in a fine silk suit and expensive-looking tie approached her. Doc Rankin, Jr., the medical director at the center. She remembered him only too well. He held out his hand, the sudden gleam in his eye unmistakable.

"Audrey McKenna, I heard you had returned. Welcome home."

She shook his hand quickly and wondered if fear of running into him this morning had caused the feeling of dread that had been with her since dawn. "Thanks, Doc. I heard you were the physician at the center."

"Yes. My father passed on, you know."

"I'm sorry to hear that." She backed up a step. "I thought you'd be practicing in some big city somewhere."

"Actually, I like it here. You know, I'm quite proud of the center's success. It took a while to catch on, of course.

When my father ran it, hardly anyone came. Now, with the day care facility on the premises, we have a full house every day."

He smiled at her. "You'll be happy to know I received your son's medical records."

"Very good." Audrey inched away, unsettled by the unrelenting gleam in his eye and more than ready to leave. "That's one less thing to worry about."

He stepped closer. "Maybe you and I can get together sometime."

Audrey pulled her shoulder bag to the front and hugged it. "Well, right now I'm really tied up with settling in and getting used to my new job. Maybe later on." She made a beeline for the door. "Good to see you again."

For a minute, she thought he might follow her. She turned around and waved, happy to see he hadn't moved. Doc Rankin had the same conservatively cut, dark brown hair he'd always had and a smile that might appeal to another woman, but his persistence had always pushed Audrey away.

She drove to the office slowly, remembering when Doc had had a crush on her. He'd pursued her mercilessly the summer she'd started dating Conner. The next summer had brought more of the same—with him showing up at unexpected places, insisting she go out with him. He'd made her feel very uncomfortable. It was easy to rationalize his behavior now; an adolescent crush made fools of many people. When she'd talked to the seniors at the center last week, they'd had only the highest praise for Doc's medical talents.

Audrey arrived at her office and learned that Conner had canceled his two o'clock appointment.

"Thanks for the message," she told Lori, as the woman breezed into her office.

She leaned back in her chair and breathed a sigh of relief, which irritated her. A fine attorney she would make if she couldn't keep her personal prejudices behind closed doors.

Lori walked to her desk. "You see Mr. Yeagher today, right?"

Audrey checked her schedule. "At ten o'clock."

"What did he decide?" Lori asked about her former client.

"He's going to go through with the countersuit."

"Good." Lori nodded and disappeared out the door.

By lunchtime, Audrey had reviewed two other cases, met with Mr. Yeagher and made an appointment for her and Conner to see Ida May again. She couldn't contact Bull Kingsley until she knew where to find him. Hopefully, Conner would tell her today.

She took advantage of her lunch break and walked to the hardware store to buy a new valve for the pump. With a little help, she found one and went to the front counter to pay for it.

"Good afternoon, Mr. Mosley. How are you?" she asked the proprietor.

He shook his head. "Been better. But when I think of little Frankie all bummed up in that accident, I count my blessings." He rang up the sale.

Frankie? "Frank Smith? Is that who you mean?"

"Bad accident."

"What happened?" Audrey's heart almost stopped in fear.

He put the valve in a bag and leaned closer. "You haven't heard? Frankie wrecked his car in the storm Saturday night. Dang thing rolled over and ended upside down in a ditch out there by the highway. Least ways, that's what the sheriff figures."

"Oh, no! What about Frank?"

"He's all banged up. They took him down to the hospital. Sheriff says he's in a coma. Got a broken leg to boot." A look of true compassion filled his eyes. "I've known Frankie since he was a little guy."

Audrey picked up her bag and remembered Frank's enthusiasm Saturday morning when he'd helped James fix her flat tires. She laid a hand on Mr. Mosley's arm. "They have good doctors at the hospital. He'll be okay." She prayed she was right. "You take care."

"One dang thing after another," he muttered, as she hurried from the store.

As soon as she reached her office, she called the hospital to check on Frank's condition. No one could tell her any more than Mr. Mosley had. For three hours she tried to work. The thought of Frank's accident preyed on her mind and prevented her from accomplishing anything. Conner's best friend was in a coma and chances were he didn't know it.

With her decision made, she packed up her briefcase and caught Lori in her office. "I'm driving out to Conner Hastings's place. I won't be long."

Lori closed the file she was reading. "Audrey, I prefer you to do your consulting in the office when possible. If Mr. Hastings can't make his appointment, that doesn't mean you should go running off to meet him somewhere. Especially in light of your past relationship. It doesn't look good for the firm."

"I understand your concern." Audrey shifted on her feet, perturbed by Lori's assumption. "You need to know that the man investigating his case has been in a terrible accident. Mr. Hastings and I need to regroup, since I plan to win this case in court."

At Lori's nod of encouragement, she hurried from the office. She'd spoken with much more conviction than she felt. With Frank out of the picture, their prospects for new leads looked dim.

THREATENING CLOUDS still filled the sky as she drove to Conner's. She parked on what looked like a solid spot in his front yard and stepped out into a quagmire. After knocking at his door and failing to get an answer, she called out his name. Conner materialized from around the side of the house.

Decked out in a sleeveless T-shirt, old jeans and knee boots covered with mud, he looked ruggedly handsome. It irritated her that her pulse was already racing. No matter what he wore or what he was doing, he set her senses on fire.

"Audrey, what's wrong?"

Her face must have given her away. "It's about Frank."

He casually wiped his hands on an old towel hanging over the porch railing. "What about him?"

There was no easy way to soften this. "Frank was in an accident Saturday night, Conner. Mr. Mosley said it happened during the storm. He's in a coma. And he broke his leg."

His face took on a haunted look of disbelief. He clutched the railing in a death grip. "Frank's in a coma? My God, I can't picture him lying helpless in a hospital."

The fact that she could read his face showed how devastating the news was. He didn't often let down his guard. The shock she saw matched her own.

Audrey couldn't resist placing her hand over his on the railing. She felt the coarseness of his skin, the tension in his fingers. She hastened to add the few reassuring words she could offer. "The hospital told me they've stabilized his condition."

"But he's still in a coma?"

She nodded, strengthening her grip when she felt his fingers tighten.

He stepped away and stared out at the woods. The clenched muscles in his jaw worked harder. "How could that happen?" He turned to her. Worry lines etched themselves deeper in his brow. "Remember all the drag racing we used to do? Frank's a damn good driver."

"That was a bad storm, Conner. With hurricane-force winds and drenching rain, I can see how somebody might swerve and end up in a ditch."

"Somebody. Not Frank."

Shadows filled his midnight eyes. She wanted to touch him, to hold his face in her hands, but she couldn't. Such a gesture would say more than she dared.

She couldn't help him. And he seemed to need to deal with this alone. "Look, I'd better get back to the office."

He gave no sign that he'd heard her. She slogged through the mud to her car, then glanced at him behind her. He was wandering toward the back of the house, his stride slow, his arms hanging loosely at his sides.

She wanted to stay to be there for him, but they'd been strangers too long for him to need her comfort. He was more of a loner now than ever. Yet she could almost feel his pain.

Audrey put the car in reverse, disturbed that the connection between them grew stronger every day. At the blast of a horn she slammed on the brakes and saw the sheriff's car on top of her back bumper, boxing her in. Her shoulders sagged in frustration.

Sheriff Parks was at her door before she could get out.

"Well, look who we have here." He leaned his arms on the top of her open door, blocking her exit. Audrey knew the sheriff best from his many run-ins with Conner. His country-boy manner hid a sharp mind. His hair was now a mix of white and black, his brown eyes as probing as ever.

"Sorry, Sheriff. I didn't see you."

"Maybe 'cause you weren't looking, little lady."

"Maybe because you came up behind me too quickly."

The sheriff bristled but failed to comment when he saw Conner approaching. A cool, cynical mask of indifference now cloaked Conner's face. He was back to normal, Audrey noted. At least on the surface.

The sheriff shifted his attention and stepped aside. He pulled a short straw from his pocket and chewed on the end of it. "Thought I'd stop around and have a few words with you, Hastings."

Audrey saw the cold shadows in Conner's eyes. He stood silently waiting for the sheriff to continue.

"You didn't happen to be out on the road Saturday night, did you?"

"Why would that concern you?"

"Come on now, boy. Don't try to lead me around the barn. Just answer the question. It's easier to do this here than haul you into town."

Conner hesitated and caught the sheriff straight in the eye with his own brand of forthrightness. "Yeah, I was out on the road."

The sheriff took a small notebook from his pocket. He twirled the straw in his mouth, staring straight at Conner. "What time would that be?"

"I don't really recall, Sheriff."

Conner's gaze never faltered, but his eyes darkened to that stormy blue Audrey recognized as anger. What was going on here? What had set off the sheriff? Why was Conner baiting him?

"Now, that is a pity." Sheriff Parks leaned closer, one hand on his hip, near his holster, his patience obviously short.

Audrey got out of the car. The silence between them was penetrating, like the cold from the mud seeping through her shoes. She had finally figured out why the sheriff was here, and she didn't like it any more than Conner did. It seemed as though the town wanted to use more than Conner's land as a dumping ground.

She watched Conner's face, waiting for some indication of where this conversation was going. She knew the second he made up his mind. His face betrayed nothing, but his eyes burned in anger and flashed at the sheriff.

"You might want to check with Jenny Covington across the road. Her car died and I drove her into Tappahannock to borrow a friend's car so she could go to church the next morning."

"What time was that?"

Conner paused for so long Audrey thought he wasn't going to answer. Silently she pleaded with him to put aside his stubborn pride and cooperate.

"Probably about six," he finally said.

"I see." The sheriff scribbled in his notebook. "And what time did you get home? If it's not too much trouble, mind you."

"Now, that I'm not quite sure about, Sheriff."

Audrey could almost hear Sheriff Parks calculating times in his head. No doubt Conner could, too.

"I'd guess about three in the morning." Conner looked pleased. "The road was flooded. The state police closed it. But don't take my word for it."

"I don't plan to." Sheriff Parks pocketed his notebook and turned to leave.

"By the way, Sheriff, why would I want to run Frank off the road? Just for the sake of argument, of course."

"I'll check it out." The sheriff removed the straw from his mouth and stuck it in his pocket. His shrewd eyes evaluated Conner. "Can't really imagine you'd be stupid enough to strike twice now, can I? Most likely Frank lost control of the car. Most likely an accident."

Conner didn't respond to the sheriff's barbed comment. Instead he said, "Most likely not an accident. Frank's too good a driver."

"Don't go looking for trouble, Hastings. I figured I owe it to Frank to do some asking, since he can't."

CONNER DIDN'T WAIT for Parks to leave before heading back to work. He picked up the pipe wrench as he passed the side of the house. He wanted to sling it as far as he could. Then take off after it and keep going. He felt like a tethered animal on too short a leash.

He had a real funny feeling about Frank. He could not believe his friend had run off the road, storm or no storm. Frank was the most conscientious driver Conner had ever seen, and he kept his cars in tip-top shape.

He lowered himself into the trench he'd dug to finish fixing the broken pipe. He was fed up with living in the substandard house, even if it was the only home he'd ever known. His decision to continue the repairs, in spite of the trial, normally provided him with an outlet for his simmering anger. Right now, though, the work would distract him from the disturbing feeling about Frank. He needed time to think, time to get beyond the sheriff's insults.

"Sheriff Parks can be a real jerk." Audrey had followed him and stood off to the side.

What he saw in her expression wasn't pity, as expected, but a sincere, controlled frustration like his own. The fire in her eyes made him ache to take her in his arms again. The damp air caused extra curls to frame her face, making her more beautiful than ever.

And reminded him of Ian. All that time in prison he'd had a son and hadn't known it. The thought doused his desire very effectively. Did she have any idea how much her betrayal hurt? He wasn't sure he could ever forgive her.

"Stay for a few minutes. I'm almost finished. Go in and get yourself something to drink."

As soon as she left, he hopped up from the trench and grabbed the shovel, furious that she'd witnessed that scene with the sheriff. He attacked the mud and flung it back where it belonged. He was disgusted with himself for needing her. And he did need her, damn it. For more than her defense skills.

Chapter Six

Once inside, Audrey fixed a fresh pot of coffee. She wasn't sure why she'd stayed, but after watching the sheriff treat Conner like dirt, she knew she couldn't walk away.

Did she feel sorry for him? Was that what this emotional confusion was all about?

She was playing with the question when Conner walked through the door. He'd finger-combed his hair and scrubbed off the mud. He strode across the room with such confidence that the idea of feeling sorry for him struck her as totally absurd and made her laugh at herself. He was the most self-contained, confident man she'd ever known.

He poured himself some coffee, padded to the kitchen table in sock-clad feet, then pulled out a chair and sat there, lost in thought. "If it had been anything but a car accident..." He turned to Audrey, a hard look on his face. "Frank doesn't have car accidents by himself."

Audrey leaned back against the counter and sipped at her coffee. She'd experienced his stubborn side before. "He's not immune to accidents on the road, Conner."

There was no dissuading him once he set his mind to something. That was one point she remembered well. What he needed was time to come to his senses.

She took her last sip of coffee and set the cup in the sink. His reaction disturbed her. *He* disturbed her.

"Whether it was an accident or not, we have a defense

to prepare. The sheriff's the one to investigate Frank's wreck, not you."

"Right." A disgusted look passed over his face. "I don't believe in coincidence. Don't you find it strange that the one person who's investigating Leona's private life suddenly ends up in the hospital?"

A terrible foreboding made her shiver. For some reason, the image of her slashed tires came to mind.

"It was a bad storm, Conner. You said yourself several roads were washed out."

His face became cool and controlled, as he focused inward on his thoughts. Audrey moved to leave. The change in his expression made her hesitate and she eased back against the counter.

"I want to take a good look at Frank's car. That'll tell us the story." He held his cup in both hands, the coffee untouched.

"The sheriff won't let you near it. You know he must have impounded it."

"That's what I'm betting on. The impoundment lot is at James's garage."

"Conner, you can't get sidetracked like this. Your trial is exactly one week away. With Frank in the hospital, you and I have a lot more ground to cover."

She picked up her jacket from the chair and headed for the door. It was impossible to make him listen to reason right now. Once the shock of Frank's accident wore off, his common sense would return. Tomorrow she would force the issue.

"I have to get back to the office."

He closed in behind her and laid a hand on her shoulder. The warmth from his fingers penetrated her thin jacket and sent flames of desire through her.

"I've got to see Frank. Do you have time to go to the hospital?"

She felt herself leaning toward him, needing more than

the warmth of his touch. Truly, she should have her head examined.

"No." Her answer seemed abrupt. "Lori's probably already wondering what happened to me."

He was so close she could see every strand of mussed hair. The changing blue of his eyes fascinated her. The lines in his brow and the curving of his mouth reflected often indiscernible emotions. His frustration was obvious to the naked eye.

She gave the first order of business one more try. "Have you located Bull Kingsley yet?"

"Not yet."

"I'll make you a deal," she offered, knowing she should pull away. "After you see Frank, go find Bull. I'll call James and ask about Frank's car." She felt the pressure of his fingers and knew she wasn't going to move. "I just wish there were some way to find out if Frank discovered any new leads before his accident."

"We'll check his computer." He seemed oblivious to the turmoil inside her. "He's a nut about documenting everything. If he uncovered anything, it'll be in his files."

"And just how do you propose to get into his house?"

"No problem." He finally released her and moved across the room. Audrey rubbed her shoulder, not knowing if she was trying to eradicate the feel of him or hold on to his heat.

He reached up to the mantel above the fireplace and turned back with a key. "I have a key, Counselor. All we have to do is unlock the door and walk in."

"Fantastic. We can go tomorrow during my lunch hour." If they could find out what Frank was up to, they might make more progress. "And you'll look for Bull today?"

"As long as you call James at the garage."

That he'd accepted a compromise pleased her. The younger man she'd known wouldn't have done that.

She found herself anticipating a trip to Frank's cottage as Conner followed her onto the porch. But in the back of her mind, doubt lingered. What if they didn't find anything? What if Ida May had an alibi and Conner couldn't find Bull? What then?

CONNOR PACED along the bank in front of Audrey's cottage late that afternoon. Where was she? Where was Ian? Why weren't they home yet?

It irritated him to realize he knew nothing about her life now. At one time, they'd known everything about each other.

He gave up pacing and sat down on the bank. Sea gulls circled overhead, across the creek, waiting for handouts. They were at the mercy of the fisherman for the easy catch they loved—just as he was at Audrey's mercy for the freedom he craved.

He watched one lone gull separate from the group. The bird flew up the creek, circled and dove for a fish. Missing, it dove again. Failure didn't force him to rejoin the group. Not this bird. He perched on Audrey's boathouse, satisfied, free to go his own way.

That's all Conner wanted, too—the freedom to go his own way, to put his degree to use and to build a life for himself.

The sound of Audrey's car had him scrambling to his feet. The sight of his son tightened his heart. That Ian existed was hard to believe.

"Conner." Audrey greeted him as she came across the side yard. "I saw your truck."

She looked stunning, radiant. The forest green suit brought out the green of her eyes. The gentle breeze teased her hair. The August sun caught her curls in a shimmering array of colors. And she had kept his son a secret.

"Hi, Conner." Ian ran across the yard and stood by Audrey. Evidently, he was reluctant to approach him.

"It's good to see you, big guy."

He kept his voice light and friendly. The last thing he wanted to do was scare the boy. Sooner or later he had to get over the urge to crush his son to him in a never-ending hug.

Ian hung his head. "You said we'd go s-norkeling."

"Ian," Audrey said, "mind your manners."

"Well." Conner held back the punch line. "I thought we could go in a few minutes, after I talk to your mom."

Ian's face lit up. "You bet. Can I, Mommy?"

"Go inside and change. You can pick up your room while Conner and I talk. Then you can go."

Ian dashed for the house.

"That's nice of you, Conner. With the bad weather, we haven't had a chance to go to the beach yet." She said it as if he were some weekend visitor.

"Nice? Audrey…"

"We need to clarify one thing. I've thought about this a great deal. You realize I have to think of Ian first."

"I don't plan to tell him I'm his father, if that's what you're worried about. That would be cruel, under the circumstances."

He couldn't let her know how much this hurt. He had no intention of injuring his son by making promises he couldn't keep. The prison term loomed closer every day.

Audrey looked relieved he hadn't given her an argument. "I agree." She lowered her eyes.

"But I do want to spend some time with him. Not too much," he added when she frowned. "I don't want him to get attached to me."

"I do want him to get to know you." She didn't add "even if it's only for a little while," but he did.

Her face looked beautiful in the late afternoon sun. The sincerity in her voice mocked his growing sense of distrust.

"Is that what brought you here? Or did you find out where Bull Kingsley is hiding himself?"

She'd become very good at using business to hide her emotions. If she thought he'd missed the light in her eye and the hope in her voice, she was crazy.

"No, but I talked to a guy who knows a friend of his.

He's looking into it for me. But that's not why I'm here. I promised Ian I'd take him snorkeling, for one thing. And I want you to go to the hospital with me tonight."

Curiosity tinged her eyes. "How was Frank when you saw him earlier?"

"That's just it. Doc Rankin has a Family Only sign posted on his door. But Frank's closest family member lives a thousand miles away, so no one's allowed in. I almost made it into the room, but Doc spotted me at the last minute."

"His condition must be worse."

"That's what I'm worried about, but since I'm not family, Doc wouldn't tell me."

"It seems odd. Doc is aware of what good friends you are, but he must know what he's doing, Conner."

"I realize that, but I can't stand the idea of Frank in there by himself, unconscious. I asked a friend of mine to find out how he's doing. Mavis is a nurse. She'll know. But I'll feel better when I see for myself. I thought having my lawyer with me tonight might be smart."

"It's not like you to want help, Conner."

She smiled that wonderful all-knowing smile of hers, and he felt his heart catch.

She could still read him so easily. "Maybe it's an excuse to spend more time with you?"

Ian zoomed out the door, the snorkeling tube bouncing along behind him. "I'm all ready." He tugged at Conner's hand.

"Hold on, sport. I have to change into my bathing suit." Conner turned back to Audrey. "Well?"

"I'll see if I can get a sitter."

Conner got his bathing suit from the truck and changed his clothes inside the cottage. When he rejoined Audrey and Ian in the yard, Ian urged him toward the beach. It seemed appropriate to be returning to the small beach with his son. Dreams of making love with Audrey here had sustained him for many nights in prison. The last time they made love had been the night before he'd lost his freedom six long years ago. Their love had been pure and innocent and blind to what lay ahead.

Ian slipped his hand in his as they walked down the dirt road to find the beach at the end. Conner had never felt prouder than he did at that moment.

"I built a big bridge today." Ian skipped beside him. "Bigger than Tommy's."

"Where was this?" Conner wanted to know it all.

"At the center. Mrs. Tompkins is my teacher."

"Is she nice?"

"Oh, yeah. She got me chocolate ice cream for a snack instead of vanilla."

"Then I know she must be nice." Conner chuckled. "How big was your bridge?" he coaxed.

Ian stopped on the road and raised his hands over his head. "This big."

"How in the world did you do that?"

"With the big blocks. I let Tommy help after his accidentally fell down." He stumbled over the word "accidentally." "I couldn't help it that it fell down."

Conner could imagine what had happened to Tommy's bridge.

"So you like the water, do you?" He let Ian's hand go as they walked single file down the path that led to the sand.

"Yep."

Ian ran ahead of him to the small beach on the Rappahannock River. In no time at all, he had his snorkeling tube ready and his goggles on. Conner waded into the water behind him.

"I can float." Ian flipped onto his back. When his legs sank a foot, he splashed to an upright position. "Can you hold your breath?" He proceeded to show him what he meant.

Conner smiled at the puffed-out cheeks and red face. "I think I can manage that."

"Then you and me can both look at the bottom. Only I get to look longer 'cause I got this." He grinned and held up the snorkeling tube, quite pleased with himself.

For an hour they explored the river's bottom together, played water tag and built a sand castle. The setting sun quickly streaked its goodbye across the sky and the heat left the air. Still, it took some fancy talking to convince Ian it was time to go home.

Once in the door, Ian had to tell Audrey everything they'd done. Conner slipped away to change into his clothes and returned to find Ian still chattering away. He stopped only when Audrey sent him off to take a bath.

She was working in the kitchen, which opened into a dining area and living room. Conner sat on a bar stool at the counter so he could watch her. The confident way she worked, the smooth way she moved around the room—he loved it all.

"It sounds to me like you two had a great time."

"Yeah."

He was surprised to find that he felt embarrassed. He hadn't guessed that one little boy could mean so much. Audrey saw Ian every day. She could never imagine how much this outing had meant to him.

Ian bounded into the room, scrubbed clean and wearing teddy-bear pajamas.

"That was fast." Audrey opened the refrigerator and took out a peeled carrot.

"I thought Conner would leave." He took the carrot Audrey held out, climbed onto the stool next to Conner and munched. "I don't have a daddy." He chattered matter-of-factly.

Conner felt his heart twist. Audrey dropped the paring knife she was using. They looked at each other across the room, their pain tangible.

"But if I did," Ian said, gazing up at Conner with deep green eyes and a dimpled smile, "I'd want him to be just like you."

THE BABY-SITTER couldn't come until ten o'clock. By the time they reached the hospital, the night shift had arrived and the visitors' lot had emptied of all but one car.

"Frank's room is on the second floor down at the west end." Conner closed the door behind her. "There are stairs near his room."

They made it to Frank's room without being spotted, and Audrey breathed a sigh of relief. They rushed over to Frank. If she hadn't known better, she would've thought he was sleeping.

"He looks awfully pale." She moved a chair closer to the bed.

"Maybe that's normal when you're in a coma." Conner leaned down and felt Frank's head. "Listen, I want to find Mavis. I'll be right back."

He squeezed her hand before walking out the door. The surprising gesture tongue-tied her. Just when he seemed focused entirely on Frank, he had to switch tactics like that. The sudden contact of skin on skin had stopped her from voicing her fear of him getting caught.

She held Frank's hand and wished the contact would wake him. There were no tubes and cords as she'd expected. Only one IV was hooked up to his arm. His right leg was in a cast suspended from a pulley.

Suddenly the door burst open. Audrey's heart caught in her throat. She was trapped. She did the only thing that came to mind, and pretended to be talking to Frank. A split second later she realized it was Conner.

"My God, Conner, don't you ever scare me like that again."

He smiled in satisfaction at having spooked her. "I didn't find Mavis. Maybe she couldn't convince her friend to stay home sick tonight."

"I'm sure Frank will be fine."

"There may be no significance to this, but the light outside the next door is flashing. I think that means the guy has signaled for a nurse. We'd better be quiet."

He kept his voice low and moved close behind her. His breath caressed her neck and distracted her.

Were it not for the almost inaudible whooshing of the door closing in the next room, they would have been caught.

"Quick, over here." Audrey pulled him by the arm.

They were behind the door when the nurse opened it. Audrey held her breath. The door now blocked their view of the room—and the nurse's view of them—but Audrey could hear the soft padding of her shoes as she crossed the room to Frank's bed.

The waiting seemed interminable. Having Conner wedged in beside her didn't help. She held his arm in a death grip, the contact as much a frustration as a comfort. A part of her refused to acknowledge their desperate situation and insisted on responding to him as though they were whiling away their time on the beach, waiting to explore each other more intimately. But inside, she was a wreck.

Audrey froze as she heard what sounded like a cart with squeaky wheels coming down the hall. The nurse left Frank's side and hurried to the door. *Please,* Audrey prayed, *don't let anyone catch us.*

Fingers wrapped around the edge of the door. Audrey caught a glimpse of the nurse hurrying out before the door closed. For several minutes, neither of them moved. She strained to hear the nurse's footsteps retreating, but could discern nothing over the noise of the cart.

"Let's get out of here." Conner squeezed her arm to him before freeing himself.

No sooner did they reach for the door than it was pushed open from the hall. A formidable-looking nurse walked in, took one look at Conner, then quickly closed the door. Audrey's heart sank.

"Thank God." Conner smiled at the woman and let his tense shoulders relax.

"My lands, son, shame on you for sneaking in here like a thief in the night and scaring poor Mavis to death."

So, this was Conner's friend Mavis.

"Yes, ma'am, I know, but I had to see Frank."

The woman turned to Audrey. "You're that nice lady lawyer helping my boy here."

"Yes, ma'am." Audrey felt foolish getting caught.

"Mavis, this is Audrey McKenna, attorney extraordinaire." To Audrey he added, "Mavis is a retired registered nurse."

"Don't be calling me 'retired,' son. These bones are strong enough to haul me in here tonight and tough enough to get me to old Doc Cranford's twice a week."

Audrey believed every word she said. Mavis stood close to six feet tall. Her short, black hair showed a lot of gray. Her skin was the color of milk chocolate. Despite the wrinkles lining her full, round face and the kindness in her smile, Mavis's eyes flashed with an energy that explained why Conner had asked her to watch over Frank.

In almost regal fashion, she walked to Frank's bed and reached for a blood pressure cuff hanging from the IV stand. Suddenly her brown eyes grew as round as saucers. "Something's wrong here. Stand back."

She grabbed a small control near the IV bag and adjusted it, her eyes still huge, her movements amazingly swift and sure.

"What is it, Mavis?" Conner hovered nearby, while Audrey braced herself against the wall.

Mavis timed the drip from the bag, then tucked in the thin blanket around Frank and timed it again. "This boy was heading for trouble for sure. You can be glad I got here. Either one of you fool with this?" She pointed to the IV apparatus.

"We haven't touched it." Audrey moved closer to the bed.

Mavis pushed Frank's hair from his face. "These things don't change by themselves. Somebody made a mighty big mistake. Look at how slow it's dripping—fifty cc's an hour, the way it's supposed to. The dial was set at two hundred cc's. Sure enough that would bloat up this boy's system and swell up his damaged brain. After two or three days he would've been dead."

Audrey gasped. Conner stood at the end of the bed, clutching the bed rail, staring at Frank. "How long has it been like that, Mavis? Can you tell?" His voice cracked with emotion.

"No way of telling." She rubbed Frank's free arm and smoothed his face. "That's the danger. Only way of telling is to look at the flow. A patient doesn't show outside signs of what's going on."

"How long before we know if he's okay?" Audrey squeaked out.

"Depends on how much extra fluid got in him." She faced Conner. "How long you been in here?"

"Not that long." Audrey hovered closer.

"A nurse came in while we were here. Why didn't she notice it?" Conner's eyes never left Frank.

"What nurse? This is my hall for the night." Mavis's eyes got big again.

"What do you mean?"

"There isn't any nurse I know of who has time to take on extra patients when she's on duty. Whoever that was, she didn't have any business in here."

Mavis continued to fuss around Frank, doing everything she could to make him comfortable. "I have to report this to Doc Rankin right away. I wish I could get old Doc Cranford in here to take a look. We're good friends. But Doc Rankin's Frank's doctor, so that's who I have to tell."

Audrey felt her face flush. It wasn't against the law to see a patient outside of visiting hours, but it could certainly be a professional embarrassment if word got out.

Mavis saw the concern on her face. "Don't you worry. I haven't seen anybody in this room tonight, understand?"

"You're a real sweetheart, Mavis."

"And I promise you one thing. I'm going to call Doris and get her in here right now, then park myself across that hall in the supply closet. I get a fine view of Frank's room from there. Nobody's going to get by Mavis again. I guarantee it."

Audrey and Conner stayed with Frank until Doris arrived twenty minutes later. Mavis, meanwhile, called Doc Rankin and set herself up across the hall.

Once they left the hospital, Conner stayed close by Audrey's side. "Frank's in danger, Audrey. Mavis can't watch him twenty-four hours a day."

"I know." She was worried, too. "Maybe he'll come out of it soon. Let's just hope and pray Mavis caught the IV in time."

AUDREY MADE A POINT of arriving early with Ian at the center the next morning. It was time to talk to Doc.

She found him outside one of the classrooms. "Doc, can you spare me a few minutes?"

Doc literally beamed. "My pleasure, Audrey. Why don't we go to my office?" He motioned for her to follow him down the hall. Once they reached his office he invited her to sit down, then took a seat, too.

Audrey got right to the point. "What can you tell me about Leona Kingsley, Doc?"

He blinked rapidly. His face turned slightly red. "I'm sure I don't know what you mean." He sounded offended she had asked.

"You know." She tried to put him at ease. "Who was she close to? What did she do in her spare time?"

"Audrey, my relationship with Leona was strictly one of doctor to volunteer. I certainly didn't know her socially."

"But it's my understanding she was here every day. Surely you must have become friends. Wasn't she your main fund-raiser?"

"Indeed she was. The lady had a way of turning straw into gold, but that's about all I can tell you."

Deciding to return to the subject of Leona later, Audrey moved on. "I'm also concerned about Frank Smith. He had an appointment to talk to you on Saturday."

"Yes," he said firmly. "He asked about Della's relationship with Leona."

"Were they friends?"

"Hardly, but they weren't enemies, either, the way the old folks told Frank. Really, Audrey, Frank's suggestion that Della might have something to do with Leona's death was totally unfounded."

"I see." She paused. "I heard what happened to him at the hospital last night."

Doc stared at his desk calendar, then abruptly waved his hand in the air, as if dismissing the problem. Or her question.

"It was nothing to be concerned about. We insist the staff regulate their routine to prevent problems, but unfortunately mistakes can happen. You may not know, but the nurse scheduled for duty last night took ill and called in a substitute. That was the problem."

Audrey decided to play dumb. "I'm sure you wouldn't allow anyone on the floor who wasn't qualified."

"Quite true. But this particular nurse tends to be careless. Unintentionally, of course. She's an older woman. Her eyesight is failing and she's not very well educated. I know you must run into people like that on a daily basis as a defense attorney."

Audrey was dumbfounded. Who was he talking about? Certainly not Mavis. "What's her name again?"

The door swung open. "Doc, I think we have a problem with—" Della Andrews's mouth popped open when she saw Audrey. "What is she doing here?"

Doc rose from his chair, the blush back in his cheeks. "Della, I believe you've already met Audrey McKenna."

"Yes, we met."

Her voice was harsh. The cold, angry eyes she'd turned on Audrey became neutral in a blink.

"Did you have a question about the school? Doc doesn't know much about that part of the center. Maybe I can help you."

Audrey took advantage of the offer. "I was asking Doc about Leona Kingsley. I know you saw her every day. What kind of person was she?"

Della's head snapped to Doc and back. "Why...she was a nice woman. We miss her contribution, of course."

"Of course." Audrey thought her response was an odd way to express loss. "Can you tell me the names of any of her friends? I'd like to talk to them."

Della scowled. "You're defending Conner Hastings, aren't you? Well, let me tell you right now, you won't get any help from me to set a murderer free." Again her tone had turned harsh.

The emotional outburst was out of sync with her lack of attachment to Leona. As tempting as it was to lash back at her, Audrey held her tongue. "I sincerely hope no one gives false testimony to set any criminal free."

Doc walked around the desk. "Audrey, you'll have to excuse us."

His eyes failed to meet hers. He touched her arm, and it was all she could do not to shrink back.

"Della and I have some things to discuss. I'm sure you understand."

Audrey stood. "I appreciate your help, Doc. We can finish our conversation at another time. Della." She nodded to the woman rather than engage in a cat fight.

And it was a cat fight, she thought as she marched out the door to her car, the conversation rolling around in her head.

They'd both been reluctant to talk about Leona. Maybe volunteers were viewed as a separate species to be left alone to function. Della's reaction to her surprised her the most. The only explanation that made sense was that Della had designs on Doc and had heard about his past infatuation with Audrey.

But none of that explained Doc's description of Mavis. Possibly he was covering up for his mistakes. Whatever the reason, the conversation left her extremely uncomfortable.

Chapter Seven

Conner slammed in the front door of Regal, Thompson and Lutz close to lunchtime. "Can you come out here a second?" His voice boomed down the hallway to Audrey in her office.

The temp Lori had brought in to answer the phones rushed through Audrey's office. "It's okay, Mandy," Audrey reassured her.

Conner stormed into her office and fixed his hands on the front of her desk. Deep furrows creased his forehead. He was definitely agitated, irritated and ready to explode. And still her skin heated and her heart beat faster.

"There's someone outside you need to speak with," Conner said, then waited expectantly for Audrey to go with him. She followed him outside. James Nelson, the mechanic, sat in his truck, which was parked behind Conner's truck. When Audrey invited him to join her in the privacy of her office, he refused to budge.

"It's got nothing to do with you, Audrey. I just don't hold with lawyering, that's all."

"James. It's just an office." Conner drummed his fingers on the roof of the truck. "Like you have at your garage."

Several merchants along First Street stared from their doorways. Customers looked their way before bypassing the shops.

Audrey walked around to James's window. She saw no

point in wasting time or testing Conner's patience further. "What is it James? What can you tell me?"

"I found something." He sat as straight as a stick, against a beaded seat cover. He stuck his balled hand out the window and slowly unrolled his fingers.

"A bullet? You found this in Frank's car?" The excitement of discovery flooded Audrey's veins.

"That I did. Right there, big as life in the left front tire. Went in through the sidewall." Pride shone in his eyes. He sent Conner a thumbs-up sign. "Conner knew what he was talking about. Frank's an ace driver. His accident was no accident."

She looked across at Conner, who was leaning against the other window. He let out a pent-up breath and beamed back at her. Finding proof that confirmed his initial suspicions had done wonders for his ego, she guessed, knowing him as well as she did. But if he thought the bullet conclusively showed a connection between Frank's accident and Leona's murder, he was wrong. The bullet merely suggested the possibility.

"I know this may sound like a ridiculous question." Audrey focused on James and took the bullet from his hand. "But I don't know much about guns or cars. Could anybody drive a car with a bullet in the tire?"

James laughed and fired up the truck. "Hardly. This bullet would've caused Frank to lose control. With the storm and all? He didn't stand a chance. He's lucky he came away with only a cracked-up head and a busted leg." He pulled away from the curb, sending them a salute as he turned onto Main Street and disappeared out of sight.

Conner followed her inside. Once they reached her office, he quickly closed the door behind them.

"This certainly gives credence to your theory."

She walked toward her desk, feeling a great deal of anticipation of holding potential proof of a relationship between Conner's case and Frank's wreck in her hand.

Conner wasn't listening. He grabbed the hand that held

the bullet, zipped her into his arms, lifted her off her feet and whirled her around in a circle. Audrey clung to his neck, enjoying his moment of excitement. With seductive slowness, he let her slide down his taut body until her feet found the floor.

Uninterested in subduing her emotions, she found the sexy mouth that had once deliciously taunted her entire body. He tasted like innocence and success.

His lips released hers. His arms wrapped her next to his beating heart. There were so many words she wanted to say, so many thoughts about future possibilities that couldn't be uttered. She held him close and savored the smell of him, the feel of him, knowing that soon, possibilities could be moot issues. Especially if she didn't get busy.

She looked up into his loving eyes and wanted to cry at the thought of losing him. "We still have a long way to go, Conner."

He gazed into her face as though trying to read her mind. He kissed her eyelids, her eyebrows, her cheeks and her nose. "You're very special to me, Audrey. I hope you know that." As tenderly as he'd spoken the words, he tucked a stray curl behind her ear.

She couldn't explain the discomfort she suddenly felt, but it was sufficient to prod her to move away. The unknown sometimes threatened a person's otherwise stable peace of mind, she reasoned, walking to her desk and pulling out her chair. In this case the unknown threatened more than she could handle. She couldn't bear to think of losing Conner again. She desperately wanted the threat erased.

"You haven't forgotten we're going to Frank's, have you?"

Audrey checked the time. "Not at all. Now is as good a time as any."

He followed her out of the door. "I'd bet my life that the same person who tried to kill Frank also killed Leona."

Audrey didn't answer. She didn't want to add that that was exactly what he was doing—betting his life.

"GOOD OLE JAMES. He's the best mechanic around. I knew he'd find something. I knew it couldn't have been an accident." Conner braked at the stop sign, then turned onto the state road toward Frank's.

"I still can't believe Sheriff Parks didn't have James examine the car, if for no other reason than to ascertain the cause of the wreck."

"Why not? Parks has more than one blind spot. Frank's accident takes a back seat to Leona's death, which makes sense. Even so, the man seems obsessed with her murder."

"You know what we have to do, don't you?"

"You got it." Conner glanced at her. "I look forward to throwing that blind spot in the sheriff's face."

Audrey reviewed her schedule in her head. "We'll go tomorrow. We also want to ask Doc and Della Andrews where they were the night Leona was killed. I had a strange conversation with the two of them this morning." She filled him in on what was said. "Something sure sounded fishy, as if they were hiding something."

"What? You think they could be involved in Leona's murder?"

"I don't know. But the picture Doc painted of Mavis was really distorted. Why would he do that?"

"Who knows? He's always been sort of strange. But I can't see him killing somebody in cold blood. If for no other reason than he's scared to death of guns."

"That's a good point. But I still want to know if they have alibis for the night of the murder. And another thing." She hated to put a damper on his enthusiasm about James's find, but she needed to state the obvious. "We have to stay objective about the bullet, Conner. It proves that someone tried to kill Frank. That's all. It couldn't have come from the same gun that killed Leona. Sheriff Parks has that one under lock and key."

"There's a connection, all right."

His deep, confident voice stroked the need burning inside her. The man never gave up. She turned sideways to see him better, to latch onto his positive outlook, to bathe herself in the luxury of being near him. From a legal perspective, it was next to impossible to share his optimism. Their inquiries led to more puzzling questions. They had yet to shake the evidence against him, and believing the bullet showed a connection didn't make it so. If only the sheriff were putting some effort into investigating the murder. They might make faster progress then.

"What we need to do right now is find Frank's notes on Leona and hope they offer something new." She reaffirmed their immediate goal as much for herself as for him.

The morning fog had cleared, leaving a refreshing blue sky that promised a beautiful afternoon. She lifted her face to the sun shining through the windshield.

If only their future held as much promise as the day, she'd be happy.

Audrey snapped to attention. She locked her hands in her lap. Her heart felt as though it might explode at the sudden insight. She believed in him. She honestly believed Conner was innocent.

How this had happened, she wasn't sure. She tried to logically assess her change of heart, but the more she tried, the more useless the effort seemed; logic and legalities would condemn him. She couldn't even attribute the change to intuition. Were that the case, she would have felt Conner's innocence from the beginning.

Her relief was so great she wanted to rationalize away the most damning evidence of all—the murder weapon. Surely the murderer had stolen Conner's gun. It was the only viable explanation. Why would anyone commit murder, then leave the murder weapon at the scene of the crime? That made no sense.

She acknowledged a humming in her heart as they turned onto Frank's road. When Conner reached over and took her hand, she made no effort to excuse the hungry longing building inside her.

She knew now something she'd refused to admit before. She'd come home to find Conner, whether it made sense or not.

CONNER PULLED to a stop in front of Frank's and she stepped from the truck. The ground was spongy beneath a thick mattress of pine needles. Tall evergreens and oaks shaded the acres of land surrounding Frank's house and reminded her of her own cottage. The cool air from the river at the bottom of the steep bank stirred her hair as she held up her head to catch the full effect.

Frank's place was as Audrey remembered it from when his parents had lived here. A wood stove and knotty pine paneling dominated the main room. Fishing poles lined half of the ceiling in neat, straight rows. Family pictures crowded every tabletop, except for the one in the corner holding Frank's ham radio.

"Where do we begin? I'm not quite sure what we're searching for."

"Notes, look for any kind of notes."

Conner was already sitting in front of the computer in the corner. He pointed to a tall bookcase along the closest wall. "You go through the papers on those shelves. I'm not sure how he organized his research or how fast he got everything into the computer, so we want to cover all our bases. Look for anything that relates to Leona. If they're dated, all the better."

The work corner was the only messy place in the room, as if this was where Frank spent his time. The bookcase was the worst. "Thanks a lot."

"Think nothing of it."

He shot her a sideways glance, along with a teasing smile that made her breath quicken. She turned away and concentrated on the collection of papers and books thrown together in the bookcase.

For a while they worked in silence, the clicking of the computer keys and the rustle of papers the only intrusions. But the position of her chair made it impossible not to see him. She watched him tap into one file after another, his attention focused. She doubted he even realized she was there.

His eyes skimmed the screen as he rapidly paged through each file. His straight back and broad shoulders leaned slightly forward in the chair. Deft fingers manipulated the keys and made her recall his natural aptitude for computers. He seemed caught up in a world of his own. Audrey found herself longing to be there with him.

In spite of her newfound belief in him, she couldn't help but wonder if she knew him anymore. A lot could happen to a person in six years. Spending time in prison definitely changed a man. Was her perception of Conner based on the man she'd known before?

Conner interrupted her thoughts when he leaned closer to the screen. His rich, dark hair tumbled carelessly down his forehead, giving him a rumpled appearance she still loved so much. Such an insignificant movement, such a small change, yet it made her heart race a little too fast.

She turned away and continued to sort folders by subject, her separate piles on the floor growing. She and Conner were there to find Frank's notes, she told herself. Any personal feelings would have to wait.

She was down on all fours, when the title drew her eyes. Curious, she pulled out the file and discovered several more with the same title. *Hastings's Horror House* was scrawled across the outside. Inside were several CD-ROMS.

She held up a CD. "What's this?"

Conner glanced at the item in her hand. "They're just demos."

"Why do they have your name on them?" Fascinated, she added, "They're yours, aren't they? What in the world are they?" She read the blurb on the envelope and learned the nature of the CD before he answered.

"It's just a computer game series. Frank likes to try out the demos."

She was losing her patience, only because she felt so dumb. The man could be so stubborn. "Why do I get the feeling I'm missing something? I know you've always been fascinated with computers, but that's a far cry from creating computer games. Where did you ever learn to do this?"

He turned toward her, his face slightly flushed. My God, he was embarrassed. She had to get to the bottom of this. "Well?"

He stared at her for a long minute. "I worked with computers in prison, all right?"

"No, it's not all right. I want to hear everything, all the details. How did you learn to create the games?" Her curiosity had gotten the best of her.

"Let's just say I discovered I have a talent for these crazy games the kids love." He turned his attention back to the computer.

This was like trying to wring the truth out of a client who didn't trust you—frustrating, aggravating and downright infuriating. But she could be just as stubborn as he was.

She stuck her face between his and the monitor. His intense blue eyes almost chased her away. "And?"

He leaned back in his chair and eyed her suspiciously. "If you must know, I got bored after I earned my degree, so I started playing around with some ideas."

She hadn't known he'd continued his studies in prison. Why wasn't that information included in her files? "You earned your degree?"

"You can do that in prison, you know." His sarcastic tone reflected her disbelief.

"Don't get your back up. Why didn't you ever mention what you were doing? I'm shocked."

"Why? Because you don't think I can make it in the

real world?" His eyes grew dark as his words became harsh.

"I didn't say that, Conner."

"But you thought it."

"No, really, I'm thrilled for you." She picked up the CDs and examined them more closely, realizing that if he'd made demos, he must be trying to sell them. "Have you found an interested buyer?"

His face softened. "I hope so. One company wanted to purchase a part of the series, but it's the whole set or nothing. You have no idea how tempting it was to accept that first offer, but it might turn out to my advantage that I rejected it. I found someone else who's as enthusiastic about the project as I am. They're test-marketing the series in California now."

She was overwhelmed with awe and admiration. He had accomplished so much, and under the most trying of circumstances. She'd always had faith in him; she knew that. When they were going together, she'd sensed the man he would become, but the surprise she was experiencing made her wonder exactly how complete her confidence in him had been.

"That's why you bought all that computer equipment." She felt like an idiot. She'd been at his house when the equipment had arrived. Why hadn't her vision of him been broad enough to ask questions then?

"Remind me sometime and I'll take you through the horror house if you like." He reached for the CDs. When she failed to let go, his hand covered hers.

She dropped the CDs and clasped his hand. Without thinking of reasons she should keep an emotional distance, she let the feel of him draw her in. She reveled in the magic of his fingers and the strength in his hand. She luxuriated in the tingling awareness brought on by his touch.

"The CDs?"

He held her captive with passion-filled eyes and an amused smile she would die for. His husky voice intruded on her private fantasy of pleasure and forced the magic moment to a close.

Her own voice, when she spoke, reflected that passion. Her tone was hushed, yet that was all she could muster. "Would you mind if I borrowed them? I have a nephew who loves computer games."

She felt him withdraw at mention of the outside world. The control had returned to his voice with his next words. "Take them. No problem."

It was difficult to resume her searching and pretend nothing had happened between them, but as he pulled away and she saw the concentration in his face once more, she forced herself to pick up the CDs and the unfiled papers and get back to work. Several minutes passed before her mind regained enough focus to concentrate—and before she realized how badly she'd slipped in her resolve to stay uninvolved. Once she did, Conner caught her attention again.

"This is curious."

Audrey moved her chair over and focused her eyes on the screen, but her attention was on Conner. "So near, yet so far away" was the phrase that ran through her head.

"Did you find something?"

"I don't know. I tried to get into this file, but he's protected it with a password. None of the other files needed passwords. I wonder if…"

He tipped back his chair and stared at the ceiling. His profile was striking, and Audrey drew back, afraid of the crazy notions forming in her mind.

"What would Frank use as a password?"

"If it's about Leona, the most obvious choice would be her name."

He lowered the chair onto all four legs. "This is the last file, Audrey. If his notes aren't here, then they have to be in those papers you're organizing."

She looked down at the long line of piles on the floor and over to the remaining mess on the shelves and groaned. "Let's hope this is the file. It could take all night to clear out the bookcase."

In a flash her mind conjured up a scene of her and Conner sorting through the papers all night. Alone. In this room. Before she could halt the flow of the obvious sequence, she saw them tangled on Frank's sofa in a passionate embrace.

"Stop it."

Conner stared at her. "Why?"

Audrey gave her head a good shake. "What I meant was, stop sounding so defeated. If we can figure out the password, we'll get in. Did you try 'Leona'?"

She scooted her ladder-back chair away and pushed herself far back on the seat until the rungs dug into her spine. The irritating pain should remind her to behave.

Conner tapped in the name and pushed Enter. "No go."

They went through a dozen words that Frank might associate with his research on Leona. In frustration, Conner typed out "murder." The screen filled with a new file.

"Bingo, we're in. Look at that, LEONA in great, big caps."

"All right!"

Conner paged down the file. "There's not much here. A lot of biographical data, a financial report, which we're already familiar with, and his interviews with the seniors at the center. The only other thing are these names. Do you recognize any of them?"

Audrey read the names aloud and searched her memory. "'Florence Jackson, eighty-one. Cornelia Stone, seventy-eight. Grace Osgood, eighty-four.' They sound familiar, but I know I've never met them."

"Look at the date." Conner pointed to the screen, his voice growing with excitement. "Frank was working on this the day he had his wreck." He reached across her and loaded paper into the printer. "I want to print this out."

She ignored his closeness, his rich male scent. She ignored the brush of his arm across her breast. But for some reason, she forgot to breathe.

The telephone rang. The unexpected intrusion jolted them both.

"Who in the world would be calling? Everyone knows Frank's in the hospital."

Conner picked up the phone. Audrey watched his face turn from relief to concern as he listened.

He slammed down the phone. "Let's go." He snatched up the printout and raced across the room. "Mavis has been trying to find us for hours. Frank is conscious."

Audrey gathered her things. "Is his mind all right?"

"She doesn't know."

CONNER TOOK Audrey back to her office under protest and hightailed it to the hospital. Now that Frank was out of the coma, he could be in greater danger than ever. It was his job to get him out of there, not Audrey's.

He took the hospital stairs three at a time. A nurse stopped him at Frank's door.

"Oh, no, you don't, buster. Can't you read?" She pointed to the sign. "You can't go in there."

"Just watch me."

He plowed past her into the room. And halted when he reached Frank's bed. With his skin pale and his eyes closed, Frank looked the same as he had the other night.

Conner pulled the chair close to the bed and took Frank's hand. His eyelids fluttered.

Conner let out a breath of relief. "Hey, old buddy, are you awake?"

"Conner?"

"Welcome back to the living."

"So I understand." Frank blinked his eyes wide-open.

"How's your leg?" Conner tapped on the cast. "And your head?"

"One question at a time, if you don't mind." Frank rubbed his head.

"We've been worried about you."

"What the hell happened?"

"What do you remember?" Hoping Frank's mind was intact, he had to ask.

"The storm. I remember the storm." Frank scrubbed his hands over his face. "I remember leaving the center. I talked to Doc Rankin and the storm hit while I was inside. I was on my way home."

He spoke slowly, hesitantly, as if searching his mind for the right words. But at least he seemed okay.

Frank zeroed in on him with questioning eyes. "So what did happen?"

"Your car went off the road, hit a ditch."

"You're kidding, right?"

"Nope. The sheriff is calling it an accident, but I had James go over the car. Somebody shot at you, Frank. James found a bullet in the tire."

His face turned whiter, his eyes wider. "Why?"

"I was hoping you might know."

"Beats me."

Frank's weakness and the heavy leg cast made him an easy target. Conner knew he wasn't going anywhere until Frank was safe.

"I don't want to upset you, Frank, but whoever tried to kill you could try again."

"Then get me the hell out of here." Frank tried to get up, momentarily forgetting the leg in the pulley.

"My thoughts exactly." Conner gently pushed him back down. "And I know the perfect place to take you."

The nurse barreled through the door and stood with her arms crossed in front of her, a look of triumph on her face. Doc Rankin closed in behind her.

"What's the meaning of this, Conner?"

"No meaning at all, Doc." He moved between Doc and Frank.

"I left strict orders that only family members were allowed to visit."

"Come off it, Doc. You and I both know that Frank's nearest relative is a thousand miles away. Why would you want to keep everyone away from Frank?"

"He's too weak to have visitors. You can see that."

"What I see is a man who was strong enough to pull himself out of a coma. No thanks to a certain nurse. Who was it, Doc? Who came sneaking in here to try to kill Frank?"

Flustered, Doc muttered incoherently. Finally he managed to say, "You have no authority to come barging in here. Disturbing everyone. Ignoring my orders." His face contorted in a series of ugly expressions. "Sheriff Parks will hear about this."

Frank stirred on the bed. "What the hell are you talking about? Someone tried to kill me again? In a coma?" His wild eyes moved from Conner to Doc. "Unhook me from this contraption, Doc. I'm checking myself out for good."

"That's not possible. You can't leave now." Doc made no move to help Frank. He waved his arms about and tried to block Conner from the bed.

Conner set to work releasing Frank's leg. Doc argued with them the whole time. He paced and ranted and got red in the face. He followed Conner down the hall and back while Conner hunted for a wheelchair and got Frank ready to leave.

As weak as he was, Frank finally blew up. "Like it or not, Doc, I'm gone. Your hospital is not a safe place for me right now."

Conner pushed the wheelchair through the hospital corridors, with Doc bellowing behind him. He only hoped the place he had in mind could keep Frank safe long enough for him to heal and regain his strength—if he could get him there in one piece without the killer discovering them.

Chapter Eight

"You have to do it, Audrey." Conner spoke urgently into the phone. "Frank can't tolerate that long a drive in my truck."

Audrey agreed to meet them at Conner's house, then hung up the phone, thankful that Frank appeared to be all right. Knowing she wouldn't be back until late, she called Helen and arranged for her to get Ian at the center and keep him for the night.

She and Conner turned into his road at the same time. A new Cadillac Seville blocked their path. It looked like the one she'd seen at Ida May's.

"Pull over close to the right," Conner called from his window. "She'll just have to go around us."

The Cadillac moved forward. But it wasn't Ida May behind the wheel. It was the handyman driving, the same one she'd seen that day at Ida May's. He passed Conner's truck, then raised a hand to wave at her.

She followed Conner into his yard, surprised to see anything left of his driveway after all the rain. Parking close to the house, she saw Ernie Covington by the porch, shuffling back and forth in typical teenaged fashion.

"Hi, Audrey," Ernie greeted her as she got out of the car.

"How are you, Ernie? You got a ride home in style, I see."

"Did you see it? Did you see that big car? I'm gonna have one just like it one of these days." His face lit up in animation.

Conner walked over from the truck. "Ernie's been doing odd jobs around the yard for Ida May."

"Where's Frank?"

"Sound asleep." He glanced over at the truck, where Frank's chin rested on his chest. "I'll wake him when we're ready to go."

"Miss Lansing pays real good." Ernie's eyes came alive.

"Conner told me what a hard worker you are. Before you know it you'll be able to buy your own car. Of course, you'll have to wait until you have your license." A weak connection was forming in her mind. "How long have you been working at the Lansing estate?"

"Since spring. Two afternoons every week." There was pride in his voice.

"I see," she said, the connection growing stronger. "Did you know Leona Kingsley, Ida May's cousin?"

"Oh, yeah." Ernie nodded. "She came out all the time."

"Do you remember the last time you saw her there?" Conner had picked up on her thoughts.

"Sure, I remember because it was the day before she got killed."

Audrey controlled herself with great effort.

"Ida May lied to you." Conner's eyes turned almost black.

"She told me she hadn't seen Leona in six months. I wonder why."

"I can think of one very good reason." His voice tightened.

"I have an appointment to see her in the morning, nine o'clock. Why don't you meet me there?"

"I wouldn't miss it."

Conner gave Ernie instructions on a few chores to do while he was gone. "What you can't load in the truck, I'll help you with tomorrow." When he saw Frank stir inside the truck, he returned his attention to him.

Audrey gave Frank a big hug when she got to the truck. "I'm so glad you're all right."

"I didn't mean to doze off, but boy, do I feel better." He leaned close and whispered in her ear. "Congratulations, little mama."

"Conner told you." Of course he would tell his best friend. She looked at Conner, the question obvious.

"Yes, he knows." His eyes dared her to object.

"My lips are sealed." Frank zipped his mouth closed. "When do I get to meet him?"

"When it's safe to come out of hiding." Conner's tone was all business. "Let's get you into Audrey's car."

It took both of them and a pair of crutches to move Frank into the back seat of the car.

Frank pointed to the truck. "Don't forget the computer."

"I don't believe this." Audrey saw Conner drag a laptop from his truck.

"I'm not an invalid, you know. Don't you two think you can shove me into a corner and keep me down. I can go right on working on the case." Frank grinned at her from the back seat.

"Let's get moving." Conner closed his door. "Take a right at the highway."

"Where are we going?" asked Audrey.

"To Mavis's. Her house is north and west of here on one of the creeks off the Piankatank."

Audrey wondered at his brusque manner, but ignored it and turned her attention to Frank. "Have you met Mavis yet, Frank?"

"Conner says I have, but I don't remember."

"You're in for a treat."

"Keep going past Saluda." Conner trained his eyes on the landscape.

"This sure as hell beats your truck, pal." Frank gave

them both a thumbs-up sign. "And it's a hundred percent better than that hospital."

"We looked for your notes on Leona," Audrey told him. "Conner managed to break into a file titled 'Leona.'" Why did Conner's accomplishment give her such a great sense of pride?

Frank smiled in amusement. "Can't keep anything secret with this guy around, not if it involves computers."

"We didn't find much."

"The article stuff's not in there. The last old gal I talked to at the center told me Leona was doing a piece on some of the people at the center."

"You mean the staff?" Audrey hadn't heard about any article.

"No, more like a human interest approach about what the center offers or what it needs. Some fund-raising gimmick."

Conner shifted in his seat to see Frank. "Why'd you have those three names at the end of the file?"

"I snagged them from Leona's desk when I interviewed the gal who worked in the office with her. You know, you see a piece of paper sticking out from underneath the blotter and you just have to look at it."

Frank never missed a trick, thought Audrey. "How do they relate to the case?" she wanted to know.

"You've got me there." Frank shook his head. "I asked Doc about them. All three were regulars at the center before they died. Heart attacks, I think he said. But Doc had a weird reaction when I asked him. Here we were having this civil conversation and he almost loses it when I read off the names."

"I had a strange conversation with Della and him, too." Audrey waited until she'd switched on her headlights and passed an intersection before continuing. "Strange enough that Conner and I want to know where they were when Leona was killed."

"Don't bother. He and Della Andrews worked late at the center that night."

Strike two suspects, thought Audrey. "What do you know about Ida May Lansing?"

"She's one of those poor little rich ladies. Grew up with money. Struck out on the family inheritance. Got stood up at the altar. The jerk she was supposed to marry swindled her out of what money she had. I did one of my first articles on him," Frank said. "Since then she's lived pretty quietly from what I hear. But I've always had this funny feeling about her. I don't know what it is."

"She's a rather pathetic figure." Audrey still remembered her surprise at seeing the worn furniture and outdated clothes.

"Take a left up ahead, Audrey." Conner pointed to a road she would have missed.

They traveled for quite a while down a two-lane, paved road. Frank, she saw in her rearview mirror, kept nodding off. The sunset disappeared and the road became unnervingly dark. Conner searched every side road for the place to turn.

"There." He gestured toward an overgrown lane that was visible only when the headlights hit it. "That's got to be it."

Audrey slowed to a crawl on the bumpy road. It looked unused. There was barely a path to follow.

"Are we lost?" Frank asked.

The same thought had occurred to Audrey. She knew the area well, but she'd never been back here.

Audrey was about to voice her doubts, when she saw a dim light through the trees. Slowly they left the bumpy lane and emerged into a cleared area that surrounded a low building.

"COME ON IN HERE, folks," Mavis called from the doorway, her regal form a silhouette against the light inside.

"I got a nice, big pot of hot coffee waiting." She switched on a spotlight so they could see the path.

Frank let them help him from the car. Once his foot hit solid ground, though, he insisted on making his way alone with the help of his crutches. Audrey and Conner walked on either side of him, just in case.

A half-moon shed enough light to reflect water off to the right of the house. The house itself appeared to stretch into the dark shadows. Mavis led them to a creekside entrance that had an old sign above the doorway that read Jock's Diner.

"You sit right here, Frank." She pulled out a chair and dragged over a second chair for his broken leg.

Audrey took in the wonderful smell of fresh coffee. She and Conner joined Frank at the table as Mavis brought them steaming mugs.

"Where's mine?" Frank looked under the tray Mavis held.

"No caffeine for you, boy. I brought you a glass of juice."

Conner and Audrey laughed at the two of them. "Frank, old buddy, I'd like you to meet Mavis. She's your guardian angel for the next few weeks."

"Oh, no!" Frank slumped against the back of the chair.

Mavis served him his glass of juice on a saucer. "You got fifteen minutes. Then my boy here needs some rest." She walked to the swinging doors.

"Before you go." Audrey stopped her. "Have you found out anything about the nurse who was in Frank's room last night?"

"My friend Abby's still asking around real quietlike." Mavis pushed the door open. "So far, that nurse just disappeared. Strange thing," she muttered as she left the room.

Audrey glanced at the dozen tables and the long counter. "Why does Mavis have a diner?" she asked Conner. "I thought she was a nurse."

"According to her son, she's the finest nurse this side of Richmond." His smile warmed her.

"So why does she have a diner?"

"Her husband used to run it before he died. Tim says she takes in all the strays along the pike and puts them to work cooking or scrubbing or serving lunch to the fishermen who dock at the pier. She keeps them busy until they can put their lives back together."

"Tim's her son?" asked Frank.

Conner nodded. "I met him in prison. He's just a kid. Got busted for drugs. Mavis swears he was set up, but the courts thought otherwise."

Audrey's respect for the woman jumped several notches. Mavis seemed to be the type of person everyone needed in his or her life—kind and strong and caring. She had to be to agree to hide Frank. Yet she must be going through her own personal hell, knowing her son was in prison.

"So who's our most likely suspect?" Frank steered them back to the case.

"It's a toss-up." Conner rested his arms on the table. "Ida May is the most obvious choice, since she's the one who benefited. Then there's Bull Kingsley."

"What do you know about Bull?" Audrey hoped he could shed some light on the elusive man.

"Well, now there's a character. He'd sell his mother to make a buck."

"That's harsh, Frank."

"Maybe. I investigated an embezzlement case for a series of articles last year. Bull's name came up over and over again. It seems he's got some shady friends. I never found any solid evidence against him, but I'd say he walks a thin line."

Conner caught Frank's eye. "If that's the case, he's gone way downhill in the past six years."

"That's right." Frank set his juice glass on the saucer. "You two used to bum around together once in a while."

"He was always a little wild, even back then, but he didn't get into any more trouble than you and I did."

"Let's not rehash that particular period, thank you." Frank lifted his cast and moved it closer to the back of the chair.

"That friend I told you about, Audrey? He found out that Bull's a regular at Charley's."

"Good old Charley's." Frank smiled at the memory.

"That's the bar on the way to Richmond, right?" It irritated her that Conner hadn't told her this before.

"That's the one. We need to pay him a visit real soon."

"Tomorrow night?"

"Sounds good to me."

"Did Ben Reilly show up yet?" Frank asked.

"No," Conner said, "but Ernie's mom found the address for his daughter. We can go see her tomorrow, if that's all right with you, Audrey. If Ben Reilly saw someone walk away with my rifle...I'll find him, if I have to turn over every rock from here to Richmond."

"Conner, why haven't you told me these things before?"

"There's nothing to tell yet."

"Withholding information from your attorney makes no sense." His attitude puzzled her. "We're pressed for time."

"Sounds downright stupid, if you ask me." Frank shrugged.

"Okay, you two, I got the point." Conner frowned. "It boils down to one thing, Frank. Whoever killed Leona tried to do you in, too."

"And I say there's no way to prove it," countered Audrey.

"But why else would someone be after me if not because of the investigation?" Frank asked. "Remember, I do have a reputation to keep up. Everyone knows Frank always gets his man."

"Make sure you get him this time, my friend." Conner looked at him seriously.

"You got that right." Frank downed the rest of his juice.

"Say, Audrey, you haven't had any more slashed tires, have you?"

Conner's face turned white. "What are you talking about?"

"Someone slashed my tires when I was at the grocery store last weekend. Frank happened to be at James's when the clerk called the garage. The whole thing was aggravating but not relevant."

"Now who's withholding information?"

Mavis burst through the swinging door and poured herself some coffee at the counter. "Um-hum, that smells good."

Conner moved over to the bar. "I don't know how to repay you for this, Mavis."

"Repay me? I owe you more than I can ever deliver, young man. You saved my Timmy. If it wasn't for you, he'd be passing his time in that prison, piling up a bunch of no-good friends and plotting ways to get in more trouble when he gets out. No, sir. You owe me nothing."

She turned to Audrey, her coffee in hand. "This young man of yours set my boy straight." She pointed her finger as she spoke. "Do you know that when Timmy gets out of that place he'll be a certified computer programmer? Conner got him to take some classes at the prison. That was the hard part—getting him started."

She stared off into the distance. "I always knew my boy had it in him to walk a straight line and earn himself an honest living like his daddy, God rest his soul. Yes sir, the hardest part was getting him started." She looked at Audrey. "That's what Conner did for me. How do you repay a man for saving your boy's life? No, sirree. There's no way to do that."

Conner shifted uncomfortably on his feet. To Audrey's amazement, his neck turned red in an honest-to-goodness blush that crept up to his face.

"I just happened to be there when he was ready, that's all."

"You think what you like, son. I know better. I know my Timmy. He doesn't cozy up to many strangers."

Mavis set down her mug. "Come on, both of you, drink up that coffee and be gone with you." She shooed them to the door.

"I just want to know one thing." Frank called to them from the table. "How come that guy's your young man and I'm just your boy?"

Mavis faced him with all her authority. "Because you need fixin', boy, that's why."

She held the door open. "Don't you worry none. Nobody will know Frank's here. Only my friends venture into this neck of the woods, and they know when to keep quiet."

Audrey and Conner said their good-nights to Frank and stepped out into the night. Once out on the paved road, Audrey found herself praying that Mavis was right, that no one would give away Frank's hiding place. But secrets were hard to keep, especially when no one knew who was after Frank. If the killer found out where he was, Frank might not survive another attempt on his life.

THE CAR SPED down the highway, its headlights piercing the black night. "Why don't we drop you off first?" Conner didn't like the idea of her driving home alone this late. "I can take your car and pick you up in the morning. After we see Ida May, you can let me off at my house."

"No, thanks anyway. I don't like to be stuck at the cottage without transportation when Ian's not there."

Mention of Ian stung like an exposed nerve. "Fine, then."

And it was fine. Her husky voice touched the essence of a fever he couldn't quite quell. The less time he had to stay close to her, the better.

She parked the car in front of his house and got out. Conner threw his head against the seat and groaned. He thought she would let the car idle long enough for him to hop out and be gone. It hadn't occurred to him she might hang around. He didn't want her to stay.

He climbed from the car, heavy with misgivings. A silent, expectant stillness hung in the air, the quiet night unlike his state of mind.

"It's a beautiful night." Audrey leaned back against the side of the car.

The porch light cast a circle of light around the car. He stayed as close to its perimeter as he could.

Audrey crossed the circle and put her hand on his arm. "You wouldn't want to invite me in, would you?"

"No, not tonight." He pulled away.

"What's going on, Conner? I know you're worried about Frank. I know we haven't yet built a credible defense. But this is something else. You've been distant all night."

She would have to ask. He prowled the ground before her, his irritation threatening to get the best of him. "How could you do it?"

He felt her eyes watching him move through the shadows of light. The silence stretched on forever.

"You're talking about Ian."

Her words broke his self-control. "I'm talking about *our* son, yes. How could you not tell me?"

Telling his best friend he had a five-year-old son who was a stranger to him had been humiliating, at best. He'd been prepared for Frank's congratulations, but not for his questions. Frank had asked things about Ian he couldn't answer.

He hadn't been a part of Ian's life. He didn't even know his own son! And Audrey's callous silence had been the cause.

"We talked about this before." Her tone bordered on exasperation. "I thought I did explain."

"Not so far as I'm concerned."

"Don't put the blame on me, Conner." Her voice got

louder. "That was your doing, not mine. You're the one who ended it."

Her anger came through clearly and pushed him to strike back. "I know what I told you. For crying out loud, I didn't want you to waste your life waiting for me to get out."

A breeze stirred the trees and twisted around their silence. He stepped out of the light, cursing his impulsive outburst. The way he put it made it sound like he'd made some great sacrifice, which was a bald-faced lie. Breaking off their relationship had been a selfish maneuver to avoid the guilt. She'd had a life to live. He couldn't have handled knowing she was waiting outside those prison gates.

"You could have told me that then. You could have given me a choice, but no, you coldheartedly forced me away."

The guilt he had desperately wanted to avoid curled around his neck and choked him. She was right. If he hadn't ended their relationship, she would have stuck by him. She was like that—loyal to the end. And if she'd been there, he would have known about his son. She was better at straightening out his head than he was.

Turning around, he saw her walking to the car. He couldn't let her leave yet, not like this. Without giving himself a chance to think twice, he caught up with her and pulled her into his arms. He hugged her close and felt her heart beat next to his. His lips captured hers quickly. His tongue tangled with hers. He explored every inch of her mouth until he felt tempted beyond endurance.

Forcing his brain to function, he ended the kiss and gently loosened his hold on her. The passion glazing her eyes fed the fire she'd ignited and almost undermined his determination to say what needed to be said.

He took her face in both his hands. "I'm sorry, Audrey." His voice cracked on her name. "I made a real mess of things."

She placed the palm of her hand on his face. The gesture was much sweeter and more loving than he deserved.

The light caught her smoldering green eyes. One small curl twisted slightly with the breeze. "I'm glad we talked this through."

"Yeah."

He felt more awkward than he'd ever felt in his life. Talk about baring your soul.

He jammed his hands in his pockets and edged away. "Listen, we'd better call it a night. Thanks for your help with Frank."

She reached for the car door hesitantly, her reluctance to leave plain to see. A lingering passion still showed in her eyes.

She climbed in and rolled down the window. "I'll see you in the morning, then."

He watched her slowly drive away, irritated with himself for being so open with her. Audrey McKenna had a way of digging into his heart. She made him want everything he couldn't have.

AUDREY WALKED back and forth across her living room early the next morning, the carpet muffling her heels. Her temper was ready to flare.

Peter had charged in with Ian five minutes before she had to leave this morning. Her first reaction of pleasure had quickly turned to disbelief when he'd begun to berate her for defending Conner. To think that her brother had been one of the main reasons she'd returned to Tabbs Corner!

"I don't care what you think, Peter. This is my job, my livelihood. You have no right to interfere. Plus," she added for emphasis, "you don't know what you're talking about."

Her brother's face showed as much anger as she felt. "I'd think you'd at least have the decency to tell me what you were doing. But no, I have to hear it at the marina."

Once again she glanced at the clock in the kitchen. If this went on much longer, Peter was going to make her late for her morning appointment with Ida May.

"You don't understand, do you?" Peter stood in front of her shaking his finger in her face. "You're risking your reputation—and mine, I might add. Conner Hastings will never amount to anything, not in this life. This is a small town, Audrey. The people who matter in this town are the ones I see every day at the marina. I have a different perspective than you do."

"Certainly not a legal perspective," Audrey couldn't help but interject.

"You should listen to me, I'm telling you. Maybe Leona was a disappointment to her family. It doesn't matter. What you're dealing with is the influential reputation of the Kingsley family—and a no-good hood they couldn't care less about. Whose side would you be on?" He stopped abruptly. "No, don't answer that."

"Everyone has the right to be represented, Peter." Her anger kept creeping closer to the surface the more he lambasted Conner. She didn't remember Peter being so vulnerable to other people's opinions. But, then, she'd never really known him as an adult. He seemed totally swayed by the prejudicial judgment of a lot of the people in town.

"But it doesn't have to be you. You're practically guaranteeing yourself a miserable life. Nobody will want to have anything to do with you."

"Or you either, is that it?"

Peter threw up his arms in exasperation. "She wasn't worth the time of day!"

Audrey stood stock-still. Something about the way he spit out the words, some change in his tone of his voice, made her instantly alert.

She swallowed and asked, "You knew Leona?"

"Unfortunately."

Tread lightly, she counseled herself. "In what respect?"

"We almost had some business dealings, that's all. That's not the point."

Audrey interrupted him. "What kind of business dealings?"

Peter eyed her suspiciously. "What does it matter? I'm standing here, racking my brains, trying to figure some way to get you to realize that defending Conner will ruin you in this town. That's the point. Whoever murdered Leona Kingsley probably did us all a favor."

"So now you're condoning murder?"

"I'm just trying to help you. You're the talk of the town. Everyone knows you and Conner used to go together. But I have to hand it to you. Even I didn't realize he was Ian's father until I saw the two of them together. How could you agree to defend him?"

An icy calm replaced the temper that had threatened to flare. "You've stepped way over the line, Peter." She picked up her briefcase and walked to the door. "Let yourself out."

Ian was drawing pictures by the shed in a pile of sand left over from ages ago. Thankfully he hadn't heard them.

"Time to go, Ian." He jumped to his feet and ran for the car, always eager to go to the center.

According to Della Andrews, Ian participated in all the activities. The staff encouraged the children to form relationships with the senior citizens who visited the day care, a concept Audrey heartily endorsed. Ian had already become friends with a Mr. Russell Vaughn, a former lawyer. Not quite comfortable with her son making friends with someone she didn't know, Audrey had asked Lori about Mr. Vaughn and received a hearty endorsement of the man.

She rolled these facts around in her head as she drove to the center. Thinking of something else helped her deal with the boiling anger. Peter's blatant efforts to persuade her to withdraw from Conner's case suggested a hidden agenda. What kind of business dealings had he had with Leona? Real estate?

She told herself her suspicions had to do with an incomplete investigation in which everyone was suspect. Peter was not someone she could easily suspect; he was family. The only way to clear up this uneasy feeling was to track down Mrs. Bracken and ask her who had tried to buy property from Leona.

She noticed her white fingers clutching the wheel and immediately loosened her hold.

On top of everything this morning, she was functioning with little sleep. She'd spent the night going over her conversation with Conner. It had killed him to admit why he'd broken off their relationship; she'd seen the pain in his eyes. And he had absolutely no idea how important his admission was to her.

She parked in front of the center and reached over to get her purse. That's when she noticed the folded piece of paper on the floor of the passenger's side.

She leaned across the seat and picked it up. It was a plain, white piece of paper, the type found in any supply store. Scrawled in what looked like a child's handwriting across the page were words that sent an icy shiver down her back: *"Make sure he dies or you'll die in his place."* The red ink had been made to bleed down the page.

She crumpled the paper and shoved it into her purse. She shook off the shiver, angry that the note had the power to affect her. She'd heard stories of threats to attorneys who worked high-profile cases, but she'd never heard of it happening in a small town that was barely a dot on the map. Obviously, some crazy had decided to come out of the closet.

But as she walked with Ian to the front door, the apprehension wouldn't go away. In the back of her mind was the fear that the killer was now after her.

Chapter Nine

Audrey kissed Ian goodbye at the door. "You have a good day, sweetheart."

"I will," he called back as he ran inside.

Della Andrews stepped outside and pulled the door closed behind her. She placed herself in front of the door and crossed her arms. Her severe look put Audrey on guard.

"Ms. McKenna, this is entirely too early to bring Ian to day care."

Della's abrupt manner and brash tone of voice were offensive. This was only Ian's third day at the center. Audrey clearly remembered the flexible hours listed in the literature she'd read. Through the glass panes she could see other children being led down the hall.

"Then I would suggest you inform the other parents, as well." She moved her eyes to the two little girls nearest the door.

Without waiting for a response, she returned to her car. She had no time to waste with pettiness, especially when Della's comments were motivated by personal jealousies rather than the center's policies.

Conner was waiting for her at Ida May's. Together they mounted the front steps and tapped on the door.

After no response, Conner said, "I think it's a lost cause."

"Her car's in the drive. Maybe she didn't hear us."

This time she banged loudly. Getting no answer, they walked around back and tried again.

"Didn't you tell me she was going on a trip?" he asked as they returned to the front.

"Yes, her bags were packed, but her plans were indefinite."

"Not anymore."

She'd anticipated getting some answers from Ida May. The woman had very good reason to want her sister dead. Her absence left a hole in the case that Audrey didn't like.

Conner turned them toward the drive, the morning sun glinting off his hair. His hand on her back as they walked to Audrey's car was reassuring after the letdown—and after the hideous note she'd found.

"If she hadn't told me she might be leaving, I'd say it looks awfully suspicious for her to disappear right now."

"What else could she say with her luggage sitting there?" He leaned against her car, his arms crossed over his chest. He didn't want to part company any more than she did.

"True. Unless we can justify some reason to bring her back, we wait."

He seemed more settled than he'd been last night. The conversation that had kept her awake most of the night still plagued her. Working on the case together was much easier than discussing their personal problems.

She'd never been sure of him six years ago. When he'd made it crystal clear that they were through, she'd taken him at his word. She'd tried to ignore the fact that they shared a son, but it had never worked. Even if Ian hadn't reminded her of him in so many ways every day, it would have been impossible to erase him from her memory. His confession last night had stunned her.

"Are you still angry with me?" She had to know.

He jerked his head toward her, his eyes wide with surprise at the change in subject. "No, I'm not angry with you."

He stretched out his arms and placed a hand on her shoulder. He traced a finger around her ear. "I could never stay angry at you, Audrey."

She tingled from his teasing touch. Pleasure rippled through her body. His deep blue eyes seemed to see into her heart.

"I just wanted to make sure."

But about the only thing she was sure of at this moment was the paralyzing effect of his touch—and the moment he stepped away.

"Are you ready to tackle the sheriff? We might as well get it over with."

For more reasons than one, she took a deep, calming breath. "I'm as ready as I'll ever be."

He opened her door and held it while she got in. "I don't look forward to this, either. I've never been one of the sheriff's favorites."

"DEPUTY, YOU WANT to give me some privacy?" Sheriff Parks barked out the demand and the deputy rushed out the door and shut it noiselessly behind him.

She and Conner hadn't discussed what they would say, but they both knew challenging the sheriff's conclusions about Frank could be a waste of time. Expecting him to change his mind was absurd.

Sheriff Parks seated himself behind his desk. "Repeat what you just said, little lady." He glowered at Audrey and chewed on his straw.

"I asked—" she enunciated slowly "—why you didn't tell James Nelson to examine Frank Smith's car after the accident."

From the chair beside her, she could feel Conner sending her the moral support she needed. She prayed he wouldn't lose his temper. He and Sheriff Parks shared a history of antagonism that dated back to before she'd come to live in Tabbs Corner with her grandfather.

The sheriff took a straw from his pocket. When he realized he already had one in this mouth, he tossed it on the desk and pushed out of his chair. "Come to the point, little lady."

His insults were truly trying her patience. "'Audrey' or 'Ms. McKenna' or 'Counselor' would be fine, *Sheriff Parks*."

"Right, right, you're a big-deal lawyer now." He popped his palm against his forehead. "How could I forget?"

Without looking to him for proof, she could sense Conner ready to pounce. She rose from her chair. "Could we stop the dramatics, please? Just answer the question."

"You're not in court now, *little* lady. You have no right to question my competence. Why, you're just an upstart."

"I have every right to—"

Sheriff Parks stomped around his desk and opened the door. "We're finished here. I'd like to say it's been a pleasure, but somehow that doesn't quite fit."

Conner stepped across the room and slammed the door shut. Audrey felt the resounding crash down to her toes.

"No, Sheriff, we're not finished. We have a little something to show you." He took the bullet from his pocket and displayed it.

"What's this?"

Audrey moved in closer. "James Nelson found this bullet in the tire of Frank's car."

Anger erupted on the sheriff's face. His cheeks turned red, his eyes grew huge. "Now just a guldurn minute. Who gave you the authority to touch Frank's car?"

"Frank did." Conner was displaying amazing control.

"That car's impounded, legally seized and retained in the custody of the county." He glared at Audrey. "Tell him. You're his lawyer."

"I don't know, Sheriff. I was at his house when you

declared Frank's wreck an accident. If that's the case, why would his car be under the jurisdiction of the county?"

The sheriff threw the other straw on the floor. "You two are asking for trouble."

"No, sir. I don't think so. The point here is not who had jurisdiction over the car. The point is this," Audrey stated. "Why didn't you examine Frank's car? You could have done it. James could have done it. Someone should have looked at it to determine the cause of his wreck. You simply assumed he had an accident. This bullet proves otherwise."

"The bullet proves nothing. No, sir. I'd say this is a mighty convenient find."

Undeterred, Audrey continued. "James Nelson will swear in a court of law that he found this bullet in the left front tire of Frank's car."

"How much did you pay him?"

"I beg your pardon?" Audrey didn't want to believe what she'd heard.

"Satisfy my curiosity. How much? Those two have been buddies for years. Everyone knows Frank and your boy here had James doctor those wrecks they called race cars."

Conner moved in. "Now you're getting nasty, Sheriff." He opened his hand and pointed to the bullet. "This bullet was found in Frank's tire. It's not a figment of the imagination. It's as real as you and me, and the person who fired it tried to kill Frank."

The sheriff's expression changed as he stared at the bullet. Incredulity turned the spiteful lines around his mouth to softer lines of amazement. "Wait a minute. Let me see that bullet."

He snatched the bullet from Conner's hand, held it closer to the light and smiled. "Ah, I'm beginning to get the picture. Interesting little .22, isn't it? Did you think I wouldn't notice? This is from the same caliber gun that killed Leona."

"That's what we've been trying to tell you," said Audrey.

The sheriff shook his head. "Yes and no. From where I stand this here bullet tells me more than what you're saying. It tells me your boy here tried to kill Frank Smith."

"What?"

Conner's mouth dropped open. "Are you out of your mind? Why would I want to hurt Frank?"

"I'd say he probably found additional proof you killed Leona Kingsley."

The angry creases on Conner's brow disappeared. His mouth assumed a neutral straight line. He'd pulled in his emotions to hide his anger and frustration, but the dark shadows in his eyes said he wasn't through.

He kept in control when he spoke, even though his eyes flashed in disbelief. "Are you blind? This is a jacket hollow point bullet."

"Yes, indeed. A mighty fancy .22 slug. It would fit just fine in your .22 Winchester Magnum."

"Which you confiscated."

"Don't ask me to believe you didn't foster some handy contacts behind bars. You could replace that old gun with a phone call." His glare cut into Conner.

Conner's jaw tensed. "Don't bet on it."

Audrey had been right. This was truly a waste of time. She couldn't understand the sheriff's attitude.

"Tell me, Sheriff, how come you're so reluctant to explain why no one examined Frank's car?"

"And you tell me, little lady, how come you're so convinced your boy here is innocent. On both counts." That said, the sheriff banged the door open against the wall and stormed out of his office.

AUDREY GRASPED the receipt for the bullet in her hand and headed for the small parking lot behind the building. Conner had gone on ahead while she got the receipt from the sheriff. It was with great relief that she left the building.

She found him standing between her car and his truck. The sun had disappeared behind some clouds. A steady wind blew in her face and chilled her arms. Or maybe the circumstances had brought on the chill.

She leaned back against her car door. "That was a useless trip."

Beside her, Conner rested his elbows on the top of her car. "Oh, I don't know. I think he was embarrassed about the bullet. He was also nervous as a polecat. I wonder why."

"That proves nothing, Conner."

His bland voice told her more than he would want her to know. He had yet to recover from the sheriff's assault. And no wonder.

"What's a jacket hollow point?" She asked not only out of curiosity but to help him forget the encounter.

"It's an expensive type of bullet normally used in competition shooting, that's all."

She mulled that over for a minute. "Do you know where you can buy this type of ammunition?" An idea formed in her head.

"Probably the same place you would buy any other ammunition. I really don't know. These bullets are way out of my league."

"Who would know?"

"Anyone can buy them, Audrey."

"So they can't be traced?"

"I wouldn't think so."

She doused the idea of tracking Frank's assailant through the sale of the ammunition and turned around and put her elbows next to his. "Something doesn't sit right, Conner. The sheriff's reaction was too extreme."

"You won't get any argument from me on that one."

"You don't think he knows more than he's saying, do you?"

"About Frank? No, Parks never had it in for Frank. And his logic was sound. Someone wanted Frank out of the way because he was getting too close to Leona's murderer. The question is who? And what did Frank do that set things off?"

"I think you're right."

"You do?"

He turned to her then. A slice of hidden pain escaped with the wind that teased his hair and crinkled his eyes. Lightly he ran the backs of his fingers down her cheek and across her chin. Audrey closed her eyes and let the sensations fill her soul.

"What do you say we take a trip out to see Frank?" He stroked her face again.

The thought of spending more time with Conner was tempting. With all her heart she wished she could. "I can't. I have to get to the office. Lori will think I've deserted her. But—" she smiled up at him "—Ian wanted me to ask you for dinner."

"He did?" He chucked her under the chin. "How about you? Do you want me to come, too?"

Thank goodness he didn't know how much. "I wouldn't ask you otherwise." She paused. "It'll give you a chance to spend time with him before we go see Bull Kingsley."

Reluctant acceptance crossed his face. "I'll settle for that." He tapped her nose. "For now."

CONNER KNOCKED on Audrey's back door that evening and held back his reaction to her when she stepped out.

"You're just in time. The weather turned so beautiful I thought we'd eat outside."

The smile she sent him fired up the aching need that was never far from crippling him.

"Ian's washing down the picnic table out front. I'm sure he could use some help."

Conner could use some help himself. She looked more beautiful each time he saw her. Her fringed cutoffs stretched across her flat stomach and threads dangled at her thighs, showing off her shapely legs. The soft curves of her breasts filled a light blue halter top. He wondered if she was trying to tempt him beyond his endurance.

"Right." He swallowed hard to clear the catch in his voice and backed up. "You know where to find me, then."

He started to leave, then stopped. "I almost forgot to tell you. I called Frank. He sounds great. Mavis's doctor friend gave him a clean bill of health. Seems he's even recovered from the shock of meeting Mavis last night. In fact—" he grinned "—he said he's considering taking up permanent residence at her house."

Audrey's laugh sounded great. "I wonder how long it'll take Mavis to recover from Frank." She slipped back inside.

When Conner rounded the corner at the front of the house, Ian was swiping up a storm with a sponge larger than his hand. "Conner!" He ran to him and hugged his leg.

Totally unprepared for such a display of affection, Conner surprised himself when he instinctively put his hand on Ian's head. The five-year-old tugged at his heart in a way that was new—and threatening, when he considered his bleak future.

Without giving in to the hesitation he felt, he picked the boy up. "You're all wet, pal."

Ian giggled and wiggled down, then hurried over to the bucket beside the table. "I got one for you, too." He grinned and held up a second sopping sponge.

Conner joined him at the table. "Let's scrub her clean, then."

There were so many questions he wanted to ask his son he didn't know where to begin. "How do you like living here on the creek, Ian?"

"I get to feed the ducks." He started cleaning one of the table legs, then paused. "See?" He pointed to a mallard swimming in the middle of the creek. "That's Donald. He's my favorite."

"How's the snorkeling coming along?" Almost the sum total of his knowledge of Ian had to do with a snorkeling tube.

"Mommy took me. But she didn't get in the water, the way you did. Will you take me again?"

"We'll see."

Conner knew he had to tread lightly. He didn't want Ian getting too used to having him around. Not when he might not be around much longer. Still, he treasured what time they did have.

Audrey appeared at the porch door. "Ian, come inside and change. Then you can help with dinner."

While Audrey attended to Ian, Conner wandered back and forth between the open kitchen and the living area, at a loss what to do with himself. He couldn't deny the contented feeling that came just from being inside Audrey's cottage. The place held a lot of good memories. He saw the fireplace tongs and recalled cool evenings and roaring fires. Those had been good times.

"You and Ian really do get along great."

He'd been so lost in his reverie he hadn't heard her come in. Now she stood too close beside him.

"He's easy to talk to, Audrey. You're doing a fine job with him."

He caressed her silky smooth cheek, loving the softness of her skin. The unexpected passion in her eyes captured him completely, and for a fleeting moment he actually believed he had the same effect on her that she had on him. Those sea green eyes taunted him and reached into his soul searching for... what?

Ian charged into the room. "Conner gets to help me."

The longing in Audrey's eyes receded. Before he could recover, she was in the kitchen, explaining Ian's job.

"And while I slice the ham, he gets to mix up the potato salad." She handed Ian a big spoon and held the stool steady while he climbed up. "But I bet Conner can slice the tomatoes, too."

In no time at all they were sitting down for dinner, a quick affair for Ian. Conner was sure he'd just taken his first bite when the boy hopped up from the table, finished with the part of his meal that hadn't ended up on the table or the ground.

Ian picked up the remains of his roll and held it up to Audrey. "Can I go down and feed the ducks?"

Audrey glanced at the pier. "All right. As long as you stay where I can see you. And no tricks."

Conner watched his son scamper down the hill and suppressed a smile. The boy was ten balls of energy rolled into one. Being around Audrey and Ian made him feel like a normal human being, a feeling he hadn't experienced in a while. And one he was afraid to get used to.

Several strands of her hair had fallen loose from her ponytail. They danced around her head in the breeze that blew across the creek from the river. He longed to reach over and capture those curls.

"I hope Bull's at Charley's tonight." She seemed unaware of the effect she had on him.

"He'd better be." More than ever he wanted to clear up Leona's murder. "I'm not sure he can do us any good, though. He never impressed me as the killer type."

He moved to an angle on the picnic bench where he could glance at Ian with a turn of his head.

"I've been thinking about tonight." He spoke slowly, knowing she wasn't going to like his suggestion. "I think I should do this alone." He remembered Bull's hangouts. They weren't the types of places Audrey should go.

She looked up from her plate and frowned. "Not without me, you don't. Don't go getting overprotective on me, Conner. I have every intention of going."

Her eyes were the purest green he'd ever seen. Framed by well-formed dark eyebrows, thick lashes and flawless light skin, they sparkled when her ire was up. Sometimes he liked to get her riled just so he could see the fire in her eyes.

"You're probably right." He watched Ian toss a crumb to the ducks.

"You don't fool me." Her voice was cool and calm and tinged with self-assurance. She continued to cut her food. "I can read you better than anyone. You're thinking you'll go by yourself, no matter what I say."

Her words were so close to his thoughts they threw him for a minute. "I'd just hate for one of your lawyer friends to see you there."

The warning sparkle stayed in her eyes. He knew it was pointless to argue with her. If he didn't take her with him, she'd go by herself, which would be worse.

"You let me worry about that. The question is not up for discussion."

Her stubbornness was written clearly on her face, the occasional twitch of her nose a dead giveaway. Conner longed to reach across the table and gently tweak that cute little nose.

Actually, he longed to do a lot more than that.

A loud splash caused Audrey to jump up and run toward the pier. "I knew it, you little devil."

Conner barely heard her. All he saw was Ian in the creek, frantically beating at the water. He raced past Audrey to save his son, his heart beating out of control in fear that Ian might drown. Without a moment's hesitation, he jumped into the creek and grabbed him.

"Are you okay?" He searched for cuts and bumps.

Ian looked at him with dazzled eyes, as bright and green as Audrey's.

"He's okay, Conner, believe me." Audrey appeared at the end of the pier and pulled Ian up. Conner followed him out of the water.

"How can you be so calm? Your son almost drowns and there you stand, Miss Calm, Cool and Collected."

Audrey's laugh made him furious.

"Kids are always getting into trouble, Conner. You should know that better than anyone."

He didn't know what to say. He'd panicked, that was for sure. He felt like an idiot. A dripping wet idiot.

Ian gestured to the water. "Want to go swimming?"

Audrey turned him in the other direction. "No, you don't, young man. You've had your swim for the day. Up the hill with you now. You were supposed to feed the ducks from the pier, not from the water, and you knew that."

Once she had Ian marching up the hill, Audrey directed her attention to Conner. "Thank you for what you did. You had no way of knowing he was playing his usual tricks. Believe it or not, he can paddle all the way across the creek and think nothing of it."

A new and different light shone from her laughing eyes, a light that made him want to take her in his arms, made him believe they'd never given up their dreams.

Still smarting from his impulsive reaction, he looked down at his wet clothes, then stared at her hard for a moment, wishing he could read her mind. "I'll grab a change of clothes from the truck before I come in."

He watched her go inside, then wandered over to his truck to pull out the extra clothes he kept behind the seat. He had to be crazy to think he could be a part of Ian's life. He sure as hell wouldn't be a good role model. He'd never known his own father, didn't even know how to act like a father, and he damn well didn't want to be responsible for corrupting his own son. Any relationship that developed between them would only bring Ian pain.

By the time he'd gone inside and changed, the baby-sitter had arrived and Audrey had Ian in bed.

"Aren't you going to kiss me good-night?" Ian stretched out his arms from his bed toward Conner.

Conner's hesitation would have gone unnoticed by anyone but Audrey. Tears threatened to flood her eyes as Con-

ner sat on the edge of the bed and hugged and kissed their
son.

"I get to go to school soon," Ian said.

Eyes so like her own widened in earnestness and
searched his father's face.

"Can we go s-norkeling one day after school?"

Audrey averted her eyes at the flash of pain on Conner's
face. She could say nothing to make it easier for either of
them.

"I hope so." Conner leaned over and kissed Ian's
forehead.

"You go to sleep now." Audrey choked out the words
from the doorway. "Debbie's right in the other room if
you need anything."

She closed the door quietly and wished she could as
easily close off her concern for Ian. He'd grown too fond
of Conner too quickly. He talked about him constantly.
Conner was his hero, a man to relate to in a way he
couldn't relate to her. If she lost the case, Conner would
go to prison. She couldn't bear to think of the pain this
would cause her son.

Chapter Ten

The phone rang as Audrey passed it on her way to the door, but no one was on the line when she answered it. The chill down her back made her tremble. She'd had three other silent calls in as many days. She hadn't given the others a second thought, but after finding the threatening note on the floor of her car this morning, the call caused her alarm.

She wasn't about to give Conner more to worry about, though. "Wrong number, I guess."

She gave the baby-sitter some last-minute instructions, and she and Conner climbed in his truck and got under way to Charley's.

"He's a great kid, Audrey."

"I think so. Of course, I'm a little biased." She tried her best to lighten the conversation and keep her concern for Ian hidden. But she couldn't resist adding, "He's also a lot like his father."

"I'll consider that your first compliment."

He reached across the seat and squeezed her hand. The feel of his coarse palm sent a rush of desire through her veins. She longed to forget about the case and focus every ounce of energy on Conner in a more personal way, but to function as his attorney she had to maintain a distance. Even knowing that didn't convince her to withdraw her hand. The connection was too fragile, too enthralling, too right.

Charley's was located on the outskirts of a small town between Williamsburg and Richmond at the end of a long, winding dirt road. The one-story cinder block building with its contiguous parking lot sat hidden amid tall evergreens and unkempt foliage. Audrey heard the beat of the music as Conner parked the truck.

By this time of night, the dinner crowd had left, the lights were dimmed and customers filled the dance floor, an unusual phenomenon for a Wednesday night as far as Audrey was concerned. She mentioned this to Conner as they made their way to a corner table.

"It must have something to do with the local colleges. Maybe it's the end of the summer session or something. A lot of students find this place. At least, they used to." He signaled to the waiter and ordered. "I guess it hasn't changed."

"I remember the big splash in the local papers when it opened." The year before she'd left, if her memory served her correctly. "Did you come here very often?"

"A few times. When you were too busy to go out with me."

In spite of the music, in spite of the loud voices, the sounds receded to background noise when he leaned across the small table and captured her hand between his palms.

"I'm sorry things got so messed up back then." His words shimmied through her, like the bass beat vibrating through the wooden floor. "Am I going to spoil the mood if I ask where you went when you left?"

"No, that's all right." More than all right, she thought, for at this moment she wanted to share everything with him. "I went to live with Aunt Nell in Stafford County. She needed some help—she was getting pretty old—and I needed a place to live."

"She didn't mind about Ian? I mean, didn't she think it was odd you were pregnant and minus a wedding band?"

She felt his hands tense and saw the blue deepen in his eyes.

"I didn't know I was pregnant when I left here, Conner. Honest. And Aunt Nell was too sweet to ask questions once my condition became obvious. Then, when Ian was born, she fell in love with him. He was the child she never had."

The waiter broke the spell when he set the drinks on the table. Conner pushed back his chair and picked up his beer.

"Do you see Bull out there anywhere?" He described Bull Kingsley.

Audrey pushed back from the table, too, as much to distance herself from their intimacy as to get a better view of the dancers and the few remaining customers seated at other tables.

"The light's really too dim to be sure."

"You're right." He rose from his chair and held out his hand. "Will you dance with me, Audrey?"

His tone and his actions implied a presumption on his part, but his question revealed a vulnerability that pulled at her heart. Conner rarely asked permission, and certainly not to dance.

He cleared his throat. "Maybe we can find Bull on the dance floor."

She linked her hand with his. "I'd be honored."

They wound their way around the scattered chairs and tables and hit the dance floor as the band shifted to a slower tempo. Conner's eyes fastened on hers. One arm reached around her and brought her close in a solid embrace. He held her hand next to his heart.

"I've dreamed of this, you know."

Oh, yes, she wanted to say, *so have I, so many times.* But she didn't dare give voice to her thoughts. The moment was too fragile. If she spoke the truth, the real world would shout its presence.

He nestled his chin against her head and led her ever so slowly through the swaying motions of the music. His hand kneaded the small of her back and caused waves of pleasure to cascade through her.

They moved as one around the dance floor, the feel of Conner's body melding with hers. The mournful song struck chords of longing deep within her soul. His heartbeat echoed through her veins like the throbbing rhythm of the bass. She felt every caress of his hands, every breath on her hair. Every sense came alive with need. She wanted the song never to end, and when the music did stop and the dancers dispersed, she wanted to cry out for them to stay.

He held her to his side as they walked casually back to the table. The band struck a new sound and he stopped abruptly.

"There's Bull." Conner rotated her slightly so she could see the dance floor.

Bull Kingsley was shorter than she'd expected, maybe five ten or eleven. He had curly blond hair and a stocky body that at the moment was glued to his dancing partner.

They sat at their table and waited for the dance to end.

"We could dance our way over to them."

His dimpled smile intimated more than dancing. Clearly, talking to Bull Kingsley had not motivated the suggestion.

"I can't think of a quicker way to lose track of him," Audrey admitted, still tingling from their turn on the dance floor. Once she was in Conner's arms again, Bull Kingsley's importance would greatly decrease.

"Oops, I'll be right back." Audrey pushed her chair from the table.

"Wait a minute. Where are you going?" Conner got to his feet.

"To powder my nose. See?" She led him with her eyes to Bull's partner, who was sashaying toward the rest room. "All kinds of things happen in ladies' rooms." She winked and smiled and started across the room.

Conner walked behind her. "I'll try to corner Bull while you're gone."

It was easy to follow the woman with the brassy red hair as she made her way across the dance floor. She wore a clinging red tank top and a tight black leather miniskirt that barely covered her rear. The silver earrings dangling down the length of her neck caught every flicker of light.

Audrey entered the rest room right behind her and deposited her purse on the counter below the mirror before helping herself to several paper towels.

She smiled at her. "Boy, it gets a little hot out there on the dance floor."

The woman was searching through her purse for something and ignored her. She cracked her gum; the sounds bounced off the tile walls.

"You're a great dancer, by the way. Are you a professional?" Audrey took out her compact and worked on the damage.

"Thanks. I did a stint in New York for a while, but it didn't pan out." She coated more mascara on her eyelashes. "They wouldn't let me use my name. Cerella." A dreamy look slid down her face. "Those jerks didn't know a thing about sex appeal. Cerella has that nice ring to it, you know? Silk and satin and sex all rolled into one. Don't you think that's better than Patsy?"

"Absolutely." Audrey held back a smile. This woman was definitely not a Patsy, although beneath all the makeup she did have a beautiful, childlike face.

"Hey, I saw you out there dancin'. You're pretty good yourself. That guy you're with? He is one sexy hunk." She brushed blush on her cheeks and checked the effect in the mirror. "Wanna switch?"

Audrey swallowed. "You mean switch dates?"

"Sure. Bull knows how to treat you right. I wouldn't cheat you or nothing. He gets a little rough sometimes, but you'd like him."

Audrey took out her brush and moved closer to the mirror. "I thought that was Bull Kingsley I saw you dancing with."

"Him and me been together about six months. He's a sweetie." Cerella stopped chewing her gum long enough to paint fire red lipstick on her mouth.

"His wife got killed, you know. You musta heard. Everybody was talking about it." She sprayed perfume on her wrists and behind her knees. "You want to know the weirdest thing of all? He was with me when she bought it. Makes you feel sorta strange and all. I couldn't let him touch me a whole week after, and Bull—he didn't understand at all."

"I can imagine." Audrey fought to keep her wits about her. Mentally, she crossed Bull Kingsley off her list.

"But it's okay now. He didn't like her much anyway." She returned the lipstick and perfume to her purse, shoved a new stick of gum in her mouth, then primped at her hair. "Sure you don't wanna switch?"

"I appreciate the offer, but I don't think so. Like you said, he's one sexy hunk."

Cerella ambled toward the door. "Yeah, hey, good luck. When you get tired of him? Toss him my way."

Once the door closed, Audrey stared at herself in the mirror before giving in to the laughter she'd been holding back. She could imagine Conner's reaction if she told him he'd been propositioned in absentia.

She felt Conner's eyes following her as she crossed the room to their table. She relayed her conversation with Cerella, omitting the woman's offer and emphasizing her role as Bull's alibi the night Leona was murdered.

"I'd still like to hear it from his mouth."

Audrey surveyed the room. The dance floor was once more filled with couples. "Where is he?"

"He disappeared out the door when his date went to the rest room."

"Maybe we can catch up with him. If he hasn't left. Let's go." She waited while he threw some money on the table, then hustled after him out the door.

Bull Kingsley was leaning against the side of Conner's

truck. A cigarette dangled from his mouth. "I understand you been asking about me."

"That's right," piped up Audrey before Conner had a chance to answer. "We want to ask you about Leona."

"Who are you?" His deep, gruff voice suggested he was not interested in verbal sparring.

"She's my lawyer."

Conner draped his arm across her shoulders, most definitely in this case an example of the male species staking out his territory.

Bull flicked his cigarette across the parking lot. "A lady lawyer, huh? You gotta be crazy, Hastings."

"Did you kill your wife?" Audrey hadn't meant to sound so blunt, but once the words were out, she waited impatiently for the answer.

"Me? Why would I do that?"

"Why don't you tell us?" Conner pulled her closer.

"The money, man, all that property. I knew what was in her will. That prissy cousin of hers gets most of it. If it'd been me? I'd have waited until the will got changed. Only makes sense."

"Do you know who murdered her?"

Bull shrugged. "Not a clue."

There was something surreal about this whole scene. Why wasn't Bull going after Conner? Audrey couldn't resist jumping in with both feet. "Doesn't it seem strange standing here talking to the man accused of murdering your wife?"

"Who, Hastings? I'd put my money on—lady, you're as crazy as that sheriff. Why would Hastings kill Leona?"

"Because she testified against him six years ago! Because without her testimony, he wouldn't have spent six years in prison. A lot of people think that's sufficient reason." When Audrey stopped, she realized she'd been shouting.

Bull lit another cigarette and glanced around the parking lot. "Cool it, lady, okay?"

Audrey had been so sure Bull had something to do with Leona's murder, she'd gotten carried away. Conner interrupted before she could ask her next question. His arm left her shoulder and he stepped close to Bull's face.

"Some friend of yours had Ernie Covington deliver a package to you a few days ago." He tapped at Bull's chest. "I don't know what games you're playing, but whatever they are, leave Ernie out of them."

Bull shrank back. "Okay, man, no problem. Just a little betting on the side. No big deal."

"As long as we understand each other."

Bull held up both hands in defense of himself. "I got your point, man. Don't worry."

Audrey moved in beside Conner. "I'm curious, Bull. Why are you so sure Conner didn't kill Leona?"

Bull considered her appeal. He glanced quickly at Conner. "That's easy. If he wanted to off somebody? He'd do it face-to-face. Whoever shot my wife is a coward."

From the mouths of babes, thought Audrey, amazed at Bull's insight into the character of the murderer, an aspect of his character that she hadn't considered.

"Would you be willing to repeat that in court?"

"For Hastings?" He slapped Conner on the back and let out a nervous laugh. "No problem, man."

Bull wouldn't make the best character witness for Conner. True, he didn't believe Conner had killed Leona, but what he just said implied he thought Conner capable of murder. The prosecution would have a field day with that one.

On the other hand, having the murder victim's husband testify for the defense could outweigh the risk. And at this point she was getting desperate.

ALL THE WAY HOME Audrey kept her mind on the trial four days away, rather than let herself relive the thrill of dancing with Conner. Something in their conversation with Bull had left questions in her mind—a slight shift in his tone of voice, the way he averted his eyes at certain points. She couldn't quite put a finger on what was bothering her.

Once they reached her cottage and she and Conner stood out front in the moonlight, her efforts to focus on the case dissolved.

How natural it felt to be standing there with him, how enticing the creek sounded with its lapping tide. The never-ending, hypnotic rhythm held the same magic as the bass on the dance floor. But the fresh air and quiet that came with it brought back visions of them swimming together on other dark, moonlit nights.

"We see Ben Reilly's daughter in the morning." He was so close she could touch him.

"Does ten o'clock sound good to you?" She noticed her shallow breathing.

"Ten's fine. We can grab some lunch at the diner in town afterward."

Audrey agreed to meet him at ten. "I'd better go in now."

"Audrey..."

His arms closed around her quickly. His hot mouth seared her lips. Nothing could have stopped her from sliding her arms around him to feel his warm body pressing hers. She caught her fingers in his hair and pulled him nearer, wanting more.

Slowly, he released her lips. "I...I'd better go."

But still he held her, close to his heart, the pounding of his as rapid as her own.

"I'd better say good-night." She managed the words in a whisper.

Gently, he let her go and she felt the loss of his heat. His eyes searched her face in the night's dark shadows, and she searched his in turn.

One small step at a time, he drew back. "Tomorrow." He turned and left her standing there.

Audrey hugged her arms to her and knew that tomorrow couldn't arrive fast enough—all the tomorrows, when he would finally be free of the charges and they could determine if the future could be theirs or not.

AUDREY TOOK another spoonful of clam chowder and stared back at the well-dressed, middle-aged woman sitting at the nearest table in the diner. From the moment she and Conner had sat down, she'd thrown icy stares of contempt across the way.

"Ben's daughter looked as if she was ready to send out a search party." Conner crumbled crackers into his chowder.

"You could tell she's afraid something terrible happened to him. I hope he's all right."

It was essential they find out if Ben had seen anyone suspicious around Conner's house. Maybe he'd even seen someone walk away with his gun. A witness who could testify to that would make the jury doubt Conner's guilt. No jury could legally find a criminal defendant guilty without proof beyond a reasonable doubt.

"And I hope the CB alert James sent out works. Somebody has to spot Ben sooner or later." Conner drank his iced tea.

"Tell me one thing." She watched him spoon the last drop of chowder into his wonderfully wicked mouth. "That message that Frank left with James? Why does he want us to bring him his boat? How can he use it with his leg in a cast?"

Conner shook his head. "You know Frank. Tell him he can't do something and the next minute he's proving you wrong."

"Sounds like somebody else I know."

He smiled and nodded in approval. "Thank you very much, Counselor. I'll remember that when we're in court. Of course," he added with a wink, "Frank has it a bit worse than I do. He has to get by Mavis."

That he could joke about his situation said a lot about him. Inside, he had to be more anxious than she was.

She pushed her bowl away and took a bite of her crab-cake sandwich. "I'm going to try Mrs. Bracken at city hall again. Every time I'm over there, I miss her."

"About the real estate deals Leona reneged on? I'll go with you."

She shouldn't have mentioned going. She couldn't imagine that Peter was involved, but she had to follow through on her brother's outburst yesterday morning. If by chance there was a connection, she'd rather deal with that on her own.

"You don't need to do that. Why don't you spend the rest of the day working on your house? I can handle Mrs. Bracken."

Conner paused with his sandwich halfway to his mouth. His head tilted to the side as he questioned what she'd said. "I'm sure you can. I'll be there for any support you might need."

"All right." She wasn't willing to argue the point.

The woman at the table got up to leave. Audrey said a little thanks that she would no longer have to feel those eyes drilling into her head. Her relief came too soon. Instead of walking toward the door, the woman turned and attacked Conner.

"What are you doing in here poisoning the air?" She waggled her finger in his face. "We don't want your kind in Tabbs Corner."

Audrey stared in surprise at the tall woman's angry face. She had neatly styled, light brown hair and wore a long-sleeved silk suit that was not only too small, but too hot for the weather.

Conner's face paled. "Excuse me?"

"You belong in jail, you murderer."

The ruckus had drawn the attention of the other diners. They gaped from their tables. All movement had stopped, as if everything had frozen in time.

Knowing that Conner would sit there and take the abuse

before he would verbally strike back at an older woman, Audrey intervened. "Can I help you with something?"

"And you!" Her venomous voice shouted at Audrey. "This is a nice, quiet town. You should pack up and leave while you can."

Audrey slid out of the booth. "Are you threatening me?"

"Sit down, Audrey." Conner reached across the table and tried to catch her hand.

"Well, well, well." Sheriff Parks strolled up beside the woman. "What's the problem, Mrs. Oglethorpe?"

"Do something about this," she demanded, and stomped her foot. "I can't understand why this murderer is allowed to walk the streets of our town." She pointed at Audrey. "And she's no better."

Audrey moved to within a hair of the woman's face. "If you have something to discuss with me, you will have the decency to discuss it in private."

Her words fueled another response. "You see what I mean?" The woman flapped her arms in the air. "Get them out of here, Sheriff, right now."

"Mrs. Oglethorpe." The sheriff took her elbow and pulled her away from the booth. "You're creating a disturbance. I'm sure we can talk about your concerns elsewhere." His implication was clear.

At Conner's urging, Audrey sat down. She found it ironic that in order to restore peace, the sheriff was forced to protect Conner's rights.

Mrs. Oglethorpe harrumphed, stood to her full height, tugged at the too-tight suit jacket and strode out of the diner with her nose in the air.

The sheriff dragged a chair up to the end of their booth. Now that the floor show was over, the other diners had lost interest in them, thank goodness, and resumed eating. Audrey gulped down some iced tea, not knowing what was coming next.

Sheriff Parks sat down and eyed Conner. "You are nothing but trouble, boy."

Conner leaned against the bench and met him eye-to-eye. "Is that a fact?"

The sheriff pulled out his ever-present straw and chewed on the end of it, his small, brown eyes more probing than ever as they darted between Audrey and Conner.

"What can we do for you, Sheriff?" Audrey wanted to avoid another public confrontation.

"I went to see Frank at the hospital this morning." He watched them.

"Why would that concern us?" Conner's face remained devoid of emotion.

"When he wasn't there, I stopped by his house. He wasn't there, either. Seems Frank Smith's disappeared. You wouldn't know anything about that, now, would you?"

"Frank? Disappeared? The man just came out of a coma. His leg's in a cast. How can he up and disappear?" Conner offered this with a straight face.

Audrey couldn't sit still. She rearranged herself on the bench, flabbergasted by Conner's control.

Sheriff Parks gazed at Conner, his eyes intent and piercing in his desire for the truth. "Maybe I should pull your bail and toss your hide back in jail for causing a disturbance, boy. That'd probably be best for all of us. Maybe I should add kidnapping charges to your troubles."

"Now, just a minute, Sheriff." Audrey stopped him. "Frank checked himself out of that hospital. He's someplace safe. There's no kidnapping involved here."

"Call it what you want. I need to talk to him."

"What about?" Conner asked gruffly.

"His accident, of course."

"You mean the bullet in his tire," Conner needled him.

The sheriff stopped chewing his straw. "Not that it's any of your business. He might know who uses those JHP bullets."

He pushed out of his chair and then leaned down to

Audrey. "That boy better be safe. For your sake." He threw the straw on the table and marched out of the diner.

Audrey let out an irritated breath. Conner was watching the front door, as if he expected the sheriff to come charging back in. Again she marveled at his self-control. First the woman, then the sheriff. He'd learned a lot in the past six years.

"Why didn't I think of that?" Conner straightened in his seat. The sudden gleam in his eye caught her attention right away. "Frank might give us some help on that bullet. Are you up to a trip to Mavis's?"

Audrey didn't hesitate. "I think a conference with my investigator would be perfectly in order."

"And just maybe," said Conner, following close behind her out of the diner, "if we can find out who uses those fancy bullets, we can catch ourselves a murderer."

Chapter Eleven

"Doc must have decided not to call the sheriff, like he threatened to do when I took Frank from the hospital." Conner slowed to allow another vehicle to pass. "Otherwise, Parks would have come looking for me sooner."

"Legally, Doc had no justification." Audrey clenched and unclenched her fingers, as she admired the way his deft hands handled the steering wheel. "Patients don't usually check themselves out of the hospital against their doctor's advice, but there's no law against it."

He maneuvered the truck onto the bumpy lane at a wide angle to allow for Frank's boat, which was hooked onto the back. His biceps bulged in his short-sleeved shirt.

"Hold on." He slowed to a crawl. "The shock absorbers in my truck don't compare with the ones in your car."

Audrey braced herself for the jerky ride. "Apparently, Sheriff Parks does believe that James found that bullet in Frank's tire."

"Not because he believed us, Audrey. Trust me. He went by the garage and talked to James yesterday after we left. The reverend who was there when James found the bullet came in to pick up his car while the sheriff was giving James the third degree."

"I see." Her spontaneous smile made her feel good. "I wish I'd been there."

"Me, too." A roguish glint sparked his eye, but his smile wasn't deep enough to show his dimple.

He eased the truck onto the smoother ground of Mavis's parking lot, pulled on the brake and faced Audrey, his eyes cloudy with concern. "That woman in the diner had no right to go after you like that."

"Or you, either." She shifted to face him. "I thought you handled yourself well."

"I'm used to that kind of harassment. You're not. I wish it hadn't happened." He played with a loose curl by her ear.

"It's over now. You have enough to worry about without adding me to the list."

"I do worry about you. I worry about how this town will treat you and Ian once the trial's over and I'm not around." He turned away.

"Look at me," she demanded.

She took his chin in her hand and forced his head around. The pain in his eyes could have made her cry if it hadn't made her angry. She would not let him give up.

"We are going to win. Whether or not you're around after the trial will be *your* choice, not the state's. You got that?"

"Yes, ma'am, Counselor, ma'am. Whatever you say."

The dimple did show this time, but the shadows of pain still lingered despite his efforts to hide them.

"Fine." She gave a quick nod. "Now, let's get the boat in the water."

She hopped from the truck. By directing him from behind the vehicle, she helped him back the boat onto the loading ramp beside Mavis's. She secured the boat in a slip while he parked the truck in the lot, before he joined her on the pier.

"This is a beautiful spot." And peaceful, she thought, loving the way the hot sun hovered above the creek. Large, overhanging trees draped the surrounding cove in privacy, and where the sun hit it, the water actually glistened.

Conner lightly took her arm and the image seemed complete. They watched a sea gull dive for his lunch. Audrey gave in to the moment and put her hand on his arm, a gesture she wouldn't have made in a different setting. She felt him tense beneath her touch, but the heat of him held her hand in place.

"Yes." He touched her hair gently. "So beautiful it hurts."

"Get on up here, you two." Mavis's voice boomed from the house and reduced the sparks between them. "I got a man inside itching to see you."

As they climbed the slight incline to the diner, Frank hobbled out the door behind Mavis. "Good grief, woman. You make it sound like I have fleas. Make way, I'm coming through."

The three of them sat at the white table under a tree beside the creek. Frank propped his cast on the extra chair and dropped his crutches to the ground. Mavis had gone inside to get drinks.

"So now you're a man, huh? That didn't take long." Conner slapped him on the back.

Frank grinned and shrugged. "What can I say? My charm wins them over every time." He gazed at his boat bobbing in the water. "Boy, isn't she a beauty? I appreciate you bringing her. I can't wait to take her out."

When Conner tried to talk him out of it, Frank shook his head and waved away his words. "Don't you get on me, too. I've got all I can handle right up there in that kitchen."

Audrey glanced over at the sixteen-foot, blue and white skiff. It was a vast improvement over the small outboard they'd puttered around in when they were kids.

She gave Frank the once-over. "You look good, Frank. Your color is back. Just promise me you won't do anything stupid."

"Deal." He made a thumbs-up sign.

Mavis sauntered down the hill with a tray of cold drinks. "Here you go, now."

The ice-cold lemonade washed down Audrey's throat like a refreshing shower on a hot, humid day. "This hits the spot, Mavis. Thanks."

Conner toyed with his glass and caught Mavis's eye. "Any word on the mysterious nurse?"

Mavis scrunched up her face. "Everybody's accounted for. One of the day nurses, though—she's missing a uniform. I think you got yourself somebody sneaking in and only pretending to be a nurse."

"I bet you're right," Audrey agreed. "The hospital is not that big. If it were one of the staff, you would know. The question is who."

"The big question." Frank rolled the cold glass across his forehead. "When we have that answer, we'll know who the murderer is."

Mavis wiped her hands on her yellow apron. "You go ahead and enjoy this nice sunshine before it gets too hot. I got work to do." She picked up the tray and started up the hill. "And keep an eye on Frank here. He's enough to try a soul."

"So tell me, what's new?" Frank said. "I know you didn't make the trip out here just to bring my boat. Not three days before the trial."

Conner wasted no time. "Do you know any sharpshooters who use JHPs?"

"Jacket hollow points?"

"That's what hit your tire."

"Wow, I'm in the big league now." He tapped his heart and raised his chin. "I can't think of anyone offhand. But there may be a way to find out."

"Please, Frank, anything is worth trying." Audrey felt encouraged by what he'd said.

"How? What do we do?" Conner wanted to know, his voice as anxious as Audrey's.

"I can tap into the gun club memberships that are involved in competition. In fact—" he scratched his broken leg "—I have a reporter friend in Richmond, a sports reporter, who might just save me some time. There're a lot of gun clubs out there. He can send me in the right direction."

"That's a fantastic idea." Audrey tried to contain her excitement at the possibility of a break. "Will it work?"

"It'll tell us if any of the members are local." Frank stretched down and picked up some rocks. "It's a good, solid start. But…"

"But what? Say it."

"You two are beating feet talking to everybody and his brother who might have had a motive to kill Leona. Other than that, it seems to me we're sitting around waiting for the killer to jump out and say, 'Here I am.'" He tossed a rock into the creek as if to emphasize his point. "We need to flush out the killer."

"How?"

"Through the press. I'm going to write an article about Leona's murder."

"There've been dozens of articles. You must have read them." Audrey remembered the scathing commentaries.

"Yeah. I've read them, and beneath every article is a presumption of Conner's guilt. No matter how objective a writer tries to be, Audrey, he can't entirely erase his personal bias. We're only human. It has to do with the way the facts are presented. It's time the public heard from someone who believes Conner is innocent. They need to see the facts from a different perspective."

"That sounds good to me," Conner encouraged.

"I don't know, Frank. Does the public need to be reminded again of the facts?"

"They need to be reminded they can think. Stay with me for a minute." He turned to Conner. "What's the worst evidence they have against you?"

"My rifle." He flinched.

Audrey shook her head. "That's a good example of what

I mean. Folks know his gun was found at the scene of the crime. Why remind them?"

"Exactly. They also know his fingerprints are on the gun. Taken separately, the facts say one thing. But listen to the evidence in a different order. You kill someone. You leave your fingerprints on the murder weapon, then toss it close to the scene of the crime for anyone to find. Come on, now. That's an obvious setup."

"You didn't think so at first," Audrey reminded him.

"No, I didn't. Because I got the information piecemeal. Present every step in order and you plant not only the possibility of Conner's innocence, but the likelihood that there's a crazy killer in this town nobody knows about. The article would make the killer believe he screwed up."

"And force him to make a move."

"Now you've got it." He threw the last rock with a powerful motion that made it skip to the middle of the creek.

"That approach in an article goes against public sentiment. Would anybody publish a piece like that?"

Audrey heard the hope in Conner's voice and crossed her fingers that Frank's idea would help.

"I'll get it published, but it may take some time." Frank gazed at his boat, then picked up his crutches and pushed himself to his feet. "I can't stand it anymore. I've got to put my hands on her." He looked lovingly at his boat. "Then we'll get down to business."

Audrey stayed at the table while Frank and Conner walked over to the boat. Her hopes soared so high she wanted to push Frank inside and get him started on his search and the article.

She considered the evidence they had gathered for the trial. They had a possible suspect who was out of reach, an unknown person angry at Leona for backing out of a deal and a missing man who might have seen someone steal the murder weapon from Conner's house. On top of that, they had an angry sheriff intent on putting Conner behind bars and a town willing to go along with him.

The one point in their favor was Bull's willingness to testify for the defense, and even the victim's estranged husband had his drawbacks.

She watched as Conner helped Frank onto the boat. Conner was a good man—tough on the outside, kind on the inside. He was a man who showed his strength of character over and over again.

She balled her hands into fists. Her jaw muscles strained. She couldn't let the jury find him guilty. Somehow they had to come up with the missing pieces.

THEY MADE IT BACK to Tabbs Corner in time to visit Mrs. Bracken at city hall. As on Audrey's previous trips, the receptionist told them she was out. This time, Audrey flat out refused to believe her.

"We can try again in the morning." Conner turned to go.

"No, we'll have a look around first."

Audrey caught the surprised expression on the receptionist's face. She coaxed Conner around the corner. "Mrs. Bracken is avoiding me, Conner, and I'm tired of playing games. She's here."

Based on the wariness in his eyes, he didn't quite believe her, but after a long pause he agreed. "Okay. You check the offices on the right of the hall and I'll check the ones on the left."

Ten minutes later Audrey found Mrs. Bracken in the file room, working behind a cabinet. The expression on her face confirmed her suspicions.

"Mrs. Bracken, you suggested the other day that you had more information that could help Conner."

Mrs. Bracken curled the file folders in her hand. Her eyes searched the room nervously. "Oh, my, I don't think so, dear."

Audrey was determined. "What is it you don't want to tell me? Please. Who are the people that were dealing with Leona?"

"Oh, my." Mrs. Bracken sat down on the edge of a folding chair.

"There you are." Conner strode across the room. His bright blue eyes focused on Audrey before turning to Mrs. Bracken. "How are you, Mrs. Bracken?"

Mrs. Bracken got up from the chair. "Why, Conner, you're a sight for sore eyes."

"My mother said to be sure and say hello the last time she wrote."

"How is the dear? Nobody deserved that wonderful man she married more than she did. Is she well?"

"Better than ever. The Florida sun agrees with her." He glanced at Audrey. "Audrey said you may be able to help us with some information about Leona."

"Oh, dear." She sat back down in the chair.

"I'm sorry to distress you like this." *But I will,* thought Audrey, *as much as I have to.* "You were extremely helpful before. I know you're reluctant to share the information, but it would be easier for you to talk about it here than in court, and it would help Conner more to have the facts now."

Mrs. Bracken took a tissue from her pocket and crumpled it in her hands. Several other pieces of tissue fluttered to the floor, but she didn't notice. "You're right, of course. You have to understand that I'm not supposed to know this. Working here, well, I pick up so much information. Rumor, mostly."

Conner put his hand on her shoulder. "Who was involved in that real estate deal with Leona, Mrs. Bracken?"

She looked up into Conner's earnest blue eyes. "Some man from Richmond. I don't know his name."

"And the other person?" Audrey asked. "You told me there were two failed deals."

"I really don't want to tell you this. Please. He couldn't have done what you're thinking."

Audrey held her ground. Guilt snaked its way into her conscience like a serpent. She hated upsetting this nice woman.

"Then there's nothing to worry about." Conner used his most soothing voice.

"You don't believe Conner killed Leona Kingsley, do you?" At the shake of her head, Audrey pushed further. "Then someone else did. Maybe this other man had something to do with her murder and maybe he didn't, but if we don't know who he is, we can't question him."

Mrs. Bracken gazed first at Audrey, then at Conner. She hung her head low to answer. "Peter."

Audrey wasn't sure she'd heard her correctly. A searing pain lodged in her stomach as she asked for clarification. "My brother?"

"Yes. I'm sorry."

Conner put his arm around Audrey's shoulders.

"Go on." Audrey dreaded what she would hear, but she had to know the full story.

Again Mrs. Bracken looked from one to the other. "Leona owned the land next to his marina. For years your grandfather talked about expanding, but every time he approached Leona about selling, she turned him down flat. When Peter took over the marina, he tried, too. This last time, Leona agreed to sell. They went all the way to settlement before she backed out. Just got up and walked away was what I heard. She didn't give him any explanation or any options. I know he'd already contracted for clearing the land."

Conner's strength helped Audrey hold on to her composure. She reached for Mrs. Bracken's hand. "I'm sure you're right. He probably had nothing to do with the murder."

Mrs. Bracken's face relaxed in relief. "I didn't want to tell you."

"I'm glad you did." Audrey studied the woman in front of her.

"You did the right thing," Conner reassured her.

"Mrs. Bracken, how long have you known Conner?"

"Why, all his life."

"Would you be willing to testify in court on his behalf as a character witness?"

"Oh, my." Several more pieces of tissue fell to the floor.

"Nobody expects you to testify, Mrs. Bracken, especially me. It's all right." Conner leaned over and patted her hand.

"You knew his mother for a long time, isn't that so?" Audrey pressed her and hoped the prodding would produce the needed results.

"Yes, that dear soul." Mrs. Bracken left the chair and faced Conner. "I owe her that much, don't I?" Holding his hand, she said to Audrey, "Yes, I'll testify in his behalf. Yes, I will."

Audrey and Conner left city hall and he drove her to her office. Numbness and shock held her in check. Why hadn't Peter been more specific about his business deal with Leona? Mrs. Bracken obviously feared he might be involved or she wouldn't have been so reluctant to tell them his name.

He pulled up behind her car and turned to her in the front seat of the truck. "Audrey, I don't know what to say."

He draped his arm across the top of the seat. She could feel his fingers touching her hair.

"We don't have all the facts yet." She hugged that thought to her.

"No, we don't." He ran his fingers over the ends of her curls. "I don't know Peter very well, Audrey. We definitely don't hit it off. I know this sounds flimsy, but I can't see him committing murder, for the simple reason that he's your brother."

His effort to make her feel better endeared him to her. "Thank you for saying that." She closed her eyes and took a deep, calming breath. "I'd better go in. I'll get in touch with you later."

The full impact hit her once she closed her office door. She collapsed in a chair and covered her face with her hands. She didn't want to think about Conner's case. Discussing this newest development with Lori was not an option. Withdrawing from the case was out of the question— her career would be ruined, leaving her and Ian without a means of support. But she'd never considered that saving Conner could mean destroying her only brother.

DELLA ANDREWS MET Audrey in front of the center, her expression as off-putting as before. "Ms. McKenna, I'd like to point out that you are late picking up your child. The center is not open twenty-four hours a day for your convenience."

The disdain in her voice slapped Audrey in the face. First the confrontation in Doc's office, then again yesterday morning. The explanation had to be misplaced jealousy, especially since Audrey had called and told the secretary she'd be late. Why Della thought she was interested in Doc, she didn't know.

"Have I done something to offend you?"

Audrey's direct approach threw her for a minute. She tossed back her hair from her face with a jerk. "I would certainly recommend you use another day care in town if there were one." Della stumbled over the words.

"That doesn't answer my question."

The woman stood straight and stiff. "If you think you can pop back into town and bulldoze everyone with your charm, you're wrong." Her voice grew louder.

"I wouldn't call that an accurate description of returning to my hometown, no." Audrey knew without a doubt that reason would never work.

Della's chest rose as she took a deep breath. "Believe me, you won't get your greedy little claws into Doc."

A car door slammed and a young mother walked toward them. Della's countenance changed immediately.

Audrey was impatient to push past the woman to get inside. Before she did, she wanted to make something perfectly clear. "I assure you, I have no designs on Doc Rankin."

The young mother reached the door and addressed Della. "Thank you so much for keeping Liz with the late class tonight. I appreciate it."

Furious, Audrey took one last look at Della, sidestepped the young mother and plowed through the door. Her comment to Della had to have put an end to this nonsense, she thought, searching the halls for the late class. She had enough on her mind without having to brace for a cat fight every day.

IAN CHATTERED all the way home about a pinecone project his class was going to do. When she asked for specifics, he told her it was a secret.

A car was parked beside the cottage when she arrived home, a car she didn't recognize. Audrey thought about the nasty note she'd received and the many silent phone calls. Her heart hammered as she backed up to leave.

"Audrey." Doc Rankin rounded the side of the house and waved to her.

She let out an exasperated breath. After the day she'd had, she didn't need this.

Doc made it to her door before she could get out. In a suit and tie, he looked out of place at the river.

"Oh, dear, I hope I didn't frighten you." He pulled a bouquet of daisies from behind his back. "Maybe these will make up for it."

"They're lovely, Doc. Thank you."

He opened her car door for her and Audrey stepped out. "Doc, what brought you out here?"

"Mommy, open the door."

Ian. She unlocked the back door and let her little boy

loose. "Go get your green bucket to use for collecting the pinecones," she told him. When he started to leave she said, "Aren't you forgetting something?"

After a quick hello to Doc, he ran over to the back shed and found his bucket.

Audrey turned to Doc, her flowers in hand. "Come in while I put these in water."

Doc followed on her heels and looked around the inside of the cottage. "This is really very quaint."

"We like it."

She put the flowers in a vase and set them on the breakfast bar. She felt compelled to be polite and offer him something to drink but didn't, hoping he wouldn't be there long enough to enjoy it.

"Now." She dried her hands. "What did you want to see me about?"

He took off his suit jacket, brushed it off, folded it with meticulous care and draped it over a chair. "Why...you know. We have to finish our conversation. I thought I would save you the trouble of making an appointment."

Audrey drew a blank. And then she remembered her parting words that day she asked him about Leona in his office, words that were said to irritate Della more than anything else.

"You have information about Leona."

She offered him a seat and then brought him some ice water, realizing she wasn't going to get rid of him quickly. If he could help with the case, she wanted to hear what he had to say.

"So what else can you tell me, Doc?"

"Leona was a very active woman." He sipped at his water, then leaned forward in his chair. "What are your plans, Audrey? What do you see in your future?"

She bit her lip to keep her patience. "Right now, my plans are to learn about Leona."

"No, no, I mean next month, next year. Certainly you

don't intend to live out here by yourself for any length of time."

"Doc, please, could we get on with this? I have a son who needs his dinner."

"You have a son who also needs a father. I'm sure you agree." He got up and walked across the room to her.

This was worse than she'd expected. Doc acted as if he were ready and willing to take on the role of the great provider.

Audrey stood. She didn't want to be rude. Doc's influence in town was great enough to make her life difficult if he so chose. But enough was enough.

She took her water glass to the kitchen sink to stall for time. After a pause long enough to get away from his last statement, she continued. "You said you have some information about Leona. I would like to hear anything you can tell me about her that you didn't mention before. But that's the only thing we're going to discuss."

Her comments didn't faze him. There was no indication he'd been put in his place. He continued across the kitchen as though he hadn't heard her.

CONNER HADN'T intended to show up at Audrey's unannounced. The news about Peter's involvement with Leona had stung him almost as badly as it had her. He wanted to tell her she should withdraw from the case, not because a conflict of interest bothered him—Audrey was the most honest person he knew—but because he couldn't stand to see what the case was doing to her.

Let's face it, chump, he told himself as he pulled up behind her car, *you brought all of this down on her head yourself.*

The extra car told him she had company. His gut tightened at the thought of a strange man in her life. He stopped himself from barging in the back door when he saw Ian over in the pine grove. He had no business interfering in her personal life. Worst of all, he had nothing to offer her.

Batting down every instinct to go inside, he wandered over to the pine grove. The minute Ian saw him the boy made a running leap into his arms.

"You can help me get pinecones." He twined his small arms around Conner's neck. "Mrs. Tompkins said I need lots."

Conner gave him a quick hug, treasuring the feeling of holding his son. They got to work picking up every pinecone within reach, then moved over to another batch on the ground. Before long the bucket was half-full.

"Mommy's going to help, too." Ian pulled some leaves off a cone, then pitched it in the bucket. "Doc Rankin came and brought some pretty flowers."

Conner saw red. "I tell you what. I should go in and say hi to your mom. Then I'll come back and help you."

It was all he could do not to race to the back door, but he made his stride long and quick and reached it fast without running. He didn't knock. He shoved open the door with a crash.

"Conner!"

Chapter Twelve

Audrey's beautiful green eyes zeroed in on him. She was standing in the kitchen, still dressed in her work clothes. A pot of something boiled on the stove.

Doc slid off the bar stool, irritation flashing across his face. He held out his hand. "Nice to see you, Conner." Sarcasm laced his voice.

Conner brought himself quickly under control. "I was out helping Ian find pinecones and thought I'd come in and say hello." He hoped he'd done a better job of controlling his own sarcasm than Doc had.

Audrey watched him from the corner of her eye. "Doc came out to talk about Leona."

"W-well, now," Doc stuttered. "I think we've covered everything." He picked up his suit jacket from the chair, shook it gently and put it on.

"Before you go, Doc, you can answer a question for me." Doc let out a deep sigh. Conner pushed on, remembering the note Frank had found on Leona's desk. "What do you know about Florence Jackson, Cornelia Stone and Grace Osgood?"

Doc's face turned beet red. "Fine ladies, every one. They were very active seniors at the center. You know they passed on."

Audrey joined them by the bar counter. "Yes, we did know that."

"What else can you tell us about them?"

"What else could there be?" Doc straightened his tie. "I must get back to the office for some late work." He took Audrey's hand. "Thank you for your hospitality, Audrey. You're very gracious. Please think about what I said."

Audrey walked him to the door. And Conner cracked his jaw muscles loose. She returned to the sink and kicked off her shoes.

"Nice flowers."

"Don't you say another word." She glowered at him. "And you might as well stay for dinner. You can cook the hamburgers while I get to work in here. Poor Ian must be starving."

"Aren't you going to tell me what Doc said about Leona?"

She whipped around, clearly angry, fire sparking from her emerald eyes. "Nothing! Not one blasted thing!"

"Oh." He had no desire to stop the silly grin that spread across his face. He couldn't resist poking fun. "So, I guess he drove all the way out here with other things in mind, right?"

Audrey swatted him with a dish towel. "Go on. Get out of here. Go light the grill for the hamburgers."

He noted a softening of the anger in her face and figured he'd better hightail it outside while he could.

Ian was sitting on the ground, playing with a video game. The green bucket sat beside him, filled to the brim. "I'm sorry I took so long, Ian. What do you have there?"

For the next ten minutes he watched Ian play the game like an expert. He caught himself wondering if proficiency in video games transferred to computer skills.

"Uh-oh, I just died."

"Then you'll just have to help me get the grill going."

Ian jumped to his feet. "I can get the charcoal." He ran to the back shed and returned with the bag. "Can I dump 'em in?"

"Be my guest." Conner moved aside so he could reach the grill.

Mistake. Before he realized what was happening, Ian had dumped the entire bag of charcoal into the grill. Charcoal dust covered the boy's hands and arms, the front of his shirt looked black not white and his face…

"Oops." Ian rolled his eyes sideways at Conner.

"'Oops' is right, young man. You must think we're making burgers for an army." Conner tried to keep things light. All he could think about was Audrey's reaction to his failure to monitor their son. "Guess we better get you washed off before you-know-who has a fit."

"Yeah. Mommy doesn't let me do the charcoal."

"Great. Now you tell me."

Every time he turned around, Conner found another example of his ineptness as a father. What did he know about kids anyway? It wasn't Ian's fault he'd emptied the bag and ruined his clothes. He should have at least suspected a five-year-old might have trouble judging how much charcoal to use. He could have helped him hold the bag. Those thoughts hadn't crossed his mind.

Ian tugged a hose out of nowhere. Water sprayed from the end. "How about this?" He smiled proudly.

Conner shook his head in exasperation. Ian's intention was good, but his method left something to be desired. Again. His tennis shoes were soaked to the point of squishing when he walked. His shorts dripped water down his legs. The charcoal-tinted shirt clung to his chest, and what clean spots had been visible on his face were a smeared gray mixture of water and charcoal dust. Yet the kid looked so earnest.

"Well, let's see. It might work." Conner was in a quandary about how to escape unscathed from this one.

He started with Ian's hands and arms and rubbed away as much dirt as possible. He ignored the dampness seeping through his own jeans and shirt and concentrated on wiping Ian's face with his hands. He didn't know what to do about the clothes.

"You're going to have to go in and change. Your mom won't like it, but, hey, that's the way the cookie crumbles."

Ian giggled just as Audrey walked out the door carrying a tray of patties. She stopped and surveyed her domain. Hers not his, he thought, reluctant to admit the regret he felt.

"Go put on some dry clothes, Ian."

Her stern voice sent Ian scrambling, but Conner noted a slight smile tilted her lips.

Ian disappeared and Conner turned off the hose. "Sorry about that." He wished he could read her face.

"Don't worry about it. Just light the grill, please."

As soon as the grill was hot, he placed the patties on the grate and returned to the house. The phone rang as he passed it and he picked it up. He could tell someone was on the line, but the person didn't answer his hello.

"Whoever called didn't say anything."

Audrey turned away to the stove. "Wrong number, then."

He moved in behind her, close enough for his breath to caress her neck. "I know you're not angry at me—well, except maybe for Ian—so how about a smile? Just a little one. For old times' sake."

He saw the color brighten her cheeks and sensed the easing of her body against him, and was ready to let his ego enjoy his success, when Ian raced into the room.

Audrey eyed her son and frowned. "Grab the catsup and mustard, please Ian. We'll eat at the picnic table."

Conner glanced at his son as he took the condiments from the refrigerator. He had on a pair of jeans and a red T-shirt—the identical outfit Conner had on himself.

Audrey passed Conner with her tray, her worried eyes fixed on Ian. "Those hamburgers are probably close to crisp by now."

He jumped to attention and took down a clean plate,

then hustled out the door to save the burgers. But the un-easiness brought on by a red shirt and a small pair of jeans cemented itself to his conscience and demanded to be heard. He couldn't let this little guy identify with him. No way. It just wouldn't work. Obviously, Audrey thought so, too.

THE NEW EMPLOYEE pulled Audrey aside when she returned from her extended lunch the next day. "Someone's waiting for you in your office."

Audrey opened her office door and saw Frank dozing in a chair. He looked world-weary and pale. "Frank! How did you get here?"

He pushed himself up straight in the chair, then chuckled. "I was just buzzing by and thought I'd drop in."

"You need to stay out of town, Frank. The wrong person might see you. It's not safe to come here until we know who the killer is."

"Audrey, you only have the weekend left before the trial. I wanted to save you some driving time."

"Please don't tell me you drove the boat over."

"All right, I won't tell you."

"Frank…"

A tiny slice of guilt passed over his face. "I tied up at your pier. Hope you don't mind."

"You know I don't, but I wish you'd just called."

"Not a chance. I didn't want to talk about this stuff on the phone. Too many ears. Besides, there's a little five-year-old I want to meet, so I arranged for James to pick me up at your place before I left Mavis's. We stopped by Conner's before coming here, but he wasn't home." He pulled over another chair, put his leg on it and rubbed his back. "James's truck is worse than Conner's."

"I was just over at the diner trying to soak up the gossip." Audrey sat at her desk. She worried about Frank being here, but she was also very glad to see him.

"So what's the latest?"

"The word is that Leona reneged on two other deals. The gossip didn't come with any names, though." She'd hoped to find someone else besides Peter who might have fallen victim to Leona's real estate whims. "I also learned that everyone thinks Ida May has a thing going with her handyman. The bad news is she won't be back until the end of next week."

"That's too late." Frank sagged back against the chair.

"We have to work with what we have, that's all. What did you find out?"

He grabbed his crutches and stood. "Conner's probably home by now. Let's hold that thought until I have the two of you together."

Eager to hear Frank's news, Audrey grabbed her purse, left a brief note for Lori and led Frank to her car. She helped him into the back seat.

As they drove through town and came close to the center, he said, "You know who the front seat's for, don't you? Aren't you going to get Ian?"

Audrey checked the time. She could easily pick Ian up early and take him with them, but she worried about his growing attachment to Conner. She didn't want them together any more than necessary.

"No, I'd rather not get him this early." She didn't miss Frank's surprised reaction in her rearview mirror.

"Okay" was all he said. "I'll see him tomorrow."

Conner was working at the computer when they walked in. A lock of hair fell across his forehead that Audrey wanted very much to brush back.

He took one look at Frank and exploded. "Are you out of your ever-loving mind?"

Frank waved away his concern. "Just grab us a beer, will you?"

Within minutes, Frank sat with his back against the side of the sofa, his broken leg extended across the cushions. His catnap in Audrey's office while waiting for her to return from lunch hadn't erased the exhaustion on his face.

Conner reappeared and held a can of beer just out of his reach. "Nobody has to tell me you drove the boat down. By yourself, no doubt. You have no business coming into town. You've got to be crazy—on both counts."

Frank rolled his eyes. He reached for the beer, but Conner yanked it away. "Don't even think about coming to the trial. If there's any trouble, you'd be a helpless target on those crutches."

Frank let out a deep sigh. His hand flopped into his lap. "You drive a hard bargain, my friend." He met Conner's dark eyes. "All right, you win."

"Good." Conner handed him the beer and began wearing down a path across the living room floor.

"You're not going to drive the boat back this evening, are you?" Audrey hoped he would say no. At the same time, she wanted to clobber him for giving Conner more to worry about.

"I'm not going to drive the boat back at all. My precious boat has officially been dumped in your lap, Audrey. If you don't mind. I figure you and Conner can take it down to my place when you have the time. After the trial would be fine."

Conner's head spun around. His hard stare said he appreciated Frank's vote of confidence that he would still be free after the trial. It also said he didn't believe it.

He sat in an overstuffed chair, at last resigned to Frank's antics. "So let's hear it."

Frank perked to attention. "First off, the editor of the local paper agreed to run the article in Tuesday's edition."

Audrey gasped. "But the trial starts Monday."

"It doesn't matter. In fact, maybe it's better. Can you see this thing hitting town after the trial starts? It might help people get their heads on straight. Besides, it's the only time the editor would run it.

"But about those JHPs." His eyes got brighter. "Ten guys in the area belong to gun clubs. They're gun clubs, remember, not hunt clubs. These guys compete nationally, maybe internationally, I don't know."

Audrey was too stunned to respond. She had to hear it all.

Conner moved to the edge of his chair. "Well, don't keep us in suspense. Tell us the rest."

Frank's grin made it clear he thought he had the upper hand. "I'm pretty sure we can forget about seven of the names. But the other three are all tied into the case. First, Bull Kingsley belongs to a gun club not far from here. He placed in two recent competitions."

Conner grimaced, but Audrey was remembering the feeling she'd had in Charley's parking lot that Bull Kingsley hadn't told them everything he knew.

"I can see Bull doing that." Conner stood and began his pacing. "He was always a competitor, and one of the best shots I know."

"You're sure these guys use jacket hollow point bullets?"

"Absolutely. I verified it with the gun club presidents before I searched each membership roster." Frank chugged his beer. "The next one you won't believe. Doc Rankin. Remember what a sissy he was about hunting when we were kids? He wouldn't get near a gun."

"He competes?"

Frank hemmed and hawed. "Well, I don't know. I only had access to the most recent competitions. I found his name on an inactive list for a club outside Charlottesville. It has to be the same guy, though. The date of the list corresponds to Doc's last three years in med school there at the University of Virginia."

"That's hard to believe." Audrey couldn't picture Doc with a gun. "The man not only hated guns, he was afraid of them."

"That may be, but his name was on the list."

Conner brought Frank another beer. Frank popped the top and took a swig. Audrey took advantage of the break to get a glass of ice water. When she came back in the room, Conner and Frank were talking in hushed tones.

"Okay, you two. I'm the one who needs the ammunition for court. No secrets."

"You have to tell her." Conner avoided her eyes.

Frank sat there for a moment, running a finger down the sweat of his beer can. She was ready to pounce on him, broken leg or not, before he frowned and said, "Peter belongs to a gun club, too. I'm sorry."

Her stomach knotted. Her throat closed. The pain was so deep she didn't think it would ever go away. "I didn't know."

"Of course you didn't."

She thought of the last time she'd seen her brother, that terrible morning at her cottage. Mrs. Bracken's reluctance to tell her about Peter's deal with Leona came to mind. And just last night Helen had called to invite her and Ian on a Sunday boat ride for a few hours with Peter and their son, Roger.

"This proves nothing, don't forget." Conner's sympathetic blue eyes caught hers across the room.

"I know."

"Don't worry. I'll keep digging, even during the trial." Frank played with his beer can. "I've been working on the article, so I haven't had a chance to roam around in Leona's files yet. I still want to do that. Those three names I found on her desk must mean something."

"They're probably related to the fund-raising article she was writing." Audrey found it easier to talk about Leona than Peter and JHPs. "Of course, they could be totally irrelevant too."

"I talked to that gal I interviewed in Leona's office and picked her brain about their computer system. Should be a cinch to get in."

"She just told you whatever you asked?" Frank's talent for drawing from people what he needed amazed her.

"She might have gotten the impression I wanted to finish the fund-raiser article."

"I wonder why she would think that. Shame on you, misleading that young girl."

"All for a good cause." Frank yawned.

"Since you're going to stay the night, we can work on Leona's files tonight." Conner nodded toward the computer.

"Not tonight, old buddy. I'm wiped out."

"Then tomorrow. Before I run you back to Mavis's."

"'We,'" Frank corrected. "I can't make that drive in your truck, not after the boat ride." He turned to Audrey. "You'll drive, won't you?"

He was putting her in a very awkward position. Tomorrow was Saturday. If she went, she would have to take Ian. She couldn't leave him at Peter's house, not now, not until Peter's involvement in the case was clarified. If she refused to go and let Conner drive her car, he would wonder why. Assuring herself the situation would be entirely different with Frank there, she agreed to go.

"It's time to get Ian." She stood. "I have to leave."

She wanted to get to the center and ask Doc about the gun club. And the first thing she would do when she got home was cancel the Sunday outing with Helen and Peter. She didn't know how she would confront Peter about what she'd learned, but she knew it had to be done, and soon.

Conner walked her out to the car. "Have I told you lately how beautiful you are?" He brushed a hand over her hair, across her ear and down to her chin.

"You look pretty good yourself." She let her fingertips skim his chest before she pulled away and got into her car.

He leaned his arms on her open window. "Frank and I'll be working on those files tomorrow. Don't look for us early." His deep blue eyes worked their way too quickly into her heart.

She started the car. "Anytime is fine."

It didn't seem likely that Leona's work at the center was

related to her murder. But Audrey knew that if it was, Conner and Frank had a better than average chance of discovering the connection.

IT WAS LATE the next evening before they left Frank at Mavis's. As Audrey turned onto the main highway, she glanced in the rearview mirror and saw Ian twisting in his seat. Conner and Frank hadn't arrived at her cottage until after dinner. Between all of their attention and the excitement at Mavis's, Ian was exhausted and antsy.

"I got lots of pinecones." Ian patted the trash bag beside him. "But I need lots more."

Conner turned in his seat to see him. "We can look down near the beach."

Audrey's heart constricted when she thought of the possibility of losing the case and never seeing Conner again, but her own feelings were secondary when she considered the pain it would cause Ian.

"If the weather's good, I'll take you down there tomorrow." She intentionally omitted Conner.

A dark, cloud-covered sky made driving more difficult now that the sun had set. The trip home would be slow.

"Reach in the side of my purse there, would you, Conner? I brought one of Ian's light-up video games to keep him busy."

Conner found the game and took it out. A paper fluttered to the floor. He handed Ian the game, then leaned down and picked up the paper.

Suddenly, Audrey realized what was on that piece of paper. "Here, I'll take that." She held out her hand, knowing the dashboard lights would make the red lettering impossible to miss.

"What in the name of...what is this?" Exasperation filled Conner's voice.

Audrey held tight to the steering wheel and darted a sideways glance at him. Shock and anger colored his face.

She tried to snatch the paper away, but he kept it out of reach. This was not a good development.

He looked back at Ian and spoke more quietly. "I could always count on you to be open with me, Audrey. Don't clam up now. This could be a serious threat. When did you get this?"

There was no point in not telling him about the note, now that he'd seen it, but pride stopped her from volunteering the information. If he thought she might be in danger, he'd want her off the case, and no one was more intent on saving him than she was.

He smacked his palm on the dash and yelled, "Tell me about the note."

"Lower your voice, Conner. You'll frighten Ian."

"No way, not until you explain this and make me understand why you didn't show it to me when you got it."

She kept her eyes on the road and relented, recalling the exact day she'd discovered the horrible note. "I found it in my car three days ago."

"And you didn't tell me?"

"You're yelling again."

"Well?"

"Your reaction right now is a perfect example of why I didn't tell you. I didn't see any point in upsetting you over nothing."

He was quiet for so long she thought maybe her answer had satisfied him. She should have known better.

He plugged on, his voice insistent. "Do you know who sent it?"

"I have no idea. It's probably somebody's idea of a joke."

"You didn't tell anyone about the note, did you? Am I right? Are you crazy?"

She checked Ian again and saw with relief he was absorbed in his game. "For your information, no, I'm not crazy. I figure the person who sent me the note is the crazy one."

"I'm not so sure about that. Have there been any other threats?"

With a sigh, she mentioned the phone calls.

"And a week ago, someone slashed your tires."

He placed his hand on her shoulder and a warm tide of passion flowed through her.

"I never considered any of these things real threats, Conner, believe me."

"You can't ignore them." He spoke softly and glanced at Ian again. "Think about it. You're on the case for less than two weeks and all of a sudden unusual things start to happen. It could very well be the killer behind every one of them, and if he is, he's been trying to scare you off from the very beginning, for crying out loud."

"Why? That doesn't make any sense." The scene he painted was not a pretty one. It frightened her and made her pause.

"Oh, it makes plenty of sense. If the killer can keep you busy worrying about slashed tires, irritating phone calls and threatening notes, he can distract you from the case. Distract you often enough and you can't possibly focus everything on my defense. Once the jury finds me guilty, nobody bothers to look for the real killer."

"I think you should have been a lawyer, Conner. Your logic is flawless." She said it nonchalantly, trying her own method of distraction, because she knew where he was going with this and she didn't like it.

He removed his hand. Already she could feel him withdrawing from her, and her regret was overwhelming.

"Don't take it so lightly, okay? The distractions haven't worked. We are asking questions and getting closer to the truth. His plan is failing right before his eyes. So, guess what happens next?"

"I don't want to hear this, Conner."

"Audrey, the man's already killed once. What makes you think he won't do it again?"

THEY REACHED the cottage as sheets of rain sluiced down her windshield. Audrey raced to the shelter of the house, and Conner followed, carrying a sleepy Ian. Together, they got him into his pajamas and tucked into bed without complaint.

"I'll fix some coffee." She closed the bedroom door and walked quietly away.

Filling the coffeemaker with water and taking out a filter became automatic motions. Conner was right behind her, but he'd closed himself off from her. More than ever she wished she could read his thoughts.

He walked to the cabinet and found an old bottle of Irish whiskey on the top shelf, and plunked it on the counter. "Make mine a little stronger."

His cold voice cut into her heart. She watched him stride across the living room to the window and wanted to run to him and reassure him again that the threats meant nothing.

Rain beat a steady rhythm against the windowpanes, as the coffee dripped. Wind whistled through unseen cracks in the cottage. The draft gave Audrey the chills.

"This isn't working, Audrey." His back was to her, his voice gruff and strained.

She dosed his coffee with whiskey, then poured her own and joined him at the window. She didn't have to read his mind to know what he was thinking. He'd grown up very poor on the outskirts of town. He'd been a victim of poverty and a victim of a lot of people's prejudices about poverty. She couldn't think of one good break he'd had in his whole life. He would see the threats as an attempt to make her a victim, too.

She handed him his coffee, letting her hand touch his fingers. They were ice-cold.

"The note and the phone calls have to be put behind us." She had to make him change his focus. "We have one full day left before the trial begins. We need to look at everything and come to a consensus about your defense."

He turned around slowly and faced her. "What about Ian? He could be in danger, too."

"There's been no threat to Ian," she emphasized. "You have to know I would have dropped the case if that were true."

"I don't agree with you."

His fear reflected so deep within his eyes she was afraid she could explain forever and he would never see her point of view.

He turned from her again. "I wish you hadn't come back."

His words stunned her to silence. She wanted to pound his chest with her knotted fists or pull his hair to knock some sense into him. She couldn't imagine a day without Conner.

The seeds of their new relationship had barely begun to sprout. Her feelings for him had grown stronger than she would have admitted before now. No matter what happened, she would never regret their time together. She couldn't even feel sorry he'd met his son.

She looked up at his face as he stared out at the wind whipping the rain into a frenzy—a frenzy too similar to her own state of mind. "You don't mean that," she insisted. *I love you* became a mantra running through her head as she waited for his answer. It seemed her whole life hung in the balance.

He set his untouched coffee on the windowsill, the action deliberate, his face again a mask of hidden feelings when he turned to her with haunted eyes and placed his hands firmly on her shoulders.

The pause seemed endless. The fingers digging into her skin set off sparks of pleasure she knew better than to deny. She placed her coffee next to his.

She wanted to snake her arms around him and rest her head on his chest. She wanted to feel the strength of him envelop her and challenge her to win the case. Some sixth sense held her back. More than anything, she wanted him to retract his last statement.

Without diverting his eyes, without flinching or loosening his hold on her shoulders, he said quietly, "I want you off the case."

Time stopped for Audrey. "But the trial's too close." The pleading tone of her voice didn't bother her. She was frantic to change his mind. "Ben Reilly could show up. We could discover new evidence against Ida May. Bull Kingsley's girlfriend could admit she lied about that night. There are so many loose ends we can't quit now." He couldn't do this; he couldn't. "You don't know what you're saying."

"I know exactly what I'm saying. You're paying too high a price for defending me. I won't have your life put in danger, and I don't like the burden we're dumping on Ian. Let's not forget that raving woman in the diner. She won't forget that his mother defended the man they believe killed Leona Kingsley in cold blood, and neither will a lot of other people. I won't do that to him and I couldn't live with myself if anything happened to you."

"You can't take me off the case!" This time she did pound his chest, furiously, hopelessly trying to force him to change his mind. "You need me!" she shouted. How could he cut her out like this?

He held on to her shoulders, the confinement frustrating. His steady gaze never left her face.

She pulled loose and backed away from him. "There's not enough time for you to get another attorney. You don't have the option of firing me." Desperately she grasped at straws.

"I can do whatever I want, and what I want right now is you off the case. This is not up for discussion, Audrey. I've managed the past six years without you. I can take care of myself." After one quick, penetrating look into her eyes, he turned and walked across the living room and out the door.

Audrey gaped at him as he left. Tears clouded her eyes as she raced to the kitchen window and watched him tramp through the rain and boost himself into the truck. Never once did he turn back.

Chapter Thirteen

"Why have you been avoiding me?"

Audrey jumped a foot and dropped the hose. The crab pot she was cleaning rolled down the hill and into the creek before she turned to face her brother.

"Peter! You surprised me."

He stood back beside the house, with his hands plastered on his hips. "I'd like an answer."

"We'll talk, okay? Just a minute. Have a seat." She pointed to the picnic table and tamped down memories of the last few times she'd shared it with Conner.

Ian had picked up the hose and was watering the creek. Since he was already wet from helping her, she decided to turn the rest of the task over to him. She called to him. He turned around to answer, the hose following his movement. Audrey ducked to avoid the spray.

"You can clean them down by the creek," she told him.

"I won't get wet. I promise."

She smiled as she helped him pull the hose down the hill. As soon as he was set, she walked up to join Peter.

Peter was straddling the bench and tapping out a song on its sides. His fingers stilled when she sat on the opposite bench. "Well, let's have it. What are you hiding now?"

She chose not to mention that Conner had fired her last night. Defensively, she admitted, she decided to use a professional approach. "As you well know," she began, "I'm investigating the murder charge against Conner, and I have reason to believe—"

"You're something else again," he interrupted. "I'm your brother, for crying out loud, not some suspect you need to question. Come off it."

So much for her attempt to keep her emotions in the background. She hoped this didn't destroy their future family relationship. "All right. Have it your way." She let her eyes skim the whitecaps forming on the river beyond the creek, then stared straight at him. "Why didn't you tell me about the real estate deal you had with Leona?"

The shock on his face was worth framing. He stuttered awkwardly before regaining control. "You just said it, the key word being 'had.' It never went through." He resumed his tapping on the bench, then stopped. "You already know that, don't you?"

"Peter, I don't want to fight about this, but I feel a responsibility to help Conner in any way I can." The conversation was becoming stickier by the minute and her patience was disappearing.

"Well, I guess we know where the cards are stacked, don't we? You'd sell out your brother for that, that—"

She pounded the table. "Stop right there!"

They both glanced at the five-year-old at the edge of the creek, merrily hosing off the three crab pots. He was as wet as the pots. Audrey felt the breeze stir and saw that the setting sun had become an orange ball. She knew she would have to call a halt to this farce of a discussion soon and take Ian inside.

"Do you know Frank Smith?" she quizzed him. "Are you aware someone tried to gun him down in the storm last week using a jacket hollow point bullet, the same kind you use in gun competitions?"

Peter sucked at the fresh air blowing in from the river, slid his other leg under the table and stared at a grease stain on the wooden slat. "I don't want things to be like this between us, Audrey. I'll admit, you're still the little sister from years ago, before I joined the army. We don't really know each other very well, do we?"

"That's true." She felt a portion of the weight on her shoulders take wing with the sea gulls in the distance. She had to give him credit for his concession, but she knew she couldn't let herself be blinded by sibling loyalty, not when it involved the father of her son.

"Please, answer my questions." She hoped her persistence didn't drive him away.

His long pause made her wonder if he would actually get up and leave without any response. If he did, what was left of her family would walk away with him.

Finally, his shoulders slumped; his eyes cleared of animosity. He folded his hands on the table and raised his head. "I didn't kill Leona Kingsley, if that's what you're getting at."

"I never truly believed you did."

For the next ten minutes, he explained what had happened. She listened with increasing relief to a story that matched what others had told her. He even included an alibi: he was playing poker in the back of the hardware store with Mr. Moseley and several other men on the night of the murder. Audrey was thankful when he included the information. She hadn't wanted to ask.

"And I didn't try to kill Frank Smith, either."

She just nodded in answer. If he hadn't killed Leona, he would have no reason to harm Frank.

She stopped talking long enough to send Ian inside for his bath. Peter waited for some response. "Thank you for being so candid, Peter. I'm really glad you told me."

He stood to leave. "Maybe now we can start over. Helen would like that." He paused. "And so would I."

"Why don't we begin with a fresh cup of coffee?" Audrey motioned him toward the cottage, relieved that they'd cleared the air.

"Sounds good to me." He followed her into the cottage. Audrey spooned coffee into the filter as sounds of Peter coaxing Ian out of the tub faded to the background. No matter what she was doing or whom she was talking with, Conner's case preyed on her mind.

She had missed Doc at the center Friday evening, but she would get him to clarify the gun club membership the first chance she got. Then there was Bull Kingsley. Had he really been with his girlfriend when Leona was shot? Where was he the night someone went after Frank?

Most important of all, she had to decide what to do tomorrow morning when Conner's trial began.

CONNER SAT behind the defense table, conscious of the capacity crowd in the courtroom behind him. He almost regretted his decision to fire Audrey, almost but not quite. With her off his case, no one would have reason to threaten her again.

He had one goal for his trial—to survive with his dignity intact. He would not grovel. He would not beg. He would call the character witnesses Audrey had planned to have testify and tell the truth as he knew it. Beyond that he had no plan of defense.

He'd never harbored a grudge against Leona because of her testimony six years ago, but no one would believe him. According to the documents he'd read, the lab had verified his gun as the murder weapon. He could not refute the gun was his. Hell, he'd carved his name on the stock when he was thirteen. The fingerprints on the gun matched his— who could argue with scientific proof? He had no witness to testify that he was miles from the scene of the crime at the time of the murder. Other than hoping to instill reasonable doubt in the jury's mind, he had no defense at all.

The smell of heather floated nearby. He allowed himself a moment of pleasure and imagined Audrey naked in his arms, saw himself sliding his hands over her soft skin, felt her response beneath his fingertips and recognized the craving deep inside.

He started when she sat beside him. Every frustration

burst to the surface. "I thought I made myself very clear, Audrey. This is no longer your case."

"Too bad, Mr. Hastings." Her eyes dared him to cross her.

He wanted to throttle her when she opened her briefcase and took out his file. "Did you hear what I said?"

She smacked her palms on the table and turned to him. "Let me ask you this. Did you submit the proper documents to the court declaring I no longer represented you?" She smiled at his silence. "That's what I thought."

Damn the woman! How was he supposed to know about that? "You should have done that, not me."

"But you fired me, remember?"

"A defendant has a right to fire his attorney, *Ms.* McKenna. I still have a few rights, or have you forgotten?"

Anger burned in her eyes when she spoke again. "I will not let your stubbornness ruin my career. Do you know what could've happened if I hadn't shown up today? I could've been disbarred. Sent to prison. I'm not into sanctimonious self-sacrifice the way you are. You'll just have to put up with me."

Dealing with Audrey's stubbornness had always been a challenge, especially when the fire in her deep green eyes drove him to distraction. He regretted not having the chance to answer her.

"All rise and come to order. The court of Judge Adrian Aldrich is now in session." The bailiff caught everyone's attention. He was a short man with round glasses and a round face. Conner remembered him from his previous trial.

Reluctantly, he stood with Audrey, seething inside, aware that together they presented a deceptive picture of unity. He wanted to boot her up the aisle and out the door. She shouldn't be here. God help him, if he only did one good thing in his life, he had to get her out of there.

The noisy courtroom immediately quieted. The judge swept into the room from his chambers, wearing the traditional black robe. He was a very tall, large man, with a square face and sharp eyes.

Conner immediately jumped to his feet. "Your Honor?"

"You may address the court, Mr. Hastings."

"Your Honor, I decline counsel and wish to represent myself." He dug his fingers into the table and prayed to all the powers that existed to hear his plea.

The judge leaned forward in his chair. He calmly examined Conner. "Very inadvisable, Mr. Hastings."

"Your Honor." Audrey sent Conner a scathing look and stood up, "May we have a moment?"

"You are Ms. McKenna, is that correct?"

"Yes, Your Honor. I am Mr. Hastings's attorney of record."

"Please advise your client of the pitfalls of self-representation, Ms. McKenna."

"Yes, Your Honor, I will."

She pulled him to his seat as she sat down. Fire burned in her eyes. Her fair skin flushed a beautiful rosy pink.

He attacked before she opened her mouth. "I don't want you here, Audrey. I don't want you at the defense table. I don't even want you in court." *Get out,* he wanted to shout, more frustrated by the need to keep his voice low. *And don't you dare let her see how much this hurts,* he demanded of himself.

Pain dulled the edges of her blazing eyes before she shifted so close she had to look down. "Well, tell me this. What is our son going to think when he grows up and learns his mother sat back and did nothing to help his father save his own life? You can't do this, Conner." Her voice shook with emotion. "You can't do this to Ian, you can't do this to me and, most important, you can't do this to yourself." She drew back and met his gaze. "I may not be experienced, but I know a lot more about criminal law than you do. Give yourself a chance. Please."

"Your Honor," roared the prosecutor.

"Sit down, Mr. Upshaw. Ms. McKenna, is this going to take all day?"

Audrey's eyes pleaded with him. She rose and faced the judge. "No, Your Honor. I apologize to the court."

"Mr. Hastings, are you ready to reconfirm Ms. McKenna as your attorney?"

Conner felt ripped in half. If there was a chance of acquittal, it would be easier to agree to keep Audrey by his side. Maybe. The town might not like her success, but at least she would win her first case. That would help her career. Once he was gone, a win would smooth her way for the future.

Her words about Ian also made him hesitate. Would the boy hate his mother when he found out the truth? He tried to imagine himself in the same position and knew with a sinking dread that she was right. He would feel justified in hating someone who allowed this to happen to his father.

Yet no matter what she said, he didn't see what he was doing as "sanctimonious self-sacrifice." Dismissing her made sense to him. Any lack of trust he'd harbored had vanished as they'd worked together to find the answers to the puzzle.

That was part of the problem. He knew she would work herself to the bone and do what had to be done to prove his innocence. Audrey believed in him. The thought overwhelmed him.

Did she really believe he had a chance? The sudden image of her in his arms blocked out every argument in his head. The thought of never loving her again was more than he could bear.

"Mr. Hastings, please answer the question," bellowed the judge.

"Yes, Your Honor."

"Is that 'Yes, Your Honor,' you'll answer the question? Or 'Yes, Your Honor,' you're ready to reconfirm Ms. McKenna as your attorney?"

The judge's comeback released some of Conner's tension. He found himself liking the man. After his first experience with Judge Bingham, he didn't think he'd ever like one of these men in black robes again. Maybe Audrey was right. Maybe he'd been acting like an idiot. Maybe there was a slim chance he'd walk away from this trial.

"Yes, Your Honor." He glanced at Audrey sitting beside him. Expectation and hope creased her forehead. Fear hid in her eyes. "I agree to have Ms. McKenna as my attorney."

"A wise decision, Mr. Hastings. Ms. McKenna, are you still willing to represent Mr. Hastings?"

Audrey jumped up to her feet. "Yes, Your Honor."

"Thank you, Ms. McKenna, thank you." The judge assumed a more formal position in his chair and placed his folded hands before him. "Bailiff, please read the charges."

Lori sat down at the table and whispered her encouragement. "Very good, Audrey. I, for one, would hate to see Mr. Hastings go down without a fight. You may have just experienced your most difficult argument of the case."

Audrey kept her voice low as the judge began the process of jury selection. "I wish that were true."

The prospective jurors filed in. "Conner, please tell me if there's someone here you feel we should challenge."

He may have agreed to have her represent him, but he hated himself for giving in. And he hated having her talk to him as though he were a stranger.

He looked over each potential juror carefully and found himself rating, on a scale of one to ten, how each would view his past offenses. He'd never broken the law as a kid. Not exactly. But he'd come close many times and aggravated a lot of people. He'd always felt so angry. Looking back, he wondered how his mother had tolerated him.

The first candidate was Dave Martin. This man hit the bad side of the scale at a booming ten. Conner leaned toward Audrey. "Get rid of Mr. Martin. He's as straitlaced and inflexible as they come. Everything is either black or white with him. Reasonable doubt isn't part of his vocabulary."

Audrey studied him, her green eyes probing his. "Okay."

Her confidence in his judgment gave Conner a satisfying boost. He sat back and admired the commanding presence of her walk across the floor to question Dave Martin, but as he remembered the soft curves beneath her suit his mind was tempted to wander.

"Mr. Martin, do you know the defendant?" Audrey used a deceptively pleasant voice.

"You bet I do. Used to chase him off my property on a regular basis when he was just a young pup."

"So you've known him for many years, is that correct?"

"I'd say so, yes."

As she considered her next question, she watched the potential juror before her, a man with bushy white eyebrows and disheveled hair, his wiry frame slumped in the chair. "Mr. Martin, can you give fair and impartial judgment to the defendant?"

His mouth formed an O. He looked at Audrey without seeing her, as if thinking hard about his answer. "The Bible says, 'An eye for an eye.' I believe that. Yes, ma'am, I do." He paused. "It also says, 'Forgive one another.'"

Audrey took a moment to look quickly at Conner before addressing the judge. "Juror is accepted, Your Honor."

Conner couldn't believe his ears. "What are you doing?" he whispered when she returned to her seat. "Dave Martin hates my guts. He's never said a decent word to me. He didn't even answer your question."

"You're right." She spoke softly, her face open and honest. "But he did more than answer the question. You heard the conflict in his statement, Conner. Mr. Martin will be hard-pressed to sentence a man to life in prison when he believes he should forgive him. We could do worse."

AUDREY SHOVED the papers into her briefcase, glowing inside from Lori's praise. It was time to pick up Ian and go home. Sitting beside Conner all day under the constraints of a formal setting was much easier than facing him now in the quiet of an empty room.

He took hold of her wrist. "Is there any way I can change your mind?"

"About representing you? No, the decision's been made. I'm here until the end of the trial, Conner. Then you can do as you please. And just for the record?" She pulled loose and walked away. "We all need somebody."

It was a spiteful statement, she knew, but his final words at the cottage still burned in her ears. She left him standing alone in the courtroom and hurried from the building before her crying heart betrayed her.

A block away she saw Ian waiting for her in front of the center. The man standing beside him made her heart flip for a moment. He was the same height as Conner and had the same coloring. From a distance she really thought it was him. The misimpression lasted only a second until she pulled the car up to the entrance and realized it was Doc Rankin.

The mistake left her with a weird feeling. *A trick of the mind,* she told herself. *Serves you right for dwelling on Conner.*

She got out of her car. "Doc, what a surprise to find you here. Where is everybody?"

She'd never seen any resemblance between the two men before, and now that she was facing Doc she couldn't see any at all.

"Della wasn't real happy about the delay." He moved closer and smiled somewhat awkwardly. "But don't you concern yourself. Everything was fine once I volunteered to stay."

"That was sweet of you to wait with Ian. I appreciate it."

"It was no trouble." Doc turned aside and watched Ian dig through his plastic case.

"Nevertheless, I appreciate it. I don't know what I would've done if Ian couldn't have stayed the extra hour."

She felt uncomfortable when he edged closer, a ridiculous reaction under the circumstances.

"I hope you haven't added baby-sitting to your list of duties." She searched for a distraction and coaxed Ian to the car. "You must have a full schedule with your practice and your responsibilities at the center."

She opened the car door and waited while Ian climbed in and buckled up. When she turned around, Doc was a foot away and closing in. He snagged her hand before she could stop him. "I'm never too busy to help you, Audrey."

The man had just done her a favor, yet his attempt to win her interest had the same effect as in the past. She felt extremely uneasy when he didn't let her hand go.

She swallowed hard and left her hand where it was. "I looked for you Friday when I came for Ian. I wanted to ask you something."

"Anything, Audrey. You have only to ask."

The surprise and pleasure on his face could have easily defeated her in her purpose. But not when Conner's future was at stake.

She worked at keeping her voice neutral. Knowing Doc's obsession with her, he would lie if he thought the answer would impress her. "Someone told me—" she decided to exaggerate "—that you're an A1 shot in those gun competitions I keep hearing about. Is that true?"

A half smile curled his lip. "Gun competitions? You know I've never been fond of guns, Audrey. As a doctor, I like to save lives, not put people at risk. They must have been talking about another Rankin."

"I was just wondering." She stepped back and thanked him profusely for his help.

With all the finesse she could manage, she reclaimed her hand and scooted around the car, then sighed in relief once she was on her way, headed toward home.

Back at the cottage, she and Ian ate dinner, and then she

read to him for a while before putting him to bed. She was fixing herself some lemonade, when the phone rang. Silence followed her hello, yet she heard breathing on the other end. There had been no indication these calls were related to the threatening note in her car. She was tired enough to let her irritation guide her.

"You have the wrong number. Please stop calling."

A raspy voice came on the line. "I have the right number, all right. I hope you do, too. Your client must die. Unless you want to take his place." The caller hung up.

The lemonade dropped to the floor. Audrey's hand flew to her mouth. She stood paralyzed for what seemed like forever. Only slowly did her brain begin to function. No one she knew in Tabbs Corner wanted Conner dead badly enough to threaten her, not like this. No one except the killer.

Fear spurred her to action. She ran through the cottage and locked all the windows and doors. In a frenzy, her hands shaking, her heart hammering, she cleaned up the lemonade, then mopped the entire floor. She washed all the dishes before loading them into the dishwasher. After folding the last tub of clothes, she ran out of chores and excuses to delay facing the threat before her.

She had a whole night alone with Ian in their isolated cottage. What was she going to do?

ON TUESDAY MORNING the air was crisp, the sky clear. The parking lot behind the courthouse was full. One had to wonder if the whole town had shut down to attend the trial.

Inside, the noisy buzz traveled down the hall. People congregated near the entrance to the courtroom in all sorts of attire. Extra guards had been added to keep order.

Audrey delayed entering the courtroom as long as possible. Conner would know something was wrong. He always did.

Lori met her by the door. "Ready?"

Audrey took a deep breath to steady herself. Any nervousness could be attributed to her trying her first case, she knew. That was fine with her. "I'm ready." She tossed back her shoulders and walked with Lori to the defense table, scanning the crowd for threatening faces.

She'd been nervous ever since she'd woken up. Everywhere she went she checked behind her to see if anyone was watching. Late last night, she'd dragged Ian from his bed, thrown her briefcase and clothes in the car and gone to Peter and Helen's for the night. It had felt better not to be alone. If they'd wondered about her midnight arrival, they said nothing, perhaps because their new ties were too delicate.

Her eyes were drawn immediately to Conner as she reached the defense table. He was dressed in a navy suit, light blue shirt and conservative tie. Shadows discolored the skin beneath his eyes and suggested his evening must have been as bad as hers.

"Good morning." She kept her tone cheerful and found herself longing for the closeness they'd once shared.

"Good morning, Counselor." His sharp blue eyes caught hers.

Audrey hid her eyes by scanning her notes to review the facts she needed clarified through testimony. She didn't care to expose the pain her eyes would reveal. He'd had his say. He didn't need her. They both knew his statement included more than her legal skills.

The bailiff called the court to order. Judge Aldrich took his seat and called for Mr. Upshaw's opening statement.

"Ladies and gentlemen of the jury," began the Commonwealth Attorney, "the state contends that on July 5 of this year, Conner Dulane Hastings did willfully, deliberately and with malice aforethought murder Leona Kingsley in cold blood by inflicting a fatal bullet wound to the back of her head."

Conner nudged Audrey's elbow. He tapped a pencil on the pad of paper before him, directing her eyes to the words he'd written. "You look beautiful" was scrawled across the page.

She covered her gasp of surprise with a quiet cough. The irritation she should feel wasn't there. She tried to return her attention to the state's opening argument, but Conner pulled her back with a loud tap on the table. "Couldn't resist" was now added to the note. She took a deep gulp of stale air, then let it out slowly.

But it was impossible to disguise her spontaneous smile. Out of the corner of her eye she could see the satisfied look on his face and it didn't help at all. A murder trial was no place to play these kinds of games, she told herself. If she wasn't careful, the state would win without a fight only because the defendant's attorney couldn't keep her mind on the trial.

Sitting next to him was more difficult this morning than it had been yesterday. There was something different about him today. She refused to try to figure out what it was and focused again on Mr. Upshaw's words.

"The state will prove beyond a shadow of doubt that Mr. Hastings had every reason to murder Leona Kingsley. Six years ago Mrs. Kingsley's testimony sent Mr. Hastings to prison. Now, I ask you folks," he said, abruptly changing his approach, "isn't it odd that less than two weeks after Mr. Hastings's release from prison and return to the area, Mrs. Kingsley was murdered? I don't know about you, but I don't believe that's coincidence."

Audrey revised her opinion of the Commonwealth Attorney. She'd talked to him twice during her preparation for trial and both times his speech had been stilted and formal. He'd toned down his style. By addressing the jury in everyday language he made them believe he was the nice neighbor next door who had a problem and needed their help.

Conner nudged her again. This time he leaned close and murmured. "You're going to clobber this guy. He won't know what hit him."

His confidence in her was daunting. Too conscious of their arms touching on the table, too affected by his whispered breath in her ear and the tantalizing shiver of pleasure it caused, she couldn't answer him.

But she hadn't missed the anxiety, even the fear, he tried to hide. When he wasn't trying to get her attention, his eyes were riveted on Mr. Upshaw; he took in every word the man said. His hand curled in a fist on the arm of the chair when he wasn't writing her messages. He was well aware he was fighting for his life.

Chapter Fourteen

"Ladies and gentlemen of the jury, I am Audrey Ann Mc-Kenna. I represent Mr. Conner Hastings, the defendant. Mr. Hastings did not kill Leona Kingsley."

Conner watched her move gracefully back and forth before the jury, pausing to make eye contact with each person in turn. Every member of the panel seemed spellbound. Even Judge Aldrich appeared impressed with the way she was handling herself. Audrey's mellow voice rose with each point of emphasis and held Conner captive.

"Imagine, if you will, that you made a mistake and paid the price," she continued. "The time arrives when you could do one of two things. Now, I admit one choice is ridiculous, but let's include it for the sake of argument."

He loved watching her work. She was spinning a strong silk web around the jury. If their final vote could be based on the effect of Audrey's opening argument instead of the state's evidence, he would win hands down. How could he ever have believed he could survive this trial without her?

"One choice would be to focus your life on the past," she went on. "The state contends Mr. Hastings did just that. The state contends Mr. Hastings returned to Tabbs Corner for the sole purpose of seeking revenge against Leona Kingsley.

"The other choice, the only one that makes sense, would be to get on with your life. After all, you spent six years in confinement, during which time you earned a college degree in computer technology. You're anxious to enjoy your freedom again. You've created competitive software that several companies want to market. You have a career waiting for you.''

Conner noted the surprised look on the jurors' faces. The O Mr. Martin formed with his mouth made him look as though he were sucking a lemon. *Good for you,* Audrey, he thought. It never would have occurred to him to use that approach.

''Now, I ask you, would you give up your freedom so quickly? Would you throw away all your hard work and accomplishments? Would you turn your back on the possibilities of a bright future? That's what the state would have you believe.'' Audrey paused, placed her hands on the front of the jury box and leaned forward. ''I submit, ladies and gentlemen of the jury—that choice makes no sense.''

Lori Thompson looked his way. From the satisfied expression on her face, he could tell she was also impressed with the love of his life. Audrey was doing an incredible job.

She used the same tactics during the rest of her speech. She led the jury down the path of opportunity and alibi and invited each one of them to examine the logic of the situation he was in.

He leaned back in his chair and flexed his fingers. Watching her defend him was fascinating; it was also draining his reserve of control.

He'd worked like a dog on the house all night to try to forget the pain he'd caused her. He'd chipped and painted and sanded and waxed until the bitter taste of yesterday's weakness had left his mouth. There were no two ways around it—he was a selfish bastard. He'd let Audrey defend him so he wouldn't have to give her up so soon. And he knew he couldn't win. Therein lay his greatest crime.

Ernie had come and helped him paint the outside of the

house. The teenager had insisted on staying to give him a hand putting up power lights at strategic spots inside. Only when Conner had forced him to accept one of his computer books and literally shoved him out the door would he leave.

But Conner had continued to work under the lights until he dropped. Finally, in that exhausted state, the acid taste of his stinging words to Audrey had subsided into a manageable pain.

Audrey returned to the defense table. He shifted close and winked, but not before drinking in the nectar in her hair. "Remind me to hire you if I ever need a lawyer," he teased. "You're terrific."

She smiled directly at him when she thanked him. It was as if heaven itself had kissed his face. Her green eyes glimmered like emeralds. Her face glowed with energy. Not seeing her smile ever again was impossible to imagine.

"Mr. Upshaw, call your first witness," the judge directed after the opening speeches.

"The state calls Sheriff Randolph Parks."

Audrey pushed her hands down flat on the table to avoid clenching them. Between the tension of her first trial and Conner's presence beside her, she was a nervous wreck. If the jurors noticed her nervousness, they would presume she was unsure of Conner's innocence. She had no intention of helping the prosecution.

The sheriff paraded forward with his head held high. The plastic straw was noticeably absent. His uniform looked as though it had just been pressed, and his silver star shone so bright Audrey caught herself wondering how long he'd spent polishing it.

The sheriff was sworn in, and he took the stand. While he answered questions regarding his credentials as a law enforcement officer, he kept his eyes on Conner. Audrey resented the man's cocky expression more than ever.

"Sheriff Parks, will you tell the court, please, what you discovered on July 5?"

"Yes, sir." He spoke very clearly. "At 11:07 p.m. on the day in question, I received a call from Mr. Bull Kingsley that he had discovered the body of his wife at the Kingsley estate. Of course I went right over." The sheriff paused and smiled.

Conner caught her attention with another whisper in her ear. "We should have asked Bull how he happened to be at Leona's that night."

"It's not too late," she murmured, suddenly calm and directed just from the sound of his voice. "I can ask him when I call him to the stand."

In addition to Mrs. Bracken and Bull as character witnesses, Audrey had lined up several people to verify Conner's accomplishments in the past six years. She'd planned to call Bull last. As the victim's husband, he would have the greatest impact.

Conner's remark now made her rethink the order. Why had Bull been at Leona's that night? If he'd killed her, he wouldn't be foolish enough to make his presence on the estate known to the sheriff. Still, when reviewing her interview notes last night, she recalled her impression that he was holding something back. What if she could break him on the stand? She decided to reorganize her defense and call Bull Kingsley first.

"I found Mrs. Kingsley, just as Bull said, at the bottom of the hill by the river. That's the Piankatank River," the sheriff added, addressing the jury directly. "She'd been shot in the back of the head with a .22." A flicker of pain crossed his face.

"And what did you do then?" asked Mr. Upshaw patiently.

"I followed procedure. We blocked off the crime scene—but naturally there wasn't any need to, the place is so big. Deputy Johnson and I searched the area. That's when I discovered the rifle. It was hidden in the woods beneath a fallen tree.''

Mr. Upshaw entered the rifle into evidence as Exhibit A and continued his questions in a steady, sure voice. "Is this the rifle?"

She felt Conner stiffen beside her. The rifle was the damning evidence. Without it, the state would have no case. If only there were someone who could testify that Conner hadn't seen or touched that rifle in six years, she could at least raise doubt in the jury's mind.

"No problem there, Mr. Upshaw." The sheriff lifted his head in confidence. "I've seen it many times. It's a .22 Winchester Magnum rifle. Belongs to Mr. Hastings, all right. Has his name carved on the stock big as life."

An excited buzz filled the courtroom and grew louder, as the judge called for order. Audrey started to take advantage of the interruption to jot down some questions, but Conner drew her attention.

The sheriff's statement seemed to have knocked the fight out of him. He'd pushed back in his chair and fixed his eyes straight ahead. His hands hung lifelessly over the arms of the chair. His face had hardened to stone.

Audrey searched for the right words to say. He'd cut her heart in half Saturday night and thrown away the pieces. She didn't want to love him. She didn't want to need him. Certainly she couldn't give in to the urge to push his chair over and force some sense into his thick head. *This trial isn't over yet,* she wanted to shout.

She tried talking to him while the judge brought quiet to the courtroom. To no avail. When Mr. Upshaw continued, Audrey pulled her mind from Conner to listen to the state's witnesses.

The medical examiner was called to the stand to testify to the results of the autopsy. Technicians verified Conner's rifle as the murder weapon and testified that the prints found on the gun matched his. When it came time to call witnesses to establish Conner's motive of revenge, Audrey found herself objecting to every other statement. They were nothing but opinions and hearsay. They made her furious.

At last the state finished with its witnesses. Audrey intentionally hit Conner's chair as she got up to call Bull Kingsley to the stand. Conner didn't budge.

Her instructions to Bull had been simple—answer yes or no whenever possible. "Mr. Kingsley, you are the husband of the deceased, is that correct?"

"Correct." Bull emphasized the stamp of his voice with a quick nod.

She approached him casually. "How long have you known the defendant?"

Conner hadn't changed, Audrey noted. He'd cut himself off from the trial. He'd given up. A desperation she'd never known crept over her and egged her on. She needed his confidence, damn him. She needed his optimism.

She turned to Bull. His face was wrinkled in concentration, as if counting up the time. "I'd say I've known Conner about twenty-one years."

She paced the floor slowly in front of Bull. His deep voice…Charley's… What was it he was hiding?

"In your opinion Mr. Kingsley, and knowing the defendant as long as you have, do you think Mr. Hastings murdered your wife?"

"No, no way," Bull stated emphatically.

"Mr. Kingsley," she continued quickly before he could expand his answer.

She made a split-second decision to follow her instincts. She didn't like what she was about to do. It wasn't common practice to intimidate your own witness. She took a deep breath and prayed for guidance.

"Mr. Kingsley," she repeated, "you were separated from your wife, weren't you?"

Bull frowned. He knew very well this was not part of the testimony they'd talked about. "I was staying at a place in Tappahannock, yeah. But it was all a misunderstanding. There was nothing official about it.''

"Why were you at Leona's estate the night she was murdered?''

"Like I said, it was all a misunderstanding. I was trying to work things out.''

"Mr. Kingsley,'' she went on, the adrenaline now flowing fast and furious, "you stand to inherit quite a lot of wealth from your wife's estate.'' She stopped her pacing directly in front of him. "Just out of curiosity—whose idea was it that you move out? Yours or hers?''

Bull shifted uncomfortably. He glanced up at the judge and then at Audrey. "Hers.'' His answer was curt, his face drawn.

"Leona was going to divorce you, wasn't she?'' Audrey pushed him, her voice a notch higher, the next questions ready and waiting to be fired at him fast.

Bull's face turned red. "I told you, no.'' He leaned forward on the witness stand and spit out the words.

"Did you kill your wife, Mr. Kingsley? Did you murder her in cold blood so you could hold on to at least part of that money?''

"I didn't give a damn about the money,'' he yelled, and jumped up and shook a finger at Audrey. "She was messing around, for God's sake. I found her sleeping with the sheriff.''

Sheriff Parks exploded from his seat. "Just a guldurn minute! You have no right...''

Chaos erupted in the courtroom. The gavel pounded through the noise.

"Order,'' shouted the judge. "Order in the court.''

Audrey was so excited she could hardly stand it. Conner, she saw, had come back to life. His face showed total disbelief. The new spark in his eye urged her on.

"Take your seat, Sheriff Parks,'' ordered the judge. "Sit down this minute or I'll hold you in contempt. That goes for you, too, Mr. Kingsley.''

Once the judge had the court back under his control, Audrey said, "Just one more question, Your Honor."

She returned her full attention to Bull. "Mr. Kingsley, why did you withhold this information during our interview?"

"You're kidding, right? And make it look like I killed her? I didn't kill her. Hell, I loved her."

For some crazy reason Audrey believed Bull had loved his wife in his own way. She dismissed him and called Sheriff Parks to the stand.

"Sheriff Parks, I remind you, you are still under oath. Were you having an affair with Leona Kingsley?"

The sheriff appeared ready to strangle her.

"Answer the question, Sheriff." The judge's demand left him no options.

"Yes." He hissed out the word.

"Let me make sure I have this right." Audrey had trouble containing her excitement. "You testified earlier that you and Deputy Johnson went to the murder scene, saw the victim's body, cordoned off the area, then searched for a weapon. Am I right so far?"

"That's what I said." His answer came out in stiff, staccato bursts.

"You also stated earlier that you found the murder weapon. Is that correct?"

"Yes." The tone shifted up a notch in frustration. His wide hand clutched the chair.

"Where exactly was Deputy Johnson when you found the murder weapon? I mean, was he on the other side of the property? Was he standing next to you? Was he six feet away from you?"

"He was in the woods on the other side of the property."

Gotcha, thought Audrey, her fervor soaring to new heights. "Could he see you when you found the weapon?"

"No, of course not, not from the other side of the estate."

"Sheriff Parks, in light of your admitted affair with the victim, would you call yourself an impartial, fact-finding representative of the state?"

The sheriff jumped to his feet. "Just what are you suggesting, little lady?"

Audrey had heard enough. She glanced quickly at Conner and saw shock on his face.

"Your Honor." She spoke loudly enough for the whole town to hear. "I move to suppress the gun as evidence based on the facts revealed in court today. I also move that all charges against my client be dismissed."

THE JUDGE WASTED no time in declaring a mistrial. He was clearly angry. His tirade against the sheriff was still ringing in Audrey's ears as she and Conner sat at the defense table, impatiently waiting for the court to clear.

Audrey had never felt so exhilarated in her life. Lori had beamed at her when she clasped both her hands and told her how proud she was to have her as a part of Regal, Thompson and Lutz.

And then there was Conner. His bewildered eyes hadn't left her since she'd called for a dismissal.

He took her hand now and held it tight. "You're a miracle worker." His voice cracked with emotion. Astonishment fringed his eyes.

Audrey almost felt embarrassed, his sincerity was so intense. "We were lucky," she told him, wishing he would pick her up and whirl her around in his arms.

"Don't underestimate yourself. I wouldn't be free right now if you hadn't maneuvered me into keeping you on." He traced a continuous circle over their entwined hands. His eyes actually twinkled.

She hated to be a spoilsport, but she wanted to make sure he understood what had just happened. "This hasn't solved your problem, Conner. Unfortunately, it's an incomplete trial. With new evidence they can charge you with Leona's murder and bring you to trial again." Expressing the possibility dropped a heavy cloud over their victory. Audrey shuddered.

"I'm not worried about that happening."

He said it with such confidence she believed him.

"But I was wrong about something. What I said before. You were right. I did need you, Audrey. I do need you."

Her heart skipped several beats. Tears of joy threatened to fill her eyes.

Conner leaned close and whispered in her ear. "I've been saving a certain bottle of wine for a special occasion. Come home with me, Audrey. Help me celebrate."

"Oh, Conner." She reached up to touch his face, then remembered where they were and lowered her hand to his. "Only if we go right now."

His face broke out in a breath-stopping smile as he helped her gather her belongings. Side by side, they began the long awaited exit from the ordeal that had brought them back together and nearly ruined both their lives.

He held the courtroom door open for her. "What made you come down on Bull like that?"

She had wondered the same thing. "I'm not sure. All along I had a feeling he was hiding something."

"They call it instinct." His hand found the small of her back. "You're a natural defense attorney, Audrey." He looked down at her with pride and pushed open the front door to the courthouse. And stopped.

They'd hoped that by waiting until after the crowd had left the courtroom they could exit the courthouse quietly, but as the door swung open they could see their mistake. Ten or twelve people congregated around the steps. Several reporters rushed forward, with cameras clicking or notebooks in hand.

"I don't want to deal with this." He pulled her back into the foyer.

"It'll be all right." Audrey plowed through the door.

No sooner had she stepped outside than two people shouted insults and shook their fists. Audrey searched the group for a familiar face and saw none. The word "Murderer!" resounded from the rear. She stepped back inside and felt the exhilaration of success collapse into a coiled knot in her stomach.

"Let's use the back exit." Conner grabbed her hand. "The parking lot is easier to reach from there."

They made their way through the courthouse halls to the back door. Audrey suddenly remembered the threatening phone call. Fear spiked the knot that had formed inside. Was the caller out there in the group? What would he do now that Conner was free?

She didn't want to tell him about the threatening call, not now when he was riding cloud nine into freedom. Maybe she'd never tell him. The call was probably a hoax anyway, she rationalized, convincing herself the only dangers awaiting them were the name-calling and the pesky reporters from the many nearby small towns.

Conner opened the back door and they saw their efforts were wasted. The reporters had circled around to meet them. The other group trailed on their heels. Audrey stepped back from the sight.

"At least we're closer to the car." Conner pulled her forward. "I'm game if you are. Take out your keys."

She held them up, as anxious as he was to leave. "Let's go."

They left the building, their heads high, and walked across the lot toward Audrey's car. The group of men continued to taunt Conner with names. The reporters pushed them to guess what kind of new evidence could surface.

Conner stayed close by her side. "I have a feeling they've read Frank's article."

Audrey checked her watch. It was twelve-thirty. "I bet you're right. The *Daily* comes out before noon. The timing couldn't have been more perfect."

They reached her car. She climbed in and surveyed the lot. "Where's your truck?"

"Around the corner."

She started the car. "Get in. I'll drive you."

After watching the group of name-callers run toward the back lot, he jumped in and said, "That's not a bad idea."

Audrey nudged the car out of its spot and through the reporters. She eased around the corner and saw Conner's truck in the farthest slot. Five men were rocking it back and forth. The sight gave her the creeps.

"Why don't we come back later for your truck? This doesn't look good."

"You can drop me off here. If I leave it, there won't be anything left of it."

He had his hand on the door handle, when she stopped him. "I'm going to pull the car up to the driver's side of the truck so you can go from one vehicle to the other."

She increased her speed into the crowd of men and watched the people scatter.

"Are you sure you haven't done this before?" He grinned as he slammed the door closed and swung up into his truck.

Her strategy took the men by surprise. Before they had a chance to regroup, she was pushing past the rowdy crowd, through the reporters and out of the lot, with Conner right behind her. She just hoped they didn't follow them.

THE ANTICIPATION of holding Audrey in his arms was hard for Conner to bear. He stayed on her bumper as they drove through town and was still there as she turned off toward his house. She stopped at the beginning of his driveway and he wondered why. Until he saw the four cars in his yard. Reporters.

Quickly he backed up, and Audrey followed suit. He pulled on the brake close to where the road met the highway and charged from his truck.

"What do you want to do?"

"We could go to my cottage. I think I can forgo the wine for now." Her smiling green eyes caressed him.

He wanted to agree. One look at the reporters scrambling into their cars changed his mind. "For some reason, I don't think that would work."

She followed his line of vision. "Oh." She put her warm hand on his arm. "There's always Frank's boat. Again no wine, and definitely none of the creature comforts I had in mind, but at least we'd be free of certain prying eyes."

Silently damning the reporters, he kissed her lightly on the mouth. "You're on."

The drive back toward town seemed like a funeral procession to Conner. Only when he and Audrey ran a yellow light did they manage to put some distance between them and the reporters.

He slammed to a stop at her cottage. Audrey ran to the truck. "I'll do a quick change of clothes and be right there."

Conner pulled out an old T-shirt and a pair of cutoffs from behind his seat and made a record change in the truck before racing down to the boat.

Audrey came down the hill in a sexy pair of shorts and halter just as he started the motor. And none too soon. The first of four cars screeched to a stop beside his truck.

"Climb aboard, Counselor. You got here just in time."

They ran the boat very slowly through the channel into the Rappahannock River, then turned and waved to the reporters standing on the pier. Once they were beyond the sandbars, Conner gave it full throttle.

Audrey by his side, the wind in his face—this was pure heaven for a man who'd thought he'd be behind bars before the sun set.

They headed toward the mouth of the river where it fed into Chesapeake Bay. Audrey tilted back her head to the cloudy afternoon sky as if she didn't have a care in the world.

Windmill Point was visible in the distance when he cut the engine and made his way over to her. "Come here,

Counselor." He couldn't resist. "I haven't thanked you properly yet."

"Yes, you have." She protested faintly, yet she turned into his arms and looked at him with searching eyes.

He ran his hands slowly over the soft curls that felt like angel-spun silk against his skin. He lifted her face and explored its beauty in detail—the high cheekbones, the delicate nose, her perfectly shaped chin, which she liked to thrust out in defiance.

"This is better than wine any day." He traced a line down the side of her neck and between her breasts to her tiny waist.

She slid her arms around his neck, her full breasts pressed against his chest. The wonderful feel of her fueled every cell in his body with a fire that could never be contained.

He crushed his mouth to hers, hungry for her fire, reveling in her unbridled response. He memorized the purr of her voice and the way she melted in his arms. He'd never felt such need. He'd never known such longing. Too much so.

He forced himself to draw his mouth away before he lost himself completely. Wrapping her in his arms, he held her close against his chest.

"My God, Audrey."

He smoothed back the hair from her forehead, then curled one loose strand around a finger and slipped it behind her ear. He wanted to keep touching her forever, but he had no inkling how she felt about him. Yes, she'd stuck with him through the trial, but they both knew that was for Ian.

"You're welcome." Her voice dipped in a husky tremor as she kissed him on the chin and pulled away.

A chilly wind skimmed across his back and drew goose bumps on Audrey's arms. "The wind's shifted." Not only that. The water had become choppy.

"It's gotten chilly." Audrey pulled on one of Frank's shirts she found stuffed in a corner of the boat.

Conner didn't like the sudden change in the weather. "We'd better head in."

It took only a few minutes to turn the boat around, but in that short time, the wind increased, dark clouds hid the sun and a cold rain pelted their faces.

"I should have checked the weather before coming out."

Audrey looked up at the sky. "These storms can hit the bay without warning. At least, that's what my grandfather used to say."

She sat close beside him by the motor, her body warm and inviting in spite of the cooler air. "We'll go to Frank's," he said. "His place is closer."

He took off across the river. "Hold on. This could get rough."

Whitecaps had formed on the surface. They bounced along the choppy water at full speed. Visibility became more difficult with each passing mile as a wispy fog settled in. It took a great deal longer than usual before they could see the entrance to Frank's cove.

"Shouldn't be long now," Conner shouted above the noise of the outboard. "We'll go in from the north side. It's trickier but quicker. I don't like the looks of this storm."

He knew from past trips that a deeper channel ran along the south entrance to the cove, yet he'd also approached it from the north. It didn't occur to either of them that in six years, even in one day, the bottom could drastically change. He was unprepared when the boat suddenly hit the bottom and the engine stalled.

THEY HAD ALMOST pushed the boat free, when the first shot rang out.

"Watch out!" His heart in his throat, he tackled her in the foot-deep water and brought her down beneath him.

"Are you crazy?" She fought to get free.

He held on to her as the rain pebbled the surface around them. The wind brought the sound of another shot. A foot away, the sand stirred to a murky brown. He felt her resistance give way as she became aware of what was happening.

"Thank God the wind's blowing in the right direction. Otherwise we wouldn't hear his shots." He pulled her closer.

"We're sitting ducks on this sandbar." She wedged in tighter against him, the feel of her body a luxury in the middle of this madness.

"I know." He fought back the panic that threatened to overtake him as he watched the flow of the water. He had to keep her safe, he had to. "But if we can get to that high bank over there, we might have a chance." He only hoped he was right.

"Then let's do it." Before he could catch her, she wiggled out from beneath him and slithered across the sand bar into deeper water.

Conner elbowed through the sand double-time to catch up. The water popped around them, inches away, the crack of the shots surprisingly loud. But the ploy was working. They swam with the current, letting it carry them farther into the cove toward the steeper bank.

The water level at the bank was normally two or three feet. With the high tide and the storm's wind, it was deeper. Conner surged ahead of Audrey and grabbed onto a protruding tree root.

"Take my hand." He wedged his feet in the maze of roots and extended his arm.

She grabbed his hand. Her nails bit into his skin. He tried to pull her up, but she started slipping away. At the last second he caught her wrist and yanked her up against him. Quickly, he swiveled around and pushed her into the bank behind him and covered her with his whole body.

Chapter Fifteen

"You're trembling."

Conner had put her life in danger; the guilt threatened to consume him. With a desperation born of fear for her, he kissed her passionately, completely.

"Well, if that doesn't warm me up, nothing will." She smiled through chattering teeth and wiped the mud from his face.

"I'd like to do more than just warm you up."

"I think our minds run on the same track."

A barrage of shots made the water hop three feet away.

He hovered closer. The feel of her against him almost interfered with his thinking. "I don't think he can get us in his sights from here."

"Maybe if we climb up the bank, we can make a run for Frank's." She made the proposal a mere inch from his ear, her breath warm against his skin.

"The sniper could be at the top." He stopped her. "He's somewhere close—that's for sure. I don't think he could see us at all from too far away, not in this weather."

Audrey searched the area ahead over his shoulder. "Then let's edge around the bank. It'll take longer, but we can make it." Her decisiveness fed his determination to succeed.

"I agree. It's our best choice." But he hated the idea of leaving her exposed for a minute. "If we can get to

Frank's—when we get to Frank's—we'll call for help. This guy definitely has an unfair advantage."

They fought to hug the bank and keep their footing in the slippery mud. Branches scratched and stabbed and slapped them in the face. The looping roots offered good handholds but left them exposed to a wind that wanted to sweep them into the water.

At last they reached the spot nearest Frank's house. Conner surveyed the area and saw nothing unusual. "I'll go first. If he sees me, you'll know to try another route."

"You will not." Audrey pushed her wet hair behind her ears. "We'll go together. One of us might need help."

Afraid that Audrey might be the one to need the help, he agreed. They climbed to the top of the bank and paused to look for the sniper. Satisfied they were safe for the moment, Conner boosted himself over and pulled Audrey up behind him.

Hand in hand, they ran from tree to tree toward the front of Frank's house. The wind clawed at their soggy clothes. The fear in Conner's heart grew fierce. When they reached the front door, he dared to let his tension ease. But his relief soon ended. He didn't have the key.

"Oh, no." Audrey slumped against the doorframe.

Conner forced his mind to function. "I think Frank keeps an extra key on the top ledge of the side window. Stay down here close to the door." He pushed her down and kissed the top of her head. "This'll just take a minute."

He dashed to the side of the house to the window. His fingers crawled along the top ledge until they found the key. A shot hit a tree three feet away, and he took off at a fast clip. He rounded the corner and caught Audrey running toward him at full speed.

She plowed into him. "I heard another shot. Are you all right?" She smoothed her hands down his face.

"Come on." He kept an arm draped around her shoulders and rushed her to the front door. "I'm fine, but I think he spotted me."

His numb fingers fumbled with the lock, and finally it clicked free—just as a bullet wedged into the doorframe, missing Conner's head by inches.

"Quick, inside." He shoved her through the door.

The next shot broke a front window.

"Stay low." They both slouched through the house. "And no lights. I'll call James."

Shivering, Audrey crouched in a corner while Conner crawled to the phone on Frank's desk. He started dialing, before he realized the phone was dead. "Damn! I think we've underestimated this guy. Looks like he cut the wires."

"But how did he know we'd come here? Even we didn't know." Audrey made herself smaller in the corner by hugging her arms around her shaking body.

"He must have been with the crowd at the courthouse that followed us to your place. I'll bet he's been watching us from the shore all along." He pushed the useless phone away. "Why don't you go into the bedroom and see if you can find some dry clothes."

"Wait a minute. Does Frank's ham radio work? James still has his. I heard it at the garage."

"You're a genius." He crossed the room.

Frank had been a ham operator since they were teenagers. James, too. They both used the radio now to monitor police calls, James for his tow truck service, Frank for a possible story.

Intermittent static filled the room as Conner scanned the frequencies. Another bullet shattered more glass and hit Frank's desk. Conner tried to concentrate, tried to remember what to do to reach James.

At last James responded. Conner identified himself quickly. "We're at Frank's. Under attack by a crazy sniper."

"I read you," James drawled. "Be right along." He didn't ask for more explanation.

His calm voice tempted Conner to give in to the hysterical laugh forming inside him. "Be careful, James. This guy shoots at anything that moves. Over and out."

Conner joined Audrey in the bedroom. He found Frank's hunting rifle and loaded it, just in case all else failed. Then he and Audrey huddled in an inside corner of the house. He kept her between the wall and him, with the gun across his lap, ready. Both prayed the sniper wouldn't come bursting through the front door.

Not thirty minutes had passed before the front room lit up. Through the whistling of the wind coming in the broken windows, they heard James's truck outside. Only it didn't sound as if James was alone.

Conner tore himself away from Audrey and crept cautiously to a window. What he saw made his heart leap in relief. Six trucks were backing up to the house at various intervals. All six had their headlights on high. One truck had spotlights and shone them through the mist into the surrounding woods. As the men climbed down from their trucks, he recognized some of his and Frank's racing friends from years ago.

"Come here, Audrey, you've got to see this."

He pulled her to him, savoring her closeness, wondering how in the world he had ever pushed her out of his life.

"See, Conner." She smiled and looked out of the broken window. "Lots of people in Tabbs Corner believe in you."

RAIN WASHED against the windshield as they drove James's truck away from the sheriff's office. Already it was getting dark. Conner held her tight beside him. The warmth of his thigh next to hers fired up her body with visions of wine and hot hands. She'd been terrified the sniper would get him when he'd left her to find Frank's key. Never did she want to leave his side again.

"The deputy seemed more responsive than Sheriff Parks would've been.

She could just imagine the picture they'd presented when she and Conner and James and his crew stormed into his office to report the sniper incident.

Conner nodded and kissed her cheek. "Deputy Johnson's a good man."

"Let's hope he catches this guy fast. I don't want to go through something like that again."

Conner hugged her to him before turning off the highway toward his house. "I want to make sure the house is locked, then I'll take you and Ian home. Those reporters could come back. I don't want you here if they do."

She'd called Helen from the sheriff's office and asked her to pick up Ian from day care. Helen had been upset when she heard what happened. "We don't have to get Ian. Helen's keeping him overnight."

"We have a whole night to ourselves?" A sly smile spread across his face. "Why, Counselor, I never realized you were such a schemer."

He slowed on the slippery, muddy road. The wind was not as strong here away from the river, but the rain continued to come down. A car came toward them on the one-lane road.

"That's Ida May's car. You don't think they had Ernie working outside today, do you?"

"Not a chance." His sea blue eyes caught hers.

"Don't let him leave. Let's make sure Ida May hasn't returned from her trip yet."

He looked at her with impatience and passion, but he stopped the truck in the middle of the road as she'd asked. Audrey jumped out with Frank's jacket over her head and ran to the Seville. Conner came up behind her and put his arm around her shoulders. She could feel the wonderful heat of his body.

The handyman cracked his window open an inch. Audrey gave the man her best smile. "Could you tell me if Ida May has gotten back from her trip?"

"Not till next week."

The handyman's wide blue eyes smiled back at her. He seemed more approachable than Audrey thought he would be, and up close he was much more distinguished looking.

She gave in to an impulse. "You don't happen to know where Ida May was the night her sister was killed, do you?"

The man actually laughed. It was a pleasant sound that made her smile again.

"Indeed I do." He looked at her with merry eyes and rolled the window down farther. "What you really want to ask is if she killed Leona. She didn't."

Conner edged in closer beside her, his shoulder feeling just right next to hers. "So can you tell me where she was?"

Again the handyman laughed. He saw Conner and leaned out more. "You see, this skunk got trapped inside the house that night. You can imagine Ida May's panic at the thought that little guy could let loose with a spray. I chased that thing for two hours. Caught him, too. Let him go outside. Unfortunately, he got me at the last minute. I spent the rest of the night in a tub of tomato juice."

He waved her closer. "Now, don't you tell anybody. This town would love to hear this. Ida May was with me through the whole night, scouring up every can of tomato juice she could find."

Audrey really liked this man. "Don't worry," she whispered through the downpour. "I won't tell a soul. Thanks."

He tipped his hat. "You clear this young man." He acknowledged Conner with a nod. "I don't care what Ida May thinks. I knew his mama and I know he didn't do what they say. What you said at the trial this morning made sense."

They thanked him and ran to the truck to pull it off to the side so he could pass. He waved to them as he left.

They got in the truck and Conner nudged it forward. "Looks like we can rule out Ida May."

"And Peter. We had a long talk. He didn't do it, Conner. He's got a valid alibi."

"That's a relief." His words rang with sincerity as he parked the truck close to the house.

"There is one thing, though." Audrey felt awkward bringing this up. Had she mentioned it earlier, they might have avoided the fiasco on the river. "I had another call last night, only this time the threat was verbal."

For long moments the only sound was the rain hitting the truck. Conner stared straight ahead. His jaw muscle jumped with tension.

"Maybe now you understand why I wanted you off the case."

His statement stung. "Would you really have preferred that I wasn't in court today?"

"Yes!" He gripped the steering wheel. Haunted eyes met hers. "If it meant putting your life in danger, you bet I would. But I'll tell you one thing. That sicko won't get a chance to threaten you again." He opened his door. "Wait here."

Audrey watched him sprint to the front door, her heart racing as fast as his feet. Hours ago they'd set off for his house with the promise of passion in the air. She'd longed to feel his body next to hers, naked and hard. Her hands ached to touch him now more than ever. She opened her door to run inside, but stopped short of getting out. Conner slammed out of the house and raced to the truck, a small bag in hand.

He pulled her close, kissed her hard and deep, then started the engine. "I'm moving into your cottage until the killer's behind bars, Audrey. We're not taking any more chances, especially after everything that's happened since the trial this morning."

She heard the slight hesitation in his voice, as if he

thought she might disagree. Not a chance. "I think that sounds like an excellent idea."

A shiver of anticipation slid down her spine.

THE RAIN HAD TURNED to a drizzle by the time they reached the cottage. The moon kept trying to peek through the clouds. Audrey led the way inside to the dark kitchen, took their jackets and hung them over a stool to dry.

She snapped on a small lamp at a corner table. The light sent the remaining shadows into hiding and surrounded her in a soft, sensuous glow. The vision stole Conner's breath away.

"We certainly took the long way to get here." Her voice quivered, as though she were nervous, yet her green eyes sparked with mischief.

"You and me? We're survivors, Audrey."

He feasted his eyes on every move she made—the way she tossed the hair from her face, the graceful lift of her arm, the gentle sway of her hips. There was a hint of desperation in her movements, the same desperation he'd been battling since the sniper took that first shot at them.

Without stepping closer, she swiveled slowly, almost in slow motion, and met him full face. His breath caught in his throat. Her green eyes burned dark with passion and longing.

He couldn't move. He'd come so close to losing her today. The desire burning inside him numbed his mind and narrowed his thinking to one question: did he dare believe she could still love him? The mistrial plagued him. Too much was unsettled. Yet her eyes kept teasing him, inviting him to do what he'd wanted to do from the first moment he saw her. Were it not for her next gesture, he might have held strong.

One by one, carefully, delicately, Audrey slipped the buttons on Frank's big shirt through the restraining holes. The fabric rustled as it dropped to the floor.

He moved closer and touched the soft skin of her cheek.

"My beautiful Audrey." The crack in his voice surprised him.

"Sh." She put two fingers to his lips. "Don't say anything."

Without any more hesitation, he swept her into his arms and buried his face in her hair, its fragrant smell an aphrodisiac. Several quick strides led him to her bedroom, and gently he lowered her onto the bed. "Are you sure, Audrey? You've got to be sure this is what you want before we go any further."

She smoothed his face with her delicate hands. He wanted to melt into the tenderness and strength of her touch. With a passionate gleam in her eye, she held both sides of his face. "I've never been more sure of anything in my life."

Her words closed the door on any restraint. He crushed his mouth to hers and drowned himself in her sweet taste. Their tongues tangled and danced to the tune of their feverish needs.

His hands roamed everywhere he could reach—her fevered cheeks, her delicate ears, her soft hair. Hating to leave her hot mouth, he let his tongue trail a blaze of fire down her throat to her breasts. He unhooked her bra and slipped it from her shoulders. Gingerly he ran his fingers over the silky smoothness of her breasts.

"This isn't fair, you know."

He circled the tip of her breast with his tongue before taking it into his mouth. Audrey arched in response, her moan of pleasure music to his ears. Her fingers clawed his back. Her hips rose to meet him.

Reveling in her response, he was reluctant to interrupt their pleasure, but when she nudged him away, he asked, "What do you mean unfair?"

"It's not fair that you're still dressed."

They both shed the remainder of their clothes and then paused, as if by removing the physical barriers between them they gave themselves permission to bask in the reality of each other's bodies.

"Dear God, I've missed you." Conner took her face tenderly and kissed every precious part of it.

They knelt on the bed, inches apart. Not quite believing this dream come true, he slid his hands down her arms, over her chest, across her breasts, to her waist and down her legs, the familiar feel of her body his most humbling experience in years. Yet he had to know she was real. He'd spent too many nights agonizing over what he'd once had and lost, and dreaming of her like this in his bed once again.

Audrey stilled his hands and began her own exploration. Her hands followed a path across the width of his shoulders and down to his chest, where she brushed at his chest hair.

He shivered at her touch. Unaccustomed to a passive role, he raised his arms to embrace her. She lowered them to his sides.

She leaned over and kissed his chest and he thought he might die. She continued her journey to his waist and around his hips. Teasing him with a touch that was lighter than he thought possible, she feathered her fingers along each thigh to his throbbing sex.

Unable to stay still any longer, he dragged them both down to the bed and scorched her skin with his hot mouth, just as hers burned him senseless. As if someone had snapped a finger to release them from the torture of their teasing, they gave in to their blinding needs, each crushing the one to the other, each frantically devouring the other.

He couldn't keep silent about his feelings. Nibbling her ear, he whispered, "I love you, Audrey. I'll always love you."

His heart stilled when she froze. For a split second he thought he'd made a complete fool of himself.

She looked up at him with filmy eyes and touched his face with her loving hands. "I love you, too, Conner. I

don't think I ever stopped loving you." She caught her
fingers in his hair and pulled him to her once more.

With a need born of separation and a desperate love
reclaimed, he branded her with his mouth and gave her his
heart. She twisted and writhed beneath him as he stroked
her. He thought he might explode if he didn't have her
now. With what sense remained, he pulled a packet from
his jeans.

"Audrey…"

He slid into her tight, hot body. Murmuring his name,
clawing his shoulders, she arched and met him thrust for
thrust. And when she cried out in ecstasy, he felt his own
world explode as he joined her in the most ultimate, incredible release of all.

Satisfied, they lay tangled together, their damp bodies
evidence of what they had shared. As Audrey curled up
inside his arm, her breath caressed his chest.

Many minutes passed before Conner thought he could
speak. He had so many things he wanted to say, things he
had no right to say, things he'd stored up inside, things of
the heart. Yet there were no words for how he felt right
now.

Audrey's slow, steady breathing told him she'd fallen
asleep. He twisted one loose curl away from her face and
kissed her forehead, wishing he could fall asleep beside
her unencumbered by the threat of danger or prison.

He slipped out of bed, wishing for a lot of other things
he couldn't have. Too many unanswered questions still
separated them, questions he was determined to resolve.

The glow from the front porch light shining through the
living room window caught his eye and reflected the glass
of a framed picture. He knew that picture. He'd avoided
the stunning eight-by-ten color photo the last time he'd
been at the cottage.

With unsteady legs, he crossed the room and picked it
up. Lovingly, he traced an outline around the two people

smiling up at him. Audrey and Ian. The two people he loved more than life itself.

Never in his wildest dreams had he imagined that Audrey could still love him. The possibility of losing her again, of losing the future they could have together, sent a shattering pain through his heart.

THE WORLD SEEMED brighter to Audrey as she picked up Ian from Helen's and took him to day care. She felt like a fairy princess imbued with a special magic. Making love with Conner had been everything she'd dreamed and more. And miracle of all miracles, he loved her! The thrill of his touch stayed with her through two morning hours at the diner, where she absorbed people's reaction to Frank's article. It encircled her like a loving cloud and encouraged her to finish her work early so she could tell Conner what she'd learned.

Of course, she acknowledged as she turned off the highway, the article was only a good excuse to spend time alone with him at his house before getting Ian.

She sensed he wasn't home before she saw the empty drive. Ernie ran out onto the road and flagged her down.

"Do you know how long Conner's gonna be gone? I'm out of paint."

Ernie had repaired half the damage to the front of Conner's house. "Maybe I can find out for you. Why don't we go to your house so I can use your phone to call a couple of places."

She phoned the garage and talked to James's assistant. No one had seen Conner. She called Mavis's and learned that Frank had hitched a ride into town with one of her customers.

"I'm sure tomorrow will be time enough to finish, Ernie. Why don't you call it a day?"

Ernie looked back at Conner's house and frowned. "I guess it's okay. James came by and Conner flew outta here like he was going to a fire. He didn't even go see Ben."

Audrey's heart stopped. "Ben Reilly? He's back? Where?"

Ernie stared at her as though she were crazy. He pointed down the road. "There he is."

Audrey was so intent on seeing a single man on the road she almost missed the couple walking arm in arm. "Thanks, Ernie," she called as she ran down the road.

"Ben Reilly!" she shouted.

This couldn't be happening. For days they'd looked for Ben in vain, and there he was right in front of her—a day too late, but never mind the trial. If Ben knew who stole Conner's rifle, they'd have their killer.

She ran down the muddy road in her heels, wishing she'd taken time to change her shoes, thinking what a foolish thought that was when she could be on the brink of discovery. If she could get a name, they could clear Conner.

"Mr. Reilly, Ben, we've been looking for you." She caught up to him in front of his house.

He stopped then and turned around, his lady friend on his arm. Ben was much shorter than Conner. He wore a white dress shirt, open at the neck, and khaki trousers, tucked inside muddy boots. His thinning, light brown hair was neatly slicked back from a heart-shaped face.

He squinted at her through thick glasses. "Is that you, Audrey? What do you know!" He left his lady friend behind and came and took her hand in both of his. "It's good to see you."

Her heart hammered she was so anxious to learn what Ben knew. "Did Ernie tell you we've been searching for you?"

"Yes, indeed—my daughter, too. Come meet my wife." He led her to his lady friend. "I'd like you to meet Delores."

Audrey shook her hand and noticed her attractive smile. "It's nice to meet you." She turned back to Ben. "I didn't know you got married, Ben."

Ben looked at his watch. "Exactly one week and two days ago. Minus five minutes."

"Oh, Benny." Delores playfully swatted him on the shoulder. "And we had the most wonderful honeymoon on my houseboat, just Benny and me." She gazed at him with love.

Audrey offered her congratulations. "Ben, this is really urgent. I understand Mrs. Hastings asked you to look after her house before she left."

"She did that." He pushed at his glasses. "I feel real bad about all that dumping. They never did it when I was around—you can bet on that."

"I guess you heard about Leona Kingsley's murder."

Something stirred in his eyes. Fear? Shock? She couldn't be sure.

"I heard." His voice was not so friendly now. He gripped Delores's arm.

"Then I guess you already know that Conner's gun was used as the murder weapon." When he didn't respond, she got right to the point. "Did you see anyone inside his house before he came back? Anyone fooling around the outside who shouldn't have been there? Somebody who might have stolen his gun?"

"No, I told you." He threw the words out to her quickly. "I never saw anyone around the place."

Delores tugged at his arm. He frowned at her, but she ignored his uneasiness and prodded him on. "Tell her, Ben."

"Hush, now."

"I'll tell her if you won't. She has a right to know."

His eyes locked with his wife's, and she gave him the sweetest smile.

"Tell me what, Ben? What do you know? What made you disappear for all this time without a word?" Her patience was running short and her curiosity was about to explode.

Delores pushed against him for encouragement. "All

right," he snipped. "The last time I saw that gun, Conner was in his backyard, aiming at something in the woods."

Audrey couldn't speak. She had her hand clamped over her mouth.

"Now, don't you go jumping to conclusions," Ben admonished. "I was scared when I heard what happened. I mean, Conner had been locked up for six years, and that can do things to a man. And at first I was sure he killed Leona, the way everybody said, but I don't think that now. So don't you go thinking it, either."

But Ben didn't know what she knew: Conner had told her the gun was already missing when he returned home from prison.

Chapter Sixteen

Audrey stumbled and slid through the mud to her car. She
crawled in behind the wheel and collapsed. Could Ben
Reilly be right?

Despair threatened to take over as she started the car
with trembling hands. Her charred heart crumbled into
ashes. She was numb with a pain she desperately wanted
gone. Had Conner lied about the gun?

Driving forced her to keep some control. Day care had
ended; Ian waited. She hugged the thought of her son to
her and reigned in her emotions as she drove down the
highway, knowing she had to get herself together before
she picked up Ian.

If Conner had lied about the gun, that meant he'd killed
Leona. Was that possible? Were her perceptions of him so
wrong? Had her love for him blinded her to the truth?

She turned into the center's parking lot and realized her
crazy thinking had almost destroyed her common sense.
Ben Reilly had to be wrong, didn't he? Someone had to
have stolen Conner's gun. Otherwise why would anyone
have been shooting at them out on the river?

She hustled into the center, anxious to get Ian and then
find Conner. But Ian wasn't in his classroom when she
arrived.

Mrs. Tompkins was lining up the children. "They're not
back yet."

"Back from where?" Ian's teacher had her totally confused.

Mrs. Tompkins looked equally baffled. "Didn't Della Andrews call you?"

"No, I haven't heard from her. Is something wrong?"

"Dear me. This is not the way to do things." Mrs. Tompkins turned the children over to her aide and pulled Audrey aside. "Della Andrews came and got Ian over an hour ago. Then, a short while later, she sent word that he was sick. She wanted Doc to take a look at him. I thought that's why you were here earlier than usual."

"But I didn't know anything about it."

"Why don't you go over to Doc's office? I'm sure Ian's fine." She placed a reassuring hand on Audrey's arm. "Maybe you can catch them before they leave."

Audrey rushed from the classroom and through the hall. She sped toward Doc's, wondering why Della had taken Ian to a doctor before calling her to get permission, then chastising herself for being so suspicious, when the woman was only trying to help her son.

CONNER SLAMMED on his brakes by the garage and rushed to Doc's front door. He'd broken every speed limit getting there after James had delivered Doc's message about Ian.

Trying to contain his fear, he accosted Doc when he opened the door. "How badly is he hurt?"

Doc Rankin ushered him inside. "He'll be fine, Conner. First, though, we need to discuss some things."

Conner followed Doc through the house to his large basement office. "What things?" he demanded. "Why didn't you call Audrey? What could be more important than seeing my..."

"Your son?"

"How did you know?"

Doc had his back to him at a bookcase and was opening a box on one of the shelves. "Medical records can be very thorough, you know."

He turned around slowly with a satisfied look on his face—and a gun in his hand.

AUDREY PULLED into the steep driveway beside Doc's house, the one that led down and around to the patient parking area in the back by his office. Ian rarely got sick, she kept telling herself, but he could have caught something from the other kids at day care. She told herself not to be overly concerned; Doc would take care of him.

The patient parking lot was empty. She thought she might have missed Della taking Ian back to the center, but realized the woman's car could be parked in the family driveway on the other side of the house.

Quickly Audrey pulled into the spot closest to the office door, growing anxious to see for herself that Ian was all right. She had no sooner stepped from her car than she heard the angry voice.

"You're out of your ever-loving mind!"

Conner? A chill crept down her paralyzed spine. What was he doing at Doc's? This wasn't right.

She forced her feet to move slowly toward the office door. The voice had come from the open window to the left of the door. Doc's office, she remembered.

Instinct stopped her from going immediately inside. She knew something was dreadfully wrong. Had she really heard Conner's voice? Where was Ian?

She edged around the bush blocking the window, pressed herself against the brick frame and peered through the miniblinds. The sun's glare cut into her eyes. She could see very little.

She shifted slightly forward to get a better look and searched the room for Ian, for Conner, her heart beating fast in worry. Where was Ian? Why was Conner here?

Conner and Doc came into her field of vision. Conner had his back to her, blocking Doc from her view. She strained to hear, but their voices were too low to catch what they said.

She moved to relieve the cramp in her leg and watched the twosome shift, cautiously, like combatants ready to attack. Suddenly she saw a gun. Fear strangled her impulse to scream.

Conner was pointing the gun at Doc, she thought at first, then realized she'd confused the two men. Doc had been the one with his back to her. Conner had been the one she couldn't see. It was Doc who was aiming the gun directly at Conner. The realization made her whole body shake.

She shifted positions as much to control the shaking as to put her ear against the screen to learn what was happening.

"I thought I got rid of you once, you see," Doc said. "But now you've returned, and that presents me with a problem."

"I'm supposed to know what that means?"

The menacing tone of Conner's voice sent more fear into Audrey's veins.

Doc moved closer to the window, the gun locked on Conner. "The robbery idea was terrific, don't you think? All I had to do was shed *my* clothes and don your...well, dress like you. Leona had no trouble thinking I was you six years ago."

Oh, my God—oh, my God! The phrase ran nonstop through her head. Doc Rankin framed Conner six years ago? Why?

"Why?" Conner asked her silent question. "Why do all that?"

"You don't know?" Doc's voice jumped an octave. "How naive."

It could have happened that way, Audrey realized, her hands shaking uncontrollably. She'd just made the same mistake herself when she'd seen Doc from the back and thought it was Conner. Ben Reilly must have done the same thing. It made sense, especially with Ben's weak eyes. Had Doc stolen Conner's gun? The idea seemed preposterous.

She moved too quickly, not thinking. Her unsteady legs gave way and she fell against the window—and cried out when she heard a shot.

"TRY THAT AGAIN and your next move will be your last," Doc spit out across the room.

Conner's left arm burned like hell. He pressed his hand against the open wound and discovered the bullet had gone all the way through his arm. He used the side of the desk for leverage to push himself up off the floor.

What the hell was going on? Where was Ian?

He should've had better sense than to lunge for Doc, but he never thought the man would shoot. He leaned against the desk and tried to stanch the flow of blood. Already he could feel his strength waning.

"I knew you would come to me someday, Audrey."

Doc's words hit Conner like a death blow. He whipped around and saw her standing in the doorway, frozen, staring at the blood dripping from his arm, the color drained from her face, her eyes wide with fright.

"I didn't expect you quite so soon, though." Doc glided toward her. "I wish you would leave now. I'll come for you later."

Conner couldn't fault the advice, but what the hell was he talking about? "Get out, Audrey. Get out," he implored, watching her bring her fear under control—and surprised when she looked at him with doubt.

She focused back on Doc. "Later?"

"Oh, yes. Later. When I finish my business. My business for you."

The guy was nuts, Conner realized. He had a madman standing there training a gun on him. Fury washed over him in a flash. Desperation squeezed his heart. It was all he could do not to charge across the room to shield Audrey. He couldn't let her get hurt.

Keep cool, he told himself. *Maintain your control—stay alert. Look for your chance to take the guy out.*

Audrey's eyes switched back and forth between the two men. "What's going on here, Doc?" Her voice trembled. She walked cautiously into the room.

Conner had to warn her. "Be careful, Audrey." He staggered away from the desk, feeling strangely drained, wanting to shove her back out the door.

Doc's eyes widened to twice their normal size. Sick adoration gushed out of him for Audrey. "This is all for you, my dear." Doc beamed a radiant smile at her. "I knew Conner wasn't the man for you. You finally understand."

"Audrey, get out of here!" Conner pleaded. "I'll find Ian. Can't you see what he's doing? Who do you think shot at us?"

"I did."

Della Andrews marched into the room, wearing a smug expression. Her words were directed at Conner, but her scowl was aimed at Doc.

"You did what?" Doc growled at her. His face went through a series of contortions. "You shouldn't have done that, Della. Everything we did was for her. I told you that. She and I are going to have a beautiful life together."

Stunned but still thinking, Conner realized he'd just discovered Doc's soft spot.

"No, Doc, I think *you* tried to hurt Audrey," Conner goaded him. "I think you're the one who kept calling her and taunting her. You left that nasty note in her car. You chased us through the storm, spraying us with bullets. You almost got us, too—did you know that, Doc?"

"That wimp?" Della screeched. She moved in on Conner as though she would punch him in his wounded arm. Instead she shoved him against the bookcase. "The only thing he's good at is wooing old ladies into leaving him all their money, then making sure they rest easily—permanently."

Audrey gasped as her hand flew to her mouth. Conner wanted to release the sigh of relief he felt but knew this was not the time. Della had just given him the biggest piece of the puzzle. He and Frank had almost figured it out from what they'd found in Leona's files.

Doc's eyes were wild. "You tried to kill Audrey?" He walked uneasily toward Audrey, clutching the gun, pointing it first at Della, then at Conner.

Della recognized the danger. She turned her attention to the man with the gun. "Calm down, Doc. She's standing right here in front of you, isn't she? She's fine."

"You weren't supposed to do that." He was whimpering now.

"I had to. We couldn't have anybody nosing around Leona's death, now, could we? She was the only one in town who might believe in Conner enough to dig deep enough to free him. And I was right. She got him off. We'd be better off if I hadn't missed."

"So you stole my gun. You killed Leona." Conner wasn't quite sure whom he was addressing, but he hoped his fishing expedition worked.

"She had to die!" Doc shouted, and turned on him. "She would have ruined everything. She was writing that frivolous article and found out about our scheme. Della's and mine. Della got a share, you know. I couldn't have that." Doc was clearly out of control.

"Frank got too close, didn't he?" Knowing the answer, Conner forced himself to keep cool. "You tried to kill him, too."

"And he botched it up real good." Della marched toward Conner. "But I'll say one thing, mister. You'll be telling me where you took Frank Smith before you die." She zeroed in on Audrey, her method of persuasion clear.

"What have you done, Doc?" Audrey's voice quivered. "What have you done with my son?"

Conner's heart took another leap. "Ian's probably not here, Audrey. Back off."

"But Mrs. Tompkins told me…"

"You heard what they said." He rushed on, trying to distract her, knowing the last place his son should be was in this room. "Doc gets his ladies to will him their money, and then he sends them to their graves. How much sicker can it get? It was there in Leona's files all the time." He moved forward a step, his blurred eyes never leaving Audrey. "I'll show you. Just take it easy," he begged.

"Stay right where you are." Della elbowed him. "We need to get on with business. Our mutual business." She stepped toward Doc, the anger clear on her face. "I knew you'd botch this up, too. Look at that." She pointed to Conner's blood on the rug. "You fool! You can't kill him here!"

"Where did you take my son?" Audrey inched toward Della, true panic ringing in her voice. "What have you done with him?"

"The kid is fine. For the moment." A deep, wicked laugh bubbled out of Della. "He's taking a nice, long nap. Finally."

Conner had never felt such rage toward a person in his life, but he took one look at the fury on Audrey's face and restrained himself. She'd reached her limit. Knowing she would go for Della, he edged along the bookcase, bound to stop her.

A strange expression formed on Doc's face. "You said you wouldn't hurt Audrey's little boy." He stepped toward Della. "You said it would be all right." Another step. "You're always telling me what to do, always telling me lies." The menacing look on his face was frightening and didn't fit the whine.

"That's because you're such a fool," Della shouted, and backed up. "Can't you see Audrey would never love a fool like you?"

"That's a lie!" Doc raged. He forgot about Conner and pointed the gun at Della.

The shot exploded in the room like a bomb.

Conner lunged for Audrey, determined to shield her from this madman, frantic to get her out of the way. He shoved her against the wall and planted himself in front of her. And froze when he saw Della move.

The woman struggled to raise herself from the floor. Conner thought she was reaching for the wound in her chest. Until she pulled out a gun from inside her jacket.

The shot was an easy one. Doc hadn't moved. Even so, Della's aim was off. The bullet hit Doc in the right side of his chest.

Della fell back, her eyes glazed in death. Doc crumbled slowly to the floor, murmuring "upstairs" as he passed out.

Conner drew Audrey to him with his good arm. Heaven had smiled down on him. She was alive and breathing and warm and wonderful. But what about their son?

Audrey looked up at him with pure panic on her face.

"He has to be here." Conner needed to reassure himself as much as Audrey.

She raced up the stairs. Conner followed more slowly, cursing the loss of blood that was draining his strength. He couldn't lose Ian, not now, not ever.

They heard the banging first. Audrey caught his eye, hope shining from her face, then turned and fled up another flight of stairs.

They found him locked in an upstairs bedroom, pounding on the door with his little fists and calling for Audrey.

Audrey hugged him in her arms as tears rolled down her cheeks.

"Where were you?" Ian swiped at his wet face. He took one look at Conner and frowned. "You're bleeding."

"I'm all right now." Conner swallowed to clear the lump in his throat as he hugged them both, his relief unspeakable.

"I thought she might have…" Audrey couldn't finish the sentence.

"I know." He'd shared her fear. Never had he felt more helpless than when he'd thought Della might have given his son drugs.

Audrey carried Ian down the stairs slowly. Conner

fought the dizziness that had taken control and leaned on her shoulder so he wouldn't fall. They left by the front door to stay as far from Doc's office as possible.

She stopped abruptly on the front porch. "Look."

Red lights flashed. Sirens screamed. Frank hobbled up the walk as fast as he could on his crutches, the sheriff's deputy on his heels. An ambulance screeched to a stop at the curb. A parade of pickup trucks blocked a section of the road.

Frank reached them and offered Conner his shoulder for support. "You just can't stay out of trouble, can you, old buddy?" His eyes were moist.

Deputy Johnson moved aside to let them pass. "I know the whole story. Frank convinced me."

"You figured it out," Conner mumbled, and swayed between Frank and Audrey.

"Don't talk," Frank insisted, and yelled, "medic, over here."

Deputy Johnson kept pace with them in the grass. "Frank dragged me out to his house to look at that computer stuff of his. It took some doing, since I don't know anything about computers. Then I saw what he was talking about. People will find it hard to believe Doc Rankin killed Leona, and then that business about the old ladies." He shook his head. "Who would've thought Doc was the greedy type?"

Even though he wasn't thinking clearly, Conner knew the deputy was wrong. Doc's obsession with Audrey, combined with his warped mind, did not equal greed, but he kept his silence. Hopefully, Doc would, too. He didn't want to see Audrey's name plastered all over the papers. She didn't need that.

"Doc's inside," Conner muttered to the deputy, fighting to stay on his feet. "If you want a statement, you'd better make it fast."

"Come with us." Two medics pulled Conner away from Audrey and Frank. "You've lost a lot of blood." They helped him onto a stretcher and wheeled him to the ambulance, as Deputy Johnson and another man ran to the house.

Through the ambulance window, Conner watched Audrey talking to Frank. Ian had his little arms around her neck as if he would never let go. He remembered the doubts in Audrey's eyes when she'd walked into Doc's office. He felt a stab of pain that had nothing to do with his wound. Where did they stand now? he wondered, collapsing onto the stretcher.

IT WAS ALMOST DARK when Peter pulled up to Audrey's cottage in a new truck. The medic had assured her Conner would be fine. She'd wanted desperately to go to the hospital to see for herself, but Ian had needed her with him. She wiped her hands on the dish towel and walked slowly out the back door. Ian flew past her before the door closed, his experience in the locked room apparently forgotten.

Conner stepped from the passenger side of the truck. And Audrey stopped in her tracks. His arm was in a sling, his face very pale.

Doc Rankin had tried to ruin their lives. He'd set Conner up with the robbery six years ago and again with Leona's murder. He'd stolen six precious years of their lives.

Conner's eyes fastened on hers across the yard. And he smiled. There was so much love shining in his eyes, she wondered how she could have doubted him.

He walked around to the driver's door and opened it to Peter as Ian scrambled inside. They said a few words and shook hands. Two weeks ago, Audrey couldn't have imagined this scene.

Ian raced back to her. "Can I ride in Uncle Peter's truck? Please, Mom? He's got a CB."

She caught Peter's nod of approval and walked over to the truck.

"How do you like my new wheels?" Peter beamed with pride.

Tongue-tied, Audrey couldn't answer for a moment. With its oversized tires and unusual height, the truck looked more like one Conner or Frank would buy.

"I like the red stripe on the side." She smiled with approval.

Ian took off for the house just as she turned to tell him he could go. He came back carrying the same type of paper lunch bag in which he'd brought home her surprise yesterday—a mama pinecone person with three little baby pinecones, all with felt hands, feet and faces, and yarn glued to their heads.

He ran to Conner. "I made you something."

The pleasure and surprise on Conner's face warmed her heart. "Do I get to look now?" He stooped to meet Ian's smiling face.

"You bet." Ian handed him the bag.

Inside were two more pinecone people, one quite large, its felt hand securely glued to the smaller cone's hand beside it.

"That's you and me." Ian grinned. "You got the biggest cone."

Conner's eyes sparkled with pleasure and joy. His face turned red and he stumbled over his words of thanks.

Audrey decided it was time to get all of their secrets out in the open. She caught Ian as he turned for the truck, then she crouched down with Conner and took both their hands.

"Remember the play school you went to when we lived with Aunt Nell? Remember when they had all the mommies and daddies visit that night? Do you remember what you asked me?"

"Yep, I member. About the daddies. I didn't know where my daddy was. You said maybe…" He glanced at the truck. "Maybe someday we'd see him." He turned his face up to hers, then tried to pull away. "Can I go in the truck now?"

She lifted his chin. "Conner is someone very, very special. You know why?"

Audrey felt Peter's hand on her shoulder.

Ian shook his head, then stopped. Pure innocence shone in his eyes as he turned to Conner with his question. "Are you my daddy?"

Conner let out a strangled breath. "You bet I am. Is that okay with you? Can I be a daddy to the best little boy in the world?"

With a squeal of delight, Ian grabbed him around the neck. A stray tear rolled down his cheek. His "You bet" stayed muffled in the folds of Conner's collar.

Audrey swiped at her cheeks and hugged them both.

Peter climbed into his truck and Ian wiggled loose. "Will you be my daddy when I come back?" He seemed caught between the urge to ride in the new truck and the need to stay with Conner.

Conner looked first at her and then at Ian. "I'll always be your daddy, big guy, and I'll be here when you get back."

Ian scurried into the truck with Peter. The CB's static filled the air as they drove off.

Audrey's eyes locked with Conner's. She longed to close the short distance between them. She wanted to touch him and taste him and feel his arms around her, but she wasn't sure he'd want her now.

"I thought..." she started to say.

"I know what Ben told you. I don't blame you for what you thought."

"But I should have known better." *Please,* she begged silently, *please forgive me for doubting you.*

"I didn't exactly give you much reason to trust me, Audrey. I'm sorry."

"You don't owe me an apology!"

"No." He paused and came closer. "I owe you my life."

I'll take it, she longed to say. Instead she ran her hand gently down his sling. "Will your arm heal all right?"

He grabbed at his arm and shook his head. Pain drew worried lines across his brow. Mischief danced in his shadowless eyes. "Not really." He pulled her to him and nuzzled her neck, then coaxed her toward the cottage. "It needs a lot more attention."

Audrey's heart sang in joy. "I'm pretty good at fixing arms...and anything else." She tripped over the words.

They stopped at the back door. He tilted up her chin and captured her with his loving eyes. A dimpled smile transformed his face.

"I may need a good lawyer to sue the guy who shot me. Do you know anyone who'd be interested?"

A breathless moment passed. Audrey's heart beat out of control. "I might have someone in mind, but she requires a lifetime commitment."

He opened the door and led her inside. "I wouldn't settle for anything less."

Outside, it looks like a charming old building near the Baltimore waterfront, but inside lurks danger... and romance.

"First lady of suspense" Rebecca York returns with

FOR YOUR EYES ONLY

Jenny Larkin has spent her life trying to make up for a mistake. But that mistake is about to cost her, for now this sightless woman has been targeted by an on-line stalker who "sees" all her guilty secrets.... And the only man who can help her is one she'll never let into her life—no matter what the risk.

Don't miss #407 FOR YOUR EYES ONLY, coming to you in February 1997—only from Rebecca York and Harlequin Intrigue!

Heartbreak RANCH

Four generations of independent women...
Four heartwarming, romantic stories of the West...
Four incredible authors...

Fern Michaels
Jill Marie Landis
Dorsey Kelley
Chelley Kitzmiller

Saddle up with Heartbreak Ranch, an outstanding
Western collection that will take you on a whirlwind
trip through four generations and the exciting,
romantic adventures of four strong women who
have inherited the ranch from Bella Duprey,
famed Barbary Coast madam.

Available in March,
wherever Harlequin books are sold.

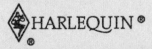

HARLEQUIN ®
®

HTBK

Ring in the New Year with babies, families and romance!

NEW YEAR'S RESOLUTION:

BABY

Add a dash of romance to your
holiday celebrations with this
delightful, heartwarming collection
from three outstanding romance
authors—bestselling author
JoAnn Ross
and
award winners
Anne Stuart and **Margot Dalton.**

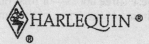

HARLEQUIN ®

Look us up on-line at: http://www.romance.net

NYRB

HARLEQUIN®

I N T R I G U E®

In steamy New Orleans, three women witnessed the same crime, testified against the same man and were then swept into the Witness Protection Program. But now, there's new evidence. These three women are about to come out of hiding—and find both danger and desire....

Start your new year right with all the books in the exciting EYEWITNESS miniseries:

#399 A CHRISTMAS KISS
by Caroline Burnes (December)

#402 A NEW YEAR'S CONVICTION
by Cassie Miles (January)

#406 A VALENTINE HOSTAGE
by Dawn Stewardson (February)

Don't miss these three books—or miss out on all the passion and drama of the crime of the century!

HARLEQUIN®

I N T R I G U E ®

WANTED

12 SEXY LAWMEN

They're rugged, they're strong and they're WANTED!
Whether sheriff, undercover cop or officer of the court,
these men are trained to keep the peace, to uphold the
law...but what happens when they meet the one woman
who gets to know the real man behind the badge?

Twelve LAWMEN are on the loose—and only
Harlequin Intrigue has them! Meet them, one per
month, continuing with

Will Biggs
#405 HERO FOR HIRE
by Laura Kenner
February 1997

LAWMAN:

There's nothing sexier than
the strong arms of the law!

LAWMAN8

Harlequin and Silhouette celebrate
Black History Month with seven terrific titles,
featuring the all-new *Fever Rising*
by Maggie Ferguson
(Harlequin Intrigue #408) and
A Family Wedding by Angela Benson
(Silhouette Special Edition #1085)!

Also available are:
Looks Are Deceiving by Maggie Ferguson
Crime of Passion by Maggie Ferguson
Adam and Eva by Sandra Kitt
Unforgivable by Joyce McGill
Blood Sympathy by Reginald Hill

On sale in January at your favorite
Harlequin and Silhouette retail outlet.

HARLEQUIN® Silhouette®

Look us up on-line at: http://www.romance.net   BHM297

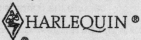

Not The Same Old Story!

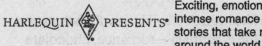 Exciting, emotionally intense romance stories that take readers around the world.

 Vibrant stories of captivating women and irresistible men experiencing the magic of falling in love!

 Bold and adventurous—Temptation is strong women, bad boys, great sex!

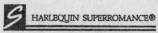 Provocative, passionate, contemporary stories that celebrate life and love.

 Romantic adventure where anything is possible and where dreams come true.

 Heart-stopping, suspenseful adventures that combine the best of romance and mystery.

𝓛OVE & 𝓛AUGHTER™ Entertaining and fun, humorous and romantic—stories that capture the lighter side of love.

Look us up on-line at: http://www.romance.net   HGENERIC